ONLY

THE ALEX CONNER CHRONICLES
BOOK THREE

Other Books by the Author

The Alex Conner Chronicles

Trust: The Alex Conner Chronicles Book One
Truth: The Alex Conner Chronicles Book Two
Forbidden: An Alex Conner Chronicles Novella

YA Epic Fantasy Novels

Eve of the Exceptionals

Keep up with Parker Sinclair:

Sign up for my newsletter here: *www.parkersinclair.net/contact*
Email: *mail@parkersinclair.net*
Webpage: *www.parkersinclair.net*
Purchase my books: *www.parkersinclair.net/buy-a-good-book*
FB group page: *www.facebook.com/groups/236408996753314/?ref=bookmarks*
Amazon Author Page: *amzn.to/1XIDwzO*
Facebook Fan Page: *www.facebook.com/ParkerSinclairbooks/*
Instagram: *@ParkerSinclairauthor*
Twitter: *@Parker_Sinclair*
Goodreads: *www.goodreads.com/author/show/9860680.Parker_Sinclair*
Blog: *www.parkersinclair.net/blog*
Youtube: *www.youtube.com/channel/UCWQE3qvMyB5DEZ9wwdz8rOQ*

ONLY

THE ALEX CONNER CHRONICLES
BOOK THREE

BY

PARKER SINCLAIR

RAWLINGS BOOKS, LLC

Only: The Alex Conner Chronicles Book Three
Copyright © 2017 by Parker Sinclair.

Rawlings Books, LLC
Visit our website at
RawlingsBooks.com

Edited by Meredith Tennant
Cover Art by Jessica Ozment
Original Photograph by Katerina Plotnikova
Interior Layout by Maureen Cutajar

The characters and events portrayed in this book are fictitious. Any similarity to real persons, living or dead, is coincidental and not intended by the author.

Paperback Edition ISBN 978-0-9984053-3-9
Epub Edition ISBN 978-0-9984053-4-6
Mobi Edition ISBN 978-0-9984053-5-3

To my sister. Beautifully magnificent things can come out of the darkest places within our chaos.

To my mother and father. She taught me how to read and he taught me how to love it.

Contents

CHAPTER 1

Loss

The writhing twists of mortal things do sicken me.
Small grey abominations, I shall teach you of salvation.
And through my eyes and by my will be free.
For fools and mules will kick and spit
And then from their knees cry holy writ,
And grasp at ghosts that cannot be.
But who are you to me?
I'll tell you girl and listen well,
For the king has come a reckoning.
And by my word you mustn't tell
Or death will come a beckoning.
~ S. A. Chamovitz

✳

"**Y**ou are the power; you belong to me," whispers through the winds in my mind, winds I've felt and loved before—winds from Avalon. Sweat drenches my chest as I toss and turn, tangled in sheets one moment and atop freshly dewed mossy ground the next.

"Do something!" Ryan's voice calls out in a rage and his ring becomes heavy, cold, and lifeless around my left ring finger.

"I'm working here, boy. Maybe you should get some air." I can barely make out Dana's voice, but I know she is closer than her distant echoes hitting my ears. Dana's power flows like warm, shallow ocean waves while something touches my lips before she encourages me to drink.

My body is wracked with seizures as the first drop travels down my throat. Valant is in a far corner of the room, grumbling and growling impatiently.

Where am I?

"You must let me try. This is in her mind, so let me near her, you fools!" Valant's footsteps echo back and forth along the floor while his ranting voice reflects his agitation at not getting close enough. Ryan is his own kind of livid. Tense waves rolling off him pulse and prickle against my skin even though I must be somewhere else, somewhere far from all of them.

"You've done enough, *Demon*. Maybe if you hadn't killed him he could help us, or at least be forced to."

What? Killed? Who died? Who is Ryan talking about? And then I am hit with unrelenting pain and a swift reminder . . . Justin, my Lestan, and I weep, falling away into darkness again.

When I wake, my head is pounding and my clothes stick to me in various places. Sandra is asleep in a chair beside my bed. Her folded arms are filled with objects: Justin's shirt, his evening primroses crushed and wilted, along with other items I am sure are his. How long have I been out and, more importantly, will it happen again?

I sit up and lightly touch her arm. Objects fly off her lap in all directions and she looks around wildly, obviously not thinking the zombie in the bed is finally awake. I smile and give her a little finger wave before croaking out my greeting.

"Hey, girlie, you know a Bloody Mary sounds mighty fine about now."

"Alex! Oh, thank god. Are you okay?"

"How long have I been out?" Please don't say long, please.

"Three days. Everyone's gone. Ryan's gone to the Council, Dana's trying to reach Vex and Terra, and Valant kept getting cock-blocked so he stormed off." Three days? Well, could be worse, but seventy-two hours have been wiped and I want answers.

"I've been trying to see what was happening to you, using some of Justin's things, but I can't see a thing—nothing. I tried before as well, I promise. When you went to Montana, I tried right away, and nothing came up. I'm so sorry. I should've known."

I grab her hand. "It's not your fault." The vision of Justin falling to the floor constricts my throat and my eyes sting with sadness.

"Do you think there's any hope that he's alive? I mean, I know what I saw, but . . ." Sandra smiles sadly, then her face freezes just before her beautiful eyes completely white out. She looks freakily eerie, even more so when her mouth moves quickly as she starts to mutter in a gravelly voice. I can barely make out her words. Before I can tell her to speak up, she launches forward and starts whispering.

Fairy fingertips tickle my toes.
Lights of the pale moonlight haunt my dreams.
Where has the boy gone, the boy who is more then he seems?
Only the King knows and he is after me.

Oh shit. I was afraid of this. The king of Avalon, Lestan's father, is coming for me, or, rather, I am being brought to him. Sandra's eyes clear. She gazes around, looking lost, until she sees me and sighs with relief.

"Oh god, I thought you were gone. I was so scared."

"Yeah, well, I'm pretty freaked out as well. We may not have much time so let's try and get some control of the situation. I can get Valant back the quickest so let's start there. Valant, help . . ." A boom rings out, shaking the bed and shattering the windows, and we're flung into complete darkness. Screams run wild inside my head. Coldness creeps into my chest and up to my throat where it tightens. This is not Valant's doing. I know, deep down, that no one can help me, no one can reach me. I'm alone. Payment for the sin is due.

Ryan! Valant! AVALON! He's taking me to Avalon. Please help me. Please find me.

An icy shock pressing against my cheek forces my eyes open. Where in the hell am I? The chilled metal sensation is coming from the side of a metal slab on which I'm lying. It reminds me of the death drawers the coroners stuff corpses into at a morgue. Is that where I am? An Avalon death room where I will be forced to see what has become of Lestan? And if so, where's the person who brought me here? His father—the king.

When I try to sit up my head spins, the sudden movement causing my stomach to follow suit, and I nearly gag, losing whatever remnants of food and drink linger within. Looking around in my shadowy confinement, I see where I've been sentenced to, the cell that is now my doom. A dirty stone floor meets my bare feet, and metal bars enclose my space within what can only be categorized as a dungeon. When I try to stand, I become woozy again and fall back down onto my new bed. A thin pad is all that lies between my body and the thick metal I'll be sleeping upon every night of my imprisonment.

Standing again, more slowly this time, I walk toward the bars and find the latch on the outside of the door. When I shoot my hand out through the bars to grab it, a fiery shock ignites on my wrist and flares up and down my arm. I bite my lip, holding back the nearly intolerable pain, expecting my power to heal me quickly, but though I try to call it forth, it does not answer and it doesn't come to aid me. Looking down, I see the cause of the assault. A bracelet, nearly black with tones of green, rests on my wrist. Is it preventing me from using my powers as well as keeping my arms and legs inside my cage?

A maniacal laugh breaks through the dank, frigid prison. Unsure how I could have missed it before, I am suddenly hyperaware of someone else close by.

"Who's there?"

Do I really want an answer? Whoever's there is either responsible for me being here or making sure I stay put until they get what they want. The answer comes in the form of a male voice, one bearing the tones of a person who holds all the cards, the control, and the kingdom.

"Alex Conner—Eila, as my foolish son so lovingly addressed you—how do you like your new home? I find it more than adequate for someone of your stature. There's only one reason you are not dead, and that is because I need something from you, Ms. Conner. Something I will get by any means necessary."

Staring out into the darkness, I can hardly make out the form speaking to me. I can't see any other cells, but I am sure they exist. The space appears unending outside my sight. Booted feet approach, and I see the king coming into view in green velvet robes and a metallic crown resembling branches on his head. As he moves closer, I can barely grasp the resemblance to the boy I knew as a child, yet there's no mistaking who he is. The only question is what he wants. Making me pay for what happened to his son is my first guess, but he's not attacking me, as I would expect him to, if that were what he wants.

"I'm sorry about Lestan, your son. I didn't mean for that to happen. I loved—I love him. Let me try to bring him back. We can work together. Is this all really necessary? I wasn't even the one who did it!"

My anger is coming purely from a place of grief and the fear of being entrapped in this place all alone. More laughter echoes around me as the king's head falls backward and his insanity becomes horrifyingly apparent. He strides forward and hovers just outside the bars where any move I make toward him will be greeted with the same fiery pain as before. Not wanting to show the king that he, or my circumstances, scare me in any way I approach the bars so we are face-to-face with only mere inches separating us.

"My son chose his fate when he failed me over and over again. And allowing himself to die at the hands of a lower being is what he deserved!" The king, Lestan's poor excuse for a father, screams his final words laced in his own spit and venom into my face, yet I refuse to take even one step back. If I'm not here to pay for what happened to Lestan or to bring him back, then why in the hell did he bring me here?

Reaching underneath my eye to wipe away his spittle from my face, I step closer to the bars of my shitty cell and stare into the king's face. Enraged to a point of blurring the lines between sanity and mania, my teeth course across each other in a painful jarring sound. Unlatching my jaw, I spit my words right back at him. "Then what does the king of Avalon, of the Fae, want from me, huh? What can I possibly have that you need?"

He stares at me, and for a second I see him searching for something. Is it my face? My eyes? As he stares, I see a flicker of recognition followed by something that could be pain, yet in an instant it's gone. It means something, but the silence in our shared space, a silence that isn't completely quiet because I can still hear the blood rushing and pounding in my ears, is an eerie quiet, one on the precipice of a vicious storm, a tragic, world-ending hurricane.

"All in due time, my dear. All I need from you I will find soon. So soon. If you think your life was full of misery before, you're in for quite a shock, because the things I can and will do to you far exceed anything you've experienced before. That I promise you, just as I promised my son the same if he didn't do as I asked. And I assure you, he fought me for a long time, and look what he became. A jealous man-child worth killing. Now what do you think will become of you, Alex? I know I'm dying to find out."

CHAPTER 2

Memories

Blinds drift back than forth as the wind shapes their destiny.
Flicker across my face–unending beams of sunlight.
Rainbows are seen upon damp eyelashes, kaleidoscopes surrounding.
Clarity of pastel colors, bright sparkles, slight heat.
Smoke rises, dancing, then disappears as it rides waves of wind and light.
Serenity fills this room.
I am happy falling asleep . . . inviting in the night.

"I have to sing again? Where are we getting these girls? Are you slumming it outside the rehab clinics?" Nic's laughing hysterically of course, which for him is a closed-mouthed, barely contained giggle that shakes his entire body and makes his brown eyes water.

"Don't smudge your man-liner with those pretty boy tears at my expense." That oughta shut him down for a few. Of course, now he produces the perfect pout before pushing me out of the way to hog the mirror so he can carefully dab at his eyes. He went for the royal blue liner tonight and, man, how it reflects magically off his warm skin tone. Maybe that means his relationship is improving; his smoky-eyed Goth phase was starting to concern me. At least he hasn't held off on the glitter that peeks in and out of his perfectly styled spikey black hair.

"Well, you should be psyched that you are on with *those* boys tonight! Now stop complaining and start thanking me and those unreliable dolls of ours. *Shots on Four* is at the top of the dance charts with this song, so buck up and don't let the crowd down. You can mimic Mayana's voice better than anyone. Now go get 'em, my little tigress." His smack on my ass wouldn't have stung so bad if he hadn't had on a thousand rings, or maybe I just need to be donning a bit more fabric. Backseam black hose under barely-there sequin shorts has to be all he had in his goody bag tonight—yeah, right. I smell a set-up.

Yanking down on the blood-red crop top that isn't going any lower even if I pop some seams, I clearly hear Shane's voice announcing the act over Rapture's insane sound system. Someone owes me for this, but I'm not sure who that would be since Shane and I own this place. Ah, the things I do for our club-goers' enjoyment. We couldn't just play Mayana's voice over the set, *no,* we had to promise live singers. The same sister singers who called not thirty minutes ago claiming their granny was ill and they were on their way to the hospital—food poisoning—thinking we couldn't hear the rambunctious chaos of party rocking carrying on in the background; priorities are spectacularly lost on those girls. Of course, I'm not one to claim perfection. Far from it.

The beginning tones of *Stay* are rattling the mirror frame in the private bathroom. I glance at my hair in the mirror; the intricate braided up-do needs a little oomph. Digging into my bag, I produce a dark feather that I weave into the braid. It shimmers like magic when I touch it. Magic. *There's no such thing as magic.* Zipping up my heels, I give myself one last lookover before taking the hallway to backstage.

Nic catches up to me, hand outstretched. "You need this, you sexy minx you, unless you just plan on shimmying around instead of actually doing what you need to be doing out there." Snatching the cordless mic from him, I spin on my heels and head for one section of the posh guest lounge behind the booth. My fingers open and close on the microphone while a shuddering intake of breath releases in a warmth that tickles a loose tendril of my hair down my chest. Composed, I slither along the wall, lightly touching the soft, pale-grey leather couches and chairs. This side is thankfully empty. The peeps from *Shots of Four,* whose clinking glasses and whoops of delight and ecstasy can be heard even over the sound system, are in the other section. Torance shifts to the left-side turntables, moving his right headphone off his ear and pushing his body down before shifting the volume to the front to send a hard-hitting beat shooting around the club. Major is quieter and deeply engrossed in the other set of tables, shifting incredible sounds of high and low into the rifts. I meet his eyes as he slowly turns; his only indication of my timing is a slight nod.

Mic up, I stride out between the tables and hit the high note Mayana made famous enough to top the chart week after week. The song is one I've known by heart since the sad beauty of it latched into the depths of my brain.

> I can't stay, not here, not for another dance in the moonlight. But can't you come, come for me, and not let me down tonight?
> Come for meeeee, You can come for meeee. Don't let me down, you won't let me down. You know I can't stay. I can't stay here alone. Please don't let me down. I want to come home. Home to you now.

Yes, at times the lyrics are agonizing to sing, but the beauty of them also reminds me of how much I still have. My friends, work I adore, even when I'm not always prepared for the slip-ups that occur every so often. Besides, I'm having fun, aren't I?

The last lyrics tear out of my heart and soul, leaving me to just dance freely, smiling at the amazing musicians on either side of me, at the crowd in a trancelike state below, and at Nic who is spinning around like a wild man in the VIP area. I swear he's taking up more space in there with his moves than the rest of the party on the opposite side.

My friends and I have an undying love of dancing. Why wouldn't we? Dance is known in many cultures to induce trance where we can escape the pressures of life, share positive vibes, and accept individuality. The diversity in the crowd fills me with pride; all are accepted and respected here. All dance on common, positive ground within the walls of Rapture.

There's a sudden flash of luminous silver light at the left side of the dance floor. A small set of stairs holds only one person, a man, blending into the darkness except for the brilliant glow coming off his hand. Can't anyone else see this? He stares at me, ignoring the beautiful mass of writhing bodies dancing around him. The dark clothing wrapped tightly around his magnificent body displays muscles one would love to touch. Is he new? Security? Why wasn't I notified? I'll have to find out who he is, for professional reasons, of course.

I try to get Nic's attention by staring at him and then back at the enigmatic man, but the music has that man-child entranced, and it looks like he brought an entire bottle of vodka up here. When I turn back around the mysterious man is gone. I stare harder, thinking that for sure he must still be there, blended into the darkness somehow with his dark hair, eyes, and skin. Sexy as hell in that tight shirt and equally fitting pants package, and now, where in the world did he go?

"Oh damn." Nic sounds as if he nearly spit out his drink. Turning back around, I see the man in black is now right in front of me, here, staring at me again with that bright silver glow, toned down a tad, sure, but still afire. A pull beyond my control has me moving toward the enigmatic man in front of me. *Shots of Four* brings in a sensuous beat and my body doesn't care who he is, only that he allows me to place my hand upon his chest and drag it down along his taut abs. My hips sway and we fall into a dance as if our bodies already know each other. Pulse racing, electrical jolts sizzle my skin as a drunken euphoria floods through me. He's so close. Every synapse in my being is firing in response to him, to his smell, and to the energy rolling off him. I'm nearly in tears with the ecstasy as we dance; our bodies become one and the music tugs and pulses throughout my being. *Shots of Four* are shamans in the dark wooing me to set myself free.

"Who are you?" I whisper into his ear. He feels warm, comfortable, and safe. I'm not used to feeling like this.

"You know who I am. Don't let yourself forget those of us who can help you. Look at me, Lex. Really look at me." Not fair that he knows my name, well part of it, when I haven't a clue of his, and what's with all of the cryptic talk? Who have I forgotten, and what help do *I* possibly need? Well, maybe a better entertainment scout, but other than that the club is doing well, my company is prospering, and San Diego is an amazing place to live. Regardless, I look into his eyes, expecting his gaze to simply make me weak in the knees, not hit me like a full-on Louisville slugger to the head.

"You know me. Don't forget me. He's trying to
all of us, even parts of you. You can't be found t
want to be. It's a trick, Alex, a trick of the Fae. Re

I pull away from him, gripping my head. Why
help, though I think I can hear Nic talking abou
Who is this man? I can't get my fingers to loosen
my head. Fae? What in the world is a Fae?

"Lex. Look at me. You trust me. We've been to hell and back.
Together. You know my name. Look at me and remember. We're coming
to help you. Dana, Sandra, she's brought more help, and we will save
you. I promise."

"Who?"

He grips my shoulders and draws me to him again. His lips are so
close to mine that I forget his words and only think of pressing them to
my own; suddenly, it hits me. My body does know him. Its reactions are
now on autopilot. It knows him and my memory of him isn't required
for my senses to remember wanting this man's skin against my own.
Wait. No, I don't know him. This is just some trick. What is happening,
why can't I remember, and who the hell are Dana and Sandra?

"Here, take this and hide it. You were taken without it, or they knew to
take it off you, but perhaps it'll work if I give it to you here in this
Dreamwalk. I'm linked to you and so is the ring. Take it, and part of me
can help you remember who you are—who we are. It'll also let you know
when you're being fooled. That was Valant's little addition. Finally doing
some good, for once." The glowing light is moving from his finger to mine.
His eyes flash to something on my head and he takes the ring back. It
shrinks in his hand to a small bead, which he places in my hair with a little
click. How in the hell did he do that? Is he some magician, a party trickster
hired by Shane or Nic? I locate the bead that is now secured to the feather
as if a part of it all along. As I touch it, a hint of memory, of the earth's life
force rushes into me—my grandmother, a fox, a knife, blood, a goddess
shifting forms in a giant tree, a boat, a bed, his lips—Ryan.

"Ryan?"

"Yes. Yes, it's me. You were taken by the Fae king of Avalon. He's
trying to make you forget us and who you really are. We thought he'd

11

you in revenge for Justin's death, but in a vision Sandra overheard
in asking you to bring *her* to him. We're trying to work it all out,
but . . ." Ryan's gaze flits around the club. Something is wrong. A wave of
electricity or understanding flows into me, one that heightens my senses
and fills me with power. Magic. It is real and I am connected to it—to all
of it. The air, water, earth, sky. It's as if I can hear every living thing
vibrating through me. Earthen power, the goddess's power surges
through me. Me. Alex Conner. Hybrid. Earthen Protector and Healer.
This, this world with Shane and Nic and my club isn't real. It's a twisted
Dreamwalk, some sort of vision. A trick conceived by Lestan's father.

Shimmers along my vision are more than mere tricks of the light;
something is changing around us.

"Vex! What's happening? I'm losing her. I need you to hold it a little
longer." With Ryan's dark eyes back on me, I spy the silver fire akin to
the ring's ablaze within them along with a shadow of regret, longing, and
fear. "You're more than this, Alex, so much more to the world . . . to
me." Fingers touch my cheek as a tear falls from my eye without warning.
Reality seeps in, in small, shattered pieces.

"I'm trapped, aren't I, in his world? Sandra came to see me." I touch
the feather in my hair again. "This. It's from them. They found me." Yes,
I remember seeing Sandra, Logan, and an eagle in my cell, but someone
else saw them as well—the king. I'd been able to speak to Sandra through
a connection we developed not long after I was taken, and the
connection had somehow brought her to me, probably through her being
a Seer. A more powerful Seer than I ever thought possible. Despite that,
and after the king nearly caught her as well, our bond weakened. I
narrow my eyes at the cursed bracelet on my wrist. No traveling out of
the Fae dimension for me. Every time I've even tried to slip my arm
through the bars in whatever basement of hell he's tossed me in, the
devil bangle scorched my arm. I have to get out of here.

"You are coming soon, right? Do you know how to get me out? What's
the plan? What do I need to do?" Ryan draws in a breath before releasing it
slowly. "You don't know how yet, do you?" Swallowing hard, I ask one
more question. His eyes look worried. "How long have I been gone? I can't
judge time here. It only feels like yesterday since I last saw you."

Ryan grabs hold of my hand. "Over two weeks, and no, we haven't figured everything out. Not yet, Lex, but we are working on it. Be careful with the Fae. Vex says they're ancient beings who believe themselves to be the true rulers of all the worlds after the gods and goddesses left. They don't view humans as equals, and even though they look like us, they aren't. They think and feel differently, and human lives don't matter to them. Remember that. The most important thing is that you don't forget and that the king doesn't get what he needs."

I lower my voice to an even softer whisper. "Because you think he'll kill me once he gets what he wants, don't you?" He pulls me closer. "He's going to kill me no matter what though, because of Justin—Lestan. He blames me for his death." Pictures from the past flip through my mind and I can't help but ask. "Why isn't he after Valant's ass? He's the trigger-happy Demon to blame, technically." Ryan manages a tight smile in response to an Alex we both used to know, a freer Alex who wasn't trapped in a crazy king's world.

"Alex?"

Either my eyes are blurry or he is. "Ryan? Ryan!" Our eyes meet, I get one last gaze at his gorgeous face, and then—he's gone.

"Come on girl! This is one of our favorite songs. Come dance with me!" Nic's voice is so real, but this isn't real. Whatever else this is, it's a trap, meaning everyone is here to get something from me. So maybe this little fakey vision has some answers for me as well.

"Coming. Pour me a stiff one, will you?" I stare into the empty space where Ryan was. A howl sounds in the distance, a mournful fading noise, and a floating light catches my eyes. The green sparkle is in the shape of a fern frond. It flares before flickering out in my palm. Vex. The fox I saved as a child that became my guide and friend, even with his lack of patience and snippy attitude. He was injured the last time I saw him and having not seen his furry face recently probably means that he hasn't returned to full foxy strength yet.

A tinkling of ice cubes hitting glass cues my palm to close hastily around the drink Nic is holding. I dance with him as if he were my real flesh-and-blood friend, and looking at him I wish it wasn't a lie. Once we'd done some damage to the carpet, we collapse onto the couch, laughing and mixing more drinks. Soon the cocktails turn to shots and a bubbly lightness floats around my head. The blends must be some sort of Fae drugging. Damn, should have thought of that possibility. I touch the feather and silver bead in my hair again lightly, not completely sure it will do anything to keep me grounded, but it's reassuring nonetheless.

"So where has Sandra been, girlie? I mean, she has seriously been MIA. I know she loves her boy toys, but damn, how much time can she spend in the fortress of sexitude."

He's asking about Sandra. Maybe she's the *her* the king wants? It's not surprising after her show of power; it can't be easy to break into Avalon. She needs to be warned. Play it cool, Alex. Try to get him to say more.

"Oh, you know her. I mean, have you dropped by her house? She always *loves* a good drop by."

Nic laughs a little too riotously, even for him, and then he leans in closer, his vodka vapors assaulting my nose. "You smell like him, that hunk of man flesh that was here earlier. What was his name? You seemed a little—cozy."

Something is definitely off with this Nic. My insides squirm, a warning that things are about to get ugly if I don't think fast. Nic's hands move smoothly to the vodka bottle and he begins to robotically pour me another drink. Even though his eyes appear to be fixed upon his cocktail concocting, he's keeping one of them trained directly upon my every move.

"I think I'm done for the night, love. Shane's around here somewhere. I'll give him my good-byes and have him come your way so you can corrupt him instead." I laugh lightheartedly and place a soft touch on his face. He's not my Nic. How I ever mistook him for one of my best friends shows the Fae king's mastery of manipulation. My worry and fear are pushed deep down, a smile plastered on my face as I kiss Nic's cheek in farewell. Yet even as I walk away, fake-Nic's eyes cause my back muscles to shiver. Does he know I'm aware? I give a little stumble to keep the act going. Ryan's ring and the feather must be helping me overcome the Fae poison after all.

Before I manage to escape the VIP section I am yanked back in and spun around to face Nic once again. Not Nic. No. A contorted, enraged version of Nic. He hisses and someone else's face appears. The king.

"Why do I have to do everything myself?"

In a flash of light, the mist machines shoot a super blast into the crowd. The king's face vanishes and there is Nic again, pulling me to the edge of the DJ booth and into the fog device's spray. My eyes close and my muscles relax, sending my head tipping backward while my cheeks ache from the broad smile as my fears slip away. Pushing aside an alien sensation, I hear the music rise and the bass takes over my body. I dance away with Nic, but why is there a nagging nibbling, warning me that I am forgetting something, somebody. But then I twirl to the music, smiling. This club is everything I hoped it would be and more. Watching the crowd dance reminds me of a collective phenomenon, as if they are merged into one body and mind, creating a harmony.

Suddenly my forgotten question returns and I pull Nic to me, whispering and giggling into his ear. "Hey, who was that guy? I mean damn!" With a broad smile and a dismissive wave of his hand his reply comes with a whisper of air upon my neck. "Nobody, sweets! He's nobody." We both laugh and I let my fascination with the stranger go. I mean, he's just a man. He'll never replace the one I really love.

When the night comes to an end, I exit the ride to my downtown loft mere minutes from Rapture. Pitter greets me at the door and I barely manage to brush my teeth before falling upon the bed calling to me. Reaching up to touch my hair, my fingertips find a feather there along with a foreign cool metal ball. With a hand still on my head I soon fall fast asleep. Feathers float to and fro in my dreams, along with silver glows of night flickering around me in the dark like tiny stars guiding me somewhere—somewhere real and not of this dream world. Coldness creeps in along with a massive ache coursing through my body. I don't ever remember a hangover like this. Actually, I've never had a hangover . . . ever.

My body's weightless fall into deep, frozen darkness jolts me awake as memories come rushing in. The cold hard bed in my Fae cell makes me shiver from more than the temperature. I've been held captive more than once in my life and this time is no different as it builds a swirling concoction of rage and fear in my soul. Tucked and woven deep within my hair, a feather tickles along my fingertips, nearly making me sob when I touch its soft smoothness. How long ago was that visit from Sandra and Logan? My god, how long have I been gone? Remembering last night, I move my hand along the feather, clamping my other one over my mouth to stop from crying out in relief when a small cool metal bead greets me and I know I have Ryan's ring once again. The carved metal band adorned with suns, moons, and stars endlessly chasing each other was secretly altered and given to me in the king's vision. How long has he been trying to steal my past from me and how close was he to succeeding before Ryan—and Vex apparently—were able to intervene? The king stole my powers from me so easily, and even Sandra's feather couldn't keep me safe. Maybe now, with Ryan's totem, I'll be able to fight the king long enough to get out of here. The best news out of this crappy-ass situation is that now at least he's shown his hand. All I have to do is play along and maybe, just maybe, I can figure out what he wants before it's too late and he weasels it from me unawares. He wants someone or something from me. Fae mind games. Ryan hit it on the nose. Every Fae I've met has treated me like a boot licker; of course they've mainly been jailers whose only duty is to keep me in line, so it's possible those outside of the dungeon think and feel differently. Too bad this bottom feeder has something the king wants, so I guess he doesn't know or have everything now does he, the jackass.

Sandra was whom he asked about in the club, well, whom "Nic" asked about. Next time I find myself in one of those Fae dreams I need to carefully and artfully use his mind-bending soldiers posing as my friends against him and find out exactly what he's up to.

What I know for certain is that I can't allow him to make me forget my life, no matter how messed up it's been. I was finally looking forward to my future . . . until, until Valant killed Justin, my Lestan. The king has shown himself to be a less than stellar father figure, even though I had thought I was down in this cell to pay for what happened to his son. Not once has he asked me to bring Lestan back. Nope, his reactions are more of a pissed-off titan who knows one of his minions failed to break me. Is that all Lestan was to him? A tool? A soldier? Honestly, that was my suspicion that night in my room. The aching in my heart and deep down in my bones when we struggled during those last moments of his life was all the proof I needed—he was being used. Used against the true character of the boy I knew in my childhood dreams. Dreams are all I thought they were, but Lestan made the reality of his existence apparent, posing as Justin for over a year.

Well, a trap to ensnare me is not what Lestan was to me. He was a savior during my times of despair. He used his powers to heal me, the same Fae powers that his father is now using to shatter my very existence. Well, the king hasn't broken me yet, and my friends have found a way to chip away at his hold on me. He apparently doesn't know whom he is dealing with. And, if I'm not mistaken, I too have at least one friend here in his world of Avalon.

CHAPTER 3

Sandra

I still hear it, so deep into my soul.
A cry for help, the voice I've known.
Along the fence line a small body I did see.
And I could hear the echoes of her screaming.

***

"That was Ryan. He reached Alex. Getting the ring to her worked. She was able to break the spell and remember who and what she is. Let's hope the king doesn't find it and destroy it because Ryan said it was a close one. She didn't remember some of us and had no recollection of who she really is."

Logan and Jax sit staring at me from my couch, their heads turning from side to side as I pace. The edges of my angled bob swing against my cheeks with my movements, tickling me in an annoying sort of way. My teeth close around my bottom lip without thinking. I'm holding something back from them, something that will seal the deal and never let us use our Seer powers to attempt to rescue her again. I've been dying to get back into the Fae world and rescue Alex, but Logan and Jax keep saying that it's too risky right now, especially since the king himself uncovered the last vision we entered in his dungeon. He somehow saw Logan and me. Ugh, that completely freaked me out. Since then my connection to my best friend has been weaker, and only the eagle Nanda-yi's link through the feather allowed us to figure out that she was losing her memories.

So, for now I will keep to myself that Ryan was able to stay joined to Alex in her dream, the ring allowing him to listen in, even though he couldn't be there. The Nic lookalike asked about me, me specifically, where I was. Am I the *her* the king was drilling Alex to bring to him? If so, why didn't it seem like it in my vision, and anyway, what in the world would he want from me? Whatever the case, if Logan or Jax sense I may be the king's target, they will never risk me returning to Avalon through my vision. Perhaps they won't even go themselves, even with the aid of Logan's mystical war eagle slash badass tattoo the Nanda-yi. No, they'll fear they'd be used in some way to set a trap for me. So for now, I'll keep this bit of information to myself. I know I can help Alex somehow, no matter the cost, and I'm the only one of us who can travel through time and space within a Seer vision. Therefore, I alone can bring her back. Keeping these two out of it will be the hard part. And what about that torture device on her wrist? Pretty certain I'll need Yi's help for that, but is that even possible without Logan agreeing?

"You're doing a whole lot of thinking and not a lot of talking over there, darling. Care to share what else is pinging around in that beautiful head of yours?"

Logan tries, not very successfully, to resist an eye roll at the loving words Jax sends my way. He's a good sport. Jax and I are totally infatuated now that we've found our way back to each other after so many years. Logan lived through all our lovey-doveyness before, when we were much younger, so it's easy enough between the three of us, even after all our years apart.

"Oh, it's nothing," I say quickly while giving an equally fast dismissive hand wave. "Just eager to get her back. Time isn't passing there as it is here, at least it seems that way to Alex; two weeks to us only feels like days to her. I guess that's good, for her anyway." The boys look at each other knowingly and I swallow away a bit of worry that they may be on to me. Instead of showing my concern, I choose to scoop up Pitter and smile devilishly at Jax. Yes, I am a Seer but I also know when to use my *other* gifts to throw someone off course. "Why don't we head to my room, love? It's late, and I'm all wound up from the anticipation of Ryan's report. Won't you come with me and help a girl—I don't know—unwind?"

Logan nearly shoves Jax off the couch, opting to be rid of the both of us rather then endure being in the same room with us much longer. See? Easy as pie.

I don't think Pitter expected me to lock him out of my room after the amazing cat massage I gave him as Jax and I walked down the hall. His little paw slashes under the door and his mews of abandonment and how-dare-yous penetrate the narrow space. Cute little guy. Alex must miss him like crazy.

"I know this isn't easy for you, Sandra, but we are going to get her back. I promise." Jax is so reassuring. His scent reminds me of our life back in Virginia when we all hung out as kids. Logan, Jax, Nora, and I were inseparable, running around the shore and dunes on the Virginia coast, back when Jax and I first fell in love. We're all years older now, and so much has transpired between us, good and bad, but this is our redo, our chance to start over. The fact that it's beginning with one hell of a shitstorm complicates things, but I also wonder if we would have ever gotten back together if I hadn't been given the push from that damn Demon Valant to seek my brother's help in the first place.

No, I know Jax has always been my destiny, and with his curse lifted now that the Demon of our pasts is dead—thank you, Alex—I know he would have come to me if I hadn't made my way to him. Despite all that is wrong falling all around us, my body can't resist Jax and I start to warm and tingle with desire as his arm wraps around me and he presses his chest against my back. His hand on my belly shoots a heated yearning deep down, one that causes me to clench my legs together and moan at his smallest of touches. Jax caresses my curves, giving each side equal attention, before moving inside my thighs and teasing his way up and around to my stomach. He finds my breasts next and his half moan half growl lets me know that he is enjoying their fullness while using his fingers to inch my shirt up before pulling it over my head. The small white-feathered wing tattoos on each of my shoulders vibrate under his touch, like a wispy tickle. I'm still getting used to their presence, but boy do they respond to Jax's touch. Turning my neck to peek behind me, I spy the inked depiction of a mighty tribal war eagle sprawled across his shoulder and down his arm. We got ours on the same day, courtesy of

Yi's magic that created an unbreakable bond between Logan, Jax, and me.

"Yes," I whisper as one piece of my clothing falls to the floor and he begins to work my soft pants off my hips. When he realizes I'm completely naked beneath, he gives a deep rumbling sigh and pulls my backside against the growing pressure in his jeans. I want nothing but to tease him a bit more before he is also undressed. He spins me around before pushing me playfully down upon the bed. Although he's only been here a couple days, this bed has gotten plenty of use already. The downy cover may never be the same again; some of those finger grip-induced wrinkles aim to stay.

Now, his turn. He pulls his tight tank up and over his sandy blond hair and I clutch the cover at my front row view of this man before me. His body, hard and tan, tempts me although I refuse to move closer to him, choosing instead to let his little strip show continue. His shorts are next, and my feet move against each other in anticipation of having his naked body against mine. With a quick unbuttoning and even faster unzip, they fall to the floor, and my smile curls up wickedly to match his.

"Touché, good sir, I must say. I most definitely like the way our minds think alike." Indeed, boxerless and without an ounce of timidity, my Jax stands before me, a god ready to give me every pleasure I desire. With one knee on the bed, he arches his body down and into mine, running one of his hands lightly up along my leg and to my center of desire, but, frustratingly, he only skims the innermost parts of my thighs, stopping and lifting away, and instead once again reaching for my breasts. Bringing his lips to devote his full attention to both of my eager nipples, his actions force a gasp from my mouth. His strength allows him to hover above my body, just out of reach, which makes me squirm and arch in hopes of having him pressed harder, and wholly, against me.

"Problem, doll?" Oh, it's game time, I see.

"Oh, not for me, but I guarantee you can't stay up there for long." On cue, I lift my back, and after letting him watch me fully wet my fingers between my lips, I reach down to hold his warm, full flesh. His breath catches and I know I have him now.

Arms trembling, his head moves into the crook of my neck where he growls into my ear. "Now you've done it, Sand. This was going to be nice and drawn out, but I am going to have to change that strategy, *right now*."

Pushing back swiftly, he hooks his arms around my legs and pulls my hips near his mouth, giving his tongue deep access to my soft, hot flesh.

No fair!

My mind is in a frenzy, fighting with wanting him to give me control and at the same time wishing he would take me any way he wants. The second thought wins out and I am mewing uncontrollably in his grasp. This is the man I've always wanted and who I've been missing all these years. The love of my life is this man who knows my body and exactly what to do with it.

Jax appears to hear my thoughts when he lifts from his thorough work at arousing me to the brink and gives me a sweet smile. Letting my hips drift slowly back down on the bedspread, he positions himself so that he's barely inside me, smothers my breasts and neck in kisses, and then drives his hard cock deeper. Madness is what this is, delicious and perfect madness. I clasp my legs around him, pushing against him and breathing heavy into each and every thrust. Lifting me slightly, he moves one hand to grab my ass and we continue our pace, our mouths crashing into each other as the intensity increases. Stars dance around my closed lids in a display of colors and the tight throbbing knot releases in ecstasy.

Throwing my eyes open, I see his gorgeous face looking at me with an expression of deep love and intimacy. I never should have waited this long to get him back into my life.

"I love you." My whisper is seductive and full of emotion.

His answer begins with a kiss. One that is soft, yet possessive and strong. "I love you too. Always have and always will."

Snuggling down next to each other, I can't seem to stop my mind from drifting back to Alex. She's trapped away in another realm, one that I know I can get to and bring her back from, but how can I go there alone and how can I lie to both Jax and my brother? There's no way they won't know if I try—all three of us are Seers, after all—and Logan has the bonus power of Yi. It's pretty much impossible for me to even concoct a way to get to her without their knowledge, especially considering how protective they are of me. I mean, really, I've shown the power I can wield. Banished that Demon as a child, didn't I? And then I ripped apart the Fae king's wards with Yi when we entered visions to uncover the past that was taken from me the night Alex disappeared. Despite the king's attempts to hide whomever took Alex, we've worked to put the pieces back together. God, our reunion in Virginia seems like forever ago, though it's barely been two weeks. All that built-up angst about bringing Logan back into my life after he forbade me to ever contact him again is all behind us now. I ignored his wishes because I needed his help to find Alex, and now Jax is back in my life too.

"Where'd you go, sweetheart?"

Proof that there's no way to hide anything from either of them, Jax knows me deep down to my very soul. Not to mention that Logan does too. Well, you know what they say about twins. That whole all-knowing connection thing we have will thwart all of my plans. I'll just have to reason with them. Yi's feather is supposed to help us know if Mr. Evil Fae is around, making it safer the next time we go to Alex. Maybe if we can bring someone else with us they'd be more willing to go for it. Maybe Ryan or . . .

"That's just what I was thinking, my little Seer vixen. Oh, I'm not interrupting anything, am I?" Jax and I both jolt upright, fingers gripping the covers tightly around us as we stare at a vision the likes of Tom Cruise's Lestat with his wicked sharp teeth and dark red eyes staring back at us.

"What in the hell, Valant! I am not a stand-in for Alex's pact Demon!"

Smirking, Valant folds his arms over his broad chest and turns his back to us. "I didn't know you were such a prude, Ms. Oman. Allow me to give you time to renew your decency and then maybe you can get your head back in the game? Or did your human needs make you forget your best friend, *Alex*, for a moment?" Demons. Valant may be helping us find Alex, but it's for his own gain. Thinking the only way she could save her mom was to make a pact with this Demon to get her murderous foster brother to tell her where he was keeping her mom only backfired on her when Greg escaped and Alex learned that her mom had never really been in danger. Oh, and that her father was actually alive; that had been one truly crazy night.

Jax is up and in his shorts before I even manage to bring my gaping jaw back to normal.

"The Demon, huh? I thought you'd be, I don't know, taller?" Failing miserably to stifle it, I unleash a laugh followed by a curious "hmmm" when Valant doesn't take the bait and retaliate. Only a shake of his head signals that he heard a single word Jax said.

"Out of respect for the fact that he is your mate and you are the best friend of my, shall we say, business partner, I will allow his petty jokes at my expense. However, once Alex is back safe and sound—for the most part, anyway—don't think for a moment that my pleasant demeanor will stick around. Now get dressed, Pamela. We have work to do." I need to unclench my hands from their death grip on my bedcover, but all I can focus on is my desire to tear the long blond hair out of Valant's shit grin-plastered head. He doesn't even look at me, instead busying himself by picking at his long sharp fingernails that match his pointy teeth.

"Interesting how you're on Alex's side this time. What's the matter? Can't you find some poor sap to soul suck lately? Why don't you pester your puppet, Greg?"

Alex and her mom, Stacy, managed to capture Greg, no thanks to Valant who was hell-bent on killing the traitor and, come to think of it, perhaps Ryan as well. Valant himself blasted Greg from the boat he was hiding on. The Earthen Protector's ego had been bruised that night, but he bucked up when he helped Alex save her father, Alexander, from, that's right, another Demon. One who had nearly fully possessed her dad, while trying to kill off Healers one by one at the bidding of someone working deep within the Earthen Protectors' sacred Council. The same Demon that came after me and mine, the Demon Alex killed in Montana, thereby freeing Jax from his curse.

"Aren't Demon puppets more *your* speed? I mean, young Jax here only recently popped his non-cursed cherry, didn't he now?"

Jax remains still with his arms crossed over that hard chest of his, all the while looking slightly amused at my banter with Valant. He is playing things so cool right now; it's one of the reasons I love him. I on the other hand am about to kamikaze dive onto Valant and kick his balls back to a hell dimension. He's been at the core of everything lately.

Yes, Greg is now jailed within the Council walls, but Alex's parents are in hiding while her dad tries to heal from the Demon possession. Alex herself is stuck in Fae town, Vex is still on the mend, and apparently Valant is my responsibility. Just peachy. Though I can't deny the Demon was the one who gave me the extra kick in the ass I needed to seek out my brother. Valant knew we needed him and Yi to help Alex. How he knew is still uncertain.

Valant makes a few impatient noises and I sigh, grabbing my clothes from Jax's outstretched hand. "Oh fantastic. Your brother, Ken, is all in a tizzy. Better hurry, Barbie, before your house gets a beating from a senseless, and unprovoked I might add, brawl." Before I can manage to get my top on, Yi's screams have up and standing while yanking my covers around me. Logan nearly kicks down the door, eyes searching and face contorted in wild fury as he looks for the invader. Yi is right behind him, flying in on strong wings and looking around wildly with his beady eyes.

Logan's own eyes nearly bulge out of his head when he gets a good look at the Demon in his sister's room. I don't have even a second to react before Yi dives at Valant, who has been almost guffawing at the scene as if it is some comedy playing out, which is his error. Yi gets a nice swipe at him and I cringe as blood—Demon blood—splatters all over my wall. Shit, I just touched up the paint in this house. What else can a girl do when it's just a waiting game? I'm a stress cleaner. Sue me.

Valant swipes at his cheek and looks at the blood on his fingers. He seems appalled at the sight. He gives me an annoyed look while pointing at my brother, as if I'm responsible for his damn safety. It's my home for god's sake and I don't want my room ruined. But I don't have time to intervene before Logan's agent training kicks in and he rushes Valant, kicking into the Demon's stomach and sending him sailing into my dresser, which thuds against the wall. Valant bounces off and falls hard to the ground.

Seeing my furniture still intact, though things are rattling around on top, I clasp my hand to my mouth to hold back the giggle that threatens to escape as I watch the Demon go down in his best suit. An answering black-and-red swirling fog consumes Valant and has me stumbling backward into Jax and pushing him away from what is about to be a serious smack down. Even as I retreat, I can't wipe the smile from my face. There must be something wrong with me. Why am I happy about watching my brother and Yi go toe to toe with Valant? Boredom? I'm a terrible sister. What if Logan gets hurt? The cyclone in my room reminds me that there's no stopping it now, so let's see what Logan can do.

Before Valant can bring his full power to bear, Yi swipes at the mist and reveals part of the Demon's form. This sudden opening lets Logan get in some good body shots, and was that a kick to the head? What is Valant doing in there? Changing into yoga pants? Yi continues to attack the mist, but even though Valant is taking some hits, he's eerily quiet. Logan seems to notice this as well, so he calls Yi back, moving away from the Demon and shouting at him to face him like the, and I quote, "fucking monster that he is."

Valant's weather show vanishes and he's fully exposed now. The Demon holds his side while his body vibrates with what looks like anguish. No, that's laughter. The bastard is just egging Logan on, and for what, to tire him out? Is he just bored as well? We're all sadists. Well, Valant surely is. Demon.

"Are you quite done with the patty cake lesson, little Oman? How about you and your parakeet there get a taste of a real beating." Spiraling power forms between Valant's long-fingered hands and is thrown at Yi first. The eagle changes his body structure, turning in mid-air into the stone-like statue he once was and merely absorbing the impact of the Demon's power before his flightless form falls toward the floor. Logan, with reflexes like a cat, quickly scoops him up with his left hand and squeezes before pressing the hard eagle totem to his right arm where Yi is absorbed and becomes his ink tattoo. Red-and-black swirls of magic race around the drawing on Logan's skin before running up his arm to his neck and then into his eyes, which flash wickedly at Valant. Holy shit. My brother's a badass. I'm the first to admit that I didn't get a single one of the fist-of-fury genes.

My glee is cut short. Valant looks totally confused and then super pissed when he sees my astonished and prideful face. He turns to Logan.

"What are you? You are not merely a human. What has the Yi done to you in your unnatural union? No one can absorb Demon power unless they are . . . a Demon as well."

What in the hell? Now my grinning cheeks fall and I look from Logan to Valant, waiting for my brother to defend himself. His answer, not the words of denial I was hoping for; instead, it's a menacing smile at the blond Demon and a holler of attack as he charges at him once again. Feigning a high hit at the Demon's head, Logan instead slides low, kicking out Valant's legs and sending him to the floor once again. In a blink, Logan pounces on the fallen Demon and proceeds to take it to him without restraint. Valant's face takes a few shots but it's Logan's arm that I'm concerned about. Yi appears to be in distress, trying to come out but unable. What has Logan done to him, or was it Valant? Whatever the case, and even if it may be nice to see someone finally getting the upper hand on Valant, especially after he posed as Greg's sidekick for nearly a year at Alex's expense, I don't like the way Yi is looking, nor is the Demon power I see radiating off Logan much of a warm fuzzy either.

Still clutching my sheet I take a step in their direction, but thank goodness I come to my senses, because now Valant's hand is on Logan's arm, inching for Yi with inky darkness oozing from his long, thin fingers. Pulling my power to me, I take their vision so they see only darkness. Jax pulls Logan off Valant and walks him to the opposite wall. My brother's eyes are cloudy white, but I know he'll only be distracted for a moment. Valant I allow to get up on his own, but I push him far from Logan and stay between the two of them.

"I don't know what that was, Valant, but if I had a guess, and trust me I'm as good at guessing as they come, I'd say you were just trying to take the Nanda-yi from my brother. Is that right? Yi is an ancient warrior against Demons, but you know that, don't you? When Logan took in your power I could tell that Yi was trying to get away from him, and who was there to scoop him up? Such a nice Demon foster parent you'd be, but no thanks. Now back off or I'll make you very unwelcome in my home." I give him a little shove, because I can, not that it moves him in the slightest. Dusting himself off and straightening his hair and jacket, Valant takes on an air of innocence while keeping his eyes on my brother whose own are narrowed at the Demon. I know Logan's allowing Jax to hold him back for now, but my man has very little real control over my twin. Unless he's hiding some tricks from me as well.

"Come now, Betty Boobs, I didn't know this would happen. Who knew your brother has demon abilities at his disposal. Now, my question is, did he have those before or after he killed a man in cold blood?"

How in the hell he knows about that I have no idea, and there we were, just getting over that dark part of our past, thank you, and I don't know what that has to do with what my brother has just done. All I know is that the look on Logan's face is of pure fury and hatred, and as much as I hate to say it, we kind of need Valant. Who knows if the magic he placed in Ryan's ring will fade if he leaves, but I can't take that chance. Plus, he may be the only one who can still travel to Alex, so I can't risk losing his help, not now.

"Logan, stop! It's okay." That's kind of an overstatement, but Valant won't hurt us with Alex gone. Annoy us to death? Maybe. Kill us with his fashion sense? Probably, but he wants Alex back, and until then, we're on the same team. Logan looks at me for a moment, then his eyes stay locked on Valant as I cross the room to Logan and touch the tattoo of Yi. The eagle calms slightly under Logan's skin, and I hope to have the same effect on my brother as well. "Logan. You're hurting Yi. Let Valant's power go. He isn't our enemy. We need him to help us get Alex back." The look in his eyes is broken and torn. Our history with Demons is a long and painful one, but Valant wasn't a part of that, and whatever just happened needs to be talked about, but not now.

The Demon power dissolves away and Yi is finally able to break free from his skin. Once he stretches his wings in the air, he lands on Logan's shoulder where he nips at him almost lovingly, and then sends a piercing screech akin to a *fuck you* to Valant who gives a you-can't-blame-a-Demon-for-trying shrug.

"Now let's start over, shall we? Logan, this is Valant. He is very sorry about his terrible manners and he will make sure he uses the door next time and won't ever try to attack us or steal our things again. Isn't that right, Valant?"

I could add that he must have forgotten about my ability to ship his ass out of this dimension, but busting his balls right in front of the boys could lead to some more senseless destruction, and I love my home. Logan's posture relaxes slightly, but Yi continues to tilt his head and stare oddly at the Demon in my room. Valant opens his mouth, perhaps to protest that he didn't start anything, but thinks better of it. Instead, his eyes meet mine and he gives the smallest of nods before he flickers away. Not a single word leaves my mouth before the doorbell rings.

"Son of a bitch!"

CHAPTER 4

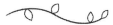

You Are Not Alone

I found serenity through the murkiness of my mind.
I reached my righteousness within the soft folds of these now restful nights.
I ended that life . . . so I could start anew.
Though you see me, though I silenced the rage
I am not who I once was–not the same.

If I didn't have to keep my mouth shut and play along right now, I would tell the damn Fae king exactly what is on my mind. It would be something poetic and beautiful, something like: *Listen, fucker! Your evil lies and treachery will not work! I can see right through your lame-ass tactics. Do you really think you can take me down with some fairy dream dust? I am Alex fucking Conner, the strongest of my kind, so stop being a pussy and give it to me straight. What in the hell do you want from me?*

But yelling into the dark, dank coldness of my jail cell will only give him the upper hand and probably have him deciding to starve me again, or maybe send his goons in to rough me up for real this time. Shit, I know I have to keep my new knowledge of what he is trying to do to me secret, but I've been down here for nearly two days since I saw Ryan, which could be weeks of worry back in my world, and the only people I have seen are the soldiers bringing me scraps for food and a medic making sure I'm not dying or dead. Their poking and prodding nearly had me choking one of them, but one's kind of helpless when Fae bodyguards on steroids overtake me and I don't have my power at my disposal.

I think it's safe to say that I'm worried his minions could tell I was on to them; Nic's eyes on my back could have burned a hole right through me. Plus, I might be using all these bold, brave words in my head, but the truth is, I only recently started reconnecting with my power in my own world, and I'm only mimicking what I've been told about my strength and heritage. I've only had a taste of what I am truly capable of a few times. Once when I was fourteen and shoved Steven into a hell dimension, another when I brought Shane back from the brink of death, and then just recently when I helped my father break free from the Demon who had possessed him, the fiend having succeeded in making my dad do terrible things before I even knew he was still alive. That was back when I thought my next step in protecting our world was to find the puppeteer behind my dad's entrapment. All of that changed the night I thought the only action I'd be seeing was to do with finally having Ryan's naked body in my bed. Boy, was I mistaken.

Okay, enough dwelling and pouting. It's time to figure out how in the hell I am going to get out of here. I can't risk my friends getting caught, which is why I warned Sandra that dream-Nic was asking about her through our barely holding on, crazy telepathy-thingy. Apparently Ryan had already told her; how he knew when he wasn't there is a mystery to me. Sandra and I agreed to lay low and not contact each other. Who knows if the king could use it against us? At least Ryan and Valant gave me another tool to help me fight the king's attempts to take my memories, my life, from me. The weight of the small metal bead where it lies attached to the feather in my hair is nearly as light as the feather itself, but I know it's there and it's saved me more than once. Touching Ryan in the Fae dream, his skin, his body pressed against me was as real as the last time we held each other; it makes sense—our minds are the reason we see, feel, and taste anything. Too bad that, for the most part, mine is being hijacked by King Douche.

The door at the top of the stairs opens. Its wood-and-stone body dragging against the floor makes my skin crawl with its grating chorus. I think I may have gotten daddy-dearests attention. He deserves the nickname. The King rarely speaks of Lestan, but he made sure that I knew he blamed me for his son's death. Although it seems he wants someone else in his world. *Who* is the puzzle, oh, and *why*. Maybe it's time to ask for forgiveness again. Ask to try to bring Lestan back? Hard to think that will work when it's pretty obvious that the king does not care. Goddess, what in the hell do I say to someone who's crazier than I am?

Footsteps, from more than one person, clump down the steps. I look at the world's worst friendship bracelet there on my wrist, ready to burn my ass to shit if I try to escape. No, I won't be busting out when the cell door opens, especially now I can no longer reach Gaia's power to send me home. That connection has been severed, though I know its raw energy flowed into me in the dream. Must have been coming through Ryan, just as it was when we stood together against the Demon in my father. Not to mention, and I mean really this is bullshit, I am a dimensional traveler, which is super cool, but when I really need to use it, can I? No, I can't. Fucking sweet.

My pity party is cut off when two medics, one a burly older woman who's been the main angel of death for me the last few days leading the march, while a new and much younger assistant follows with her head down. I try to get a better look at the newbie but not only is her face hidden by long red hair, it also appears to be shifting. She's using a cloaking spell. Well, I'm familiar with that trick. I've used it on many occasions. Wonder rises to the surface, along with curiosity about what's going on here and if her companions know what she's doing. I keep my mouth shut for now. Something pokes at my awareness, something calming and reassuring, but also teeming with suppressed vengeance.

Behind them at first, and now flanking the two women, are the Fae soldiers meant to keep me in line. I'm up now, on my tippy toes trying to see behind them for the king in his velvety cloak. I'm all for a cool cloak, hell, he can wear a dress for all I care, but his attitude is in major need of a makeover. Of course I can't talk; wearing the same jeans and T-shirt I was taken in and barely getting a chance to bathe is rather appalling. Not seeing him anywhere, I ease back down on my feet and make eye contact with Doctor Evil.

"What's the drill today m'lady? More needles and feel-ups? If I didn't know better, I'd say you have a thing for me, eh, Flean? Can I call you

Flea for short? I just love a good nickname." I give the hag my sweetest smile laced with all of my built-up intent. "Does your boss know? I mean, I don't think he'd like that. I mean, just look at this love dungeon he keeps me in. You know he wants me all to his little self." I crook my little pinky to show her what I think of the king's manhood, which earns me a sneer from the good doc. She wastes no time barking orders for my cell to be opened and my instant restraint. What they miss, and I do not, is the smirk on Red's face.

"It's your lucky day, Miss Conner. I've brought you a lovely concoction, one so strong you won't be able to break free ever again. Oh, it may have taken us some time, but we've engineered this beauty just for you. I can't say how much we love having you around. It's given us quite the challenge."

Damn it, they did know. Not wanting to show my cards by admitting that I was found out, I don't fight the beefcakes when they restrain my hands behind me. Hey, my arms may be held back but I could still cock one hell of a hip at her.

"Oh, and here I thought the Fae believed themselves all-knowing and far above we mere humans. Maybe you've been wrong all these millennia and your older-than-dirt asses need a nice swift enema to clear out those sticks up your asses." Looking over each shoulder in turn, I give the soldiers a little Alex Conner love as well. "I mean, am I right, guys? Guys?" With the force that I have come to expect from these douchebags, I am slammed against the back of the cell, and one even takes the time to grab hold of my jaw, shoving the back of my head against the wall with a crack. Through their muffling grasp I don't hold back one bit.

"Hit a sore spot, eh boys? No offense, ya know. After this is all said, done, and over with I'm sure we'll share a nice drink and a few laughs over this whole misunderstanding. Though not with you, Tean. Nope, you suck man! My fucking head hurts now, do you know that? You hurt me and for that I will not cheers you one bit, you cretin, no sir. Not one clink of the glass, or goblet, or whatever you freaking Faes call it."

"Enough, you little smart-mouthed bitch. Your fun time is over. Our king always gets what he wants, and I am always going to find a way to help him." With a last dashing smile from the doc she plunges the needle into my arm and a burning sensation blossoms from the injection site. Damn, that stings. "Now you see, Glena, nothing to fear from this human. After today, you and the boys can handle her yourselves. She'll never fully regain her strength after this liquid gift. Now come on in here, Glena. I'll let you clean her up a bit. That was a big needle for such a measly girl."

Now that hurts my feelings. After giving Tean a swift back kick that forces him to loosen his grip, I am able twist away from his arm. With my right hand free, I jab Den in the throat with my fist and then the nose with the heel of my hand before he has a moment to react. Just like that, now I'm able to get my hands on the good doc. No magic needed for this one. Nope, none . . . at all . . . crap, the drugs work quickly, and my outstretched hands fall short before they hit their mark around the older Fae medic's throat. Shit. Grabbing me not so delicately, the soldiers pick me up and toss me onto the hard cell bed. The loss of control over my body brings back memories of my abusive foster dad's home. Tears burn their way down my face, yet I can hardly register their existence as the numbness reaches my mouth and cheeks. Damn it. I will get out of this. This will not be my fate. Not after all I've been through and fought to survive, to move on from, and to become someone and something more. An Earthen Protector in the fight against evil; someone who protects the earth and those who can't protect themselves from the vile magics of my world and many others. But it all seems like a faraway life, something not of my own to live or have lived. Unable to move but still able to hear and see, I watch the sinister doctor leave, confident that I will not be a danger to Glena. If my eyes could shoot fire into the good doctor's ass she would be scorched from head to toe.

Frightened and pissed off, I am left alone with Red working diligently on the injection site. Once again a needle pricks my skin and the sensation of fluid rushing into my vein shoots up my arm. What the hell is she giving me now? Moving her hair back from her face, the medic positions herself in a way that allows me to see her fully. Once again her face fluctuates from beauty to plain. The beauty is the true girl in this cell, and not the plain-looking Glena she poses as. Knowing it's not just the drugs messing with my sight, I study her face. There's something familiar about her that I can't put my finger on.

35

"Alex, don't be afraid. I am an ally and I promise I can help free you. However, you must promise to help me in return. My name is Verus. I am Lestan's sister."

The princess? How can she want to help me? Why wouldn't she want me dead? This is not in a million years who I thought would come to my aid. I'm still hoping he'll show soon. That is, if he even knows I'm here.

"Don't worry," she whispers. "I know my father is the one truly responsible for Lestan's death. He has proven many times that he doesn't care about us—his children—only himself. Maybe part of him did once, but he's been lost to his madness for far too long. The last year Lestan was doing his bidding, our father turned his controlling insanity onto me. He vowed to cast me out of the kingdom and tear my rightful place from me unless I marry a man. He won't accept my true love and he has threatened to harm me, to kill me even. Please, we can assist each other. Will you promise to help me, please?"

Not being a fan of anyone who tells a person who to love, let alone who to be attracted to, I'd help this girl in an instant if I weren't worried about this being some sort of trap. Perhaps sensing my unease, Verus reaches out to me slowly, words tumbling from her lips. "We don't have much time since they have already injected you. I can fight it off for a while but we must hurry. Please, trust me."

Once her hand touches my face, a fog settles in, obscuring my vision. Verus and my cold, dirty cell disappear. My mind slips into something new, foreign, and the brightness of a warm sunny day is nearly blinding. I'm unexpectedly in a body that is not my own. Looking down, I see a beautiful floral skirt, and soft, pale, freckled hands lie in my lap. A wild red strand of hair flies into my line of sight and tickles my cheek. It's as if I'm watching a scene from a movie and I'm the lead. Delicate fingers grab my hair and tuck it gently behind my ear. Not my ear. Verus's ear. I have slipped into her body, into this, what? Memory. A beautiful Fae girl, whom my own lips lovingly call Misa, sits on soft green grass next to me. I touch the small green blades with my fingertips and raise my head to the sun, basking in its warming glow. I smile and send a prayer of thanks to the goddess.

Misa's hand trails along my arm and I lean in, kissing her soft lips, touching her hair. Well, this is new. Foreign thoughts and emotions spark within my soul. My chest tightens and aches for her, driving a need to take in every part of her appearance. Her shining, nearly black hair that falls straight to her shoulders, the almond shape of her beautiful brown eyes, the paint stains on her hand that I now hold, and the shape of her small frame in her sundress—this is true. An unwavering love, one so entirely obvious to me, real, and evermore heartbreaking if Verus's father is indeed forbidding it. This is a vision unlike any I have been in before. With her magic I have become Verus, and I'm able to take in everything she experienced in this moment. Sensing eyes on me, I look up to see Verus herself sitting a mere ten feet away, alone on an intricately carved bench. She's able to come into her memories as part of the backdrop, watching with a smile, though tears fall unhindered as both pain and happiness are reflected on her face. Forbidden love, one worthy of Shakespeare or Disney, but this has more of a Joss Whedon no-happily-ever-after dramatic flair to it. This is her gift, sending me here, to a time within her own life, a time that proves this part of her tale is undeniably true.

Even though this body is not mine, and the fluttering heart beating wildly while I look at the woman next to me isn't mine at all, it is nice to feel in control of movement and to have contact with someone again. Moments after the thought leaves my mind the surroundings change and I'm somewhere else entirely. Here I sit, in a hard chair within a cool room. My skin misses the free open space and the warmth of the sun. But the chill isn't from the change in location alone. No, I am frightened, sad, and when my eyes slide to the right I see the reason for my fear. Verus has brought me to dinner with Daddy. Thoughts scream inside my head, thrashing and gnashing at my skull, demanding that I tear him apart. Confusion grips my head like a vise. The pressure is unyielding as an unknown force turns the lever and I swear I can feel my skull cracking. My mind meshing with Verus's has created a vacuum of reverberating anger, hers and mine both aching to burst out and take the king down. Yet instead, tears not of my own fall silently down my face and I glance at the empty seat across from me while Verus's heart and mind say one name in such a painfully heartbroken voice—Misa.

"I don't know why you are crying, my dear. A man of great wealth and power, someone who will make your family even stronger and kept in the many riches you are accustomed to, will make you his bride. How can that not make you happy? I, for one, know I will be."

Murmurs of agreement sound around me and I realize for the first time that we are not alone. Others eat along with us. The two men either side of me make me wary. Is Verus being guarded at dinner, and for whose protection? Looking around, I see Verus on a cushioned bench by the fire across the room. Shoulders tense and hands clenched, she sits, watching herself relive this moment.

Lips, mine but not mine, answer him but I don't raise my head to give him the satisfaction of looking upon my suffering. "But I don't love him. I love . . ."

With a strike of his fist upon the thick wood table, a blow hard enough to rattle solid metal dishes and vicious enough to bring glasses crashing to the floor, the king keeps his daughter from uttering her final word.

"You love who? That lowly waif of a *girl*? That pitiful artist with nothing to her name? She doesn't even have a mother or father. An orphan, living off you, disguised as your friend and you dare tell me she is more than such? You are a disgrace, daughter. She must have put a spell on your poor dulled mind. No daughter of mine will engage in such an insult. A woman and a man alone join together in this world, my world. Do you hear me? How dare you try to bring her to my house, to eat my food under the guise of friendship, and then to try and throw this in my face when I've already promised you to Char. You are *my* child. I am the reason you are in this world, daughter, and I am the only reason you are *still* in this world."

With Verus's hair creating a veil around my sight, my eyes widen at the mixture of the bright oranges and reds of a sunrise. The vision stirs and fans the surging force that's been simmering throughout my body along with photograph-like memories of a woman who can only be Verus's mother. My face lifts. I know this show will reveal her intent on defying her father—but at what cost?

"You cannot tell me who to love, *Father*. You may have been able to control Lestan with your lies and manipulations, but you cannot control me." Standing, my hands touch the shoulders of the two men on either side of me. So far they've stayed relatively quiet, yet once these borrowed hands touch them, they rise, grabbing their knives from the table. With a flick of their wrists, the knives are thrown at the king, each one burying in the wood of his chair, barely missing his face on either side. Verus has them under her control, and just by simply touching them as she touched me. Why does this girl need me when this is the power she controls?

The answer comes in a resounding yell when the king retrieves the knives from his chair and throws them back, striking their marks with their sharp ends, pinning the two men under Verus's spell to the table by their hands. Two faces reflect the confusion about what has happened, and they begin to plead with the king for forgiveness, words flying around about never turning against his wishes, of their families needing them, literally begging the man who rules their world for their lives. Both voices are full of fear, for they must know he cares for no one but himself and his power. Steven was such a man. But look what happened to him. The higher they are, the farther they fall.

Hollering out, the king summons his soldiers to remove everyone from the dining room, aside from his daughter. Screams lead to bloody hands wrapped in napkins and then to a scuffling of hurried feet. The closing door marks the beginning of her father's sentencing. I ache to move, to get Verus out of here, yet my muscles won't respond. I'm paralyzed once again with my eyes held open, forcing me to watch what will happen next.

Without missing a beat, and bereft a care for the blood pooling and dripping from his table, the king begins to eat once more, tearing into a hunk of bloody meat and raking his fork and knife sharply against his plate. "You may have the abilities of your mother, but you will never have your freedom from me. Don't forget. Banishment or death are your only choices. You see what your brother chose, allowing that Demon to take his life. If you choose banishment, know that she will not be coming with you. Your Misa will not be going anywhere—not even her chest will be allowed to rise and fall with her breath. Am I understood?" Blood drips from the corner of his mouth as he gives me a fearsome and calculating smile. "Don't be stupid, Verus. You will marry Char or I will ensure that you never see Misa again." An icy dread fills me. I know the look of pure evil and that is exactly what I am up against. Lestan's twisted father is all the clearer now.

Oh Lestan, my Lestan, my Justin, did he truly allow himself to be killed to escape his father? Did he think he was saving me by disappearing, by dying? He mustn't have known all of what the king wanted from me, because if he had, he would have known that his "sacrifice" would unleash another wave of horror into my life. Verus is showing me what this man is capable of, and if I can help her, I will.

As the vision fades, I reach out to grab Verus's hand. It must have been hard for the princess to show me one of the best days of her life followed so closely by the worst. From her trembling, she seems to have relived every part of it all over again by showing it to me. A spectacular display of power, yes, but as with us all, at a cost.

Ignoring her tears, she speaks quickly and quietly. "Try not to move too much. You're supposed to be drugged up, remember? Play the part in case someone comes to check on us." I nod and move my hand from hers, letting it rest by my side on this shitty bed. "Will you help me? Together we can break you free, and my Misa."

"Of course I want to help you, but I'm worried about what help I can possibly be when I have no access to my Earthen abilities. I can barely keep from forgetting who I am thanks to yo . . . to his wickedness." I stay away from saying "your father" after what I've just witnessed. She doesn't need the reminder. I also hold on to my questions about her brother. I am not the only one in here who must grieve the loss of someone I loved.

"There are ways around the different prisons my father has built to confine you. I can help you when he tries to put you in the dream world where you'll forget your past, and I may also be able to help you reconnect to the goddess's energy, for we will need it to escape this place, all three of us."

"So you choose banishment? Do you really think he won't come after you once he finds out what we've done? He was able to take me away from some very powerful friends back in my world. How will you keep him from finding you? That is, assuming we can get out of this hellhole. Sorry. I'm sure this is a lovely place, aside from your leadership issues. At least, it was when I visited Lestan, but that was long ago."

The look on Verus's face is unnerving but not calculating or evil. No, it looks similar to the one I saw in the mirror when I knew what I had to do to be rid of Steven. It's a look that makes me quiver.

"Oh, he won't find me. He won't be finding anyone. Before I leave this 'hellhole,' as you say, he's going to die. Misa and I are only leaving to find my mother, to bring her back to her rightful place here in the kingdom where she will fix all he has wrought upon our lives and our people." Her mother is alive? Lestan always thought her dead. I click quickly through the times Lestan and I spoke of losing a parent and think about how things are so different now. My father is alive, and it seems Lestan's mother is as well. In Verus's vision, the king spoke of banishment or death. He must have banished their mother from the kingdom and, instead, told his children she had died. Oh man, the Fae king's asshole-chocked evilness just keeps getting sicker and sicker.

"Lestan and I thought our mother died from a rare illness when we were both very young. Turns out it was another one of my father's lies. He gave it away during one of his tirades about his arrangement for me to marry Char. Our mother knew what he was before we did, and he feigned her death to replace the truth. If anyone dares to defy the great king of Avalon, they either mysteriously disappear or are executed. She knew the truth of our father's madness while others still believe the lie that his ability to keep things orderly are due to his intelligence and charm." Verus stands, pretending to rummage for something in the medical bag, and the power radiating off her body causes her to quiver slightly as she continues. "The majority of the Fae people have no idea, not a single notion of how insane he really is. They only see that he provides them with what they need to survive. They do not see how subtly he has them all under his control, nor do they know that anyone who opposes him are dealt with swiftly and unbeknownst to any who would care. There's more I could tell you about Avalon, but we don't have much time. We have a king to overthrow and you and I are going to make sure he knows who's responsible for the last breath he'll ever take."

Oh, I *like* her. She reminds me so much of myself and maybe a little of my foster sister, Chey. With all of her spirit, I find myself believing in her confidence in getting us out of here. How, though, is something I can't wait to hear.

41

"Okay, Verus. I'm in. What's the plan?"

Her smile has a touch of impishness and of relief. "Firstly, I will be the one giving you the dream potion, which is how they immerse you in the world they are building to make you lose yourself and to trick you into getting what they want. I won't inject you with the memory-taking part though, so you will need to put on your best act in the dreams. They must not know that you are no longer under their influence, and when you are back in your cell you must continue the lie. No matter what they do, because they will try to trick you every step of the way, you must not break. You must live in the lies to fool them all."

It's like being asked to go undercover. I only hope I don't get lost in the façade or get amnesia or something like Crockett in *Miami Vice*.

"I will be seeing you daily and have been charged to watch you for a time. My duty is to make sure the potion is functioning. I've been working on how we can get access to your powers back and how to build you up. We will be protected. No one will know what we are doing. Misa is an artist, yes, but what Father doesn't know is that she can change surroundings to appear one way when they are not at all what they seem. It's as if she creates a stage, showing them what they want to see while we are doing quite the opposite. It's how I have fooled them all and become their assistant Glena."

I take a gulp, wondering what lengths Verus may have gone to for this to work.

"And the real Glena?"

A dark, fleeting look of regret crosses Verus's face, but for only a moment. "We had to do what was necessary." She searches my eyes for the shock I suspect is plain to see. Then she gives a hearty laugh. So the Fae have jokes. Good to know. "She is happy, with plenty of riches to keep her and her family in good fortune forever. Of course, she had to return home as someone else, and they have all given their oath to keep the secret, but once Father is dead, she will be free again."

Now that's a much better outcome than the finger across the throat I got of her and Misa as they disposed of the real Glena and plotted their next move. Do you blame me? My experiences with Fae so far have been wicked and cruel, to say the least, though never with Lestan. It was Justin who attacked me that night, and now I am left to wonder if my Lestan had existed within the skin and bones that was my boyfriend. I want to speak his name to Verus, but this is all too much to take in as is; we will have to speak of him later, and when we do, I'll need to prepare for the hope that I can somehow bring him back to inevitably shatter all around me.

"Oh, and to show my good faith and promise of a trustworthy partnership, I have brought you these." Verus opens her palm to reveal two small wooden hairpins. Serenity and Chaos, the charmed fighting staffs Dana made for me. "Misa left exact duplicates in my father's vault, minus the embedded power yours have. Who made these for you? I must meet him."

"Her," I reply. "Dana, the Mistress of Potions and Weaponry, to be exact. Thank you for bringing them. It's nice to know I have some sort of protection now. Though I won't be able to use them properly with this thing on." I narrow my eyes at my wrist and she touches it lightly.

"We have a plan for that, but in the meantime hide the pins well—as well as those." Her eyes move to the feather and silver bead hidden in my hair. "Your friends have sent you powerful objects that will serve us well. Should my help falter at any time, or if anything should happen to me, I hope these magics can hold for just long enough." She touches the bead-adorned feather where I had thought it out of sight and tucks it away for me before taking my hand. "If you trust me well enough now, I have an idea." Oh boy, this should be good. "I can make a shallow piercing in a spot no one can see, and we will place the pins in there. You will just have to keep them from being pushed out since they will be a shallow and oddly placed piercing. Can you do that? I mean, I have heard rumors of your abilities, so perhaps this is something you can ensure?"

"How, when I have *this* keeping me from drawing any power from Gaia?" Our eyes drop to my wrist.

"I can help with that temporarily. Just be ready."

Well, okay then. If I can tap into my healing abilities, can I keep my body from healing too quickly, and instead have it form protection around the staffs, taking them in as a part of me that must stay? Is that not in fact exactly what I did to Steven, making his body break apart, forbidding him to heal while I returned him to the earth where he was then shifted to another dimension? Hell ya, I can.

I nod to Verus and pretend to scratch at an area at the bottom of my hairline. There, in case they show through my skin, my hair can cover them. She gives a smile of agreement and then turns me over slightly, giving her access to the area.

"This may hurt a bit."

The princess digs around in her pack, eventually producing a large gauge sterile needle. I focus on anything but what is going to happen next, choosing to hide within my mind as a way to brace for the pain. She breaks through the skin on my right side first, piercing it with the needle and then replacing the metal with one of the pins. Ah, Chaos. Fitting that she chose that one first. There's no Serenity in my life at this moment, barely ever has been. She dabs where warmth is leaking. The blood may not stop without my assistance since we daren't risk a bandage that someone else may notice.

"Okay." She grips my wrist and an icy pool floods my skin. Without hesitation, I send a touch of healing to the site, not much, just enough to stop the bleeding. Once I can tell the blood has coagulated just enough, I will my skin to form a callus, allowing the staff to become one with me. It's easier than I thought, though why not, the staffs are a part of me, almost an extension of my hands.

Just as I'm thinking everything is hunky dory, I hear heaving sounds of struggled breath demanding my attention, so I steal a glance over my shoulder only to nearly jump off the bed in shock at the sight of Verus. Her face is breaking out in beads of sweat as her hand holds the magical shackle on my wrist. She's taking in the power that keeps me from using my abilities; all that pain and fire is rushing into her, and her face is softly contorting in pain from her will to keep it together. I make a move to help her but abandon that plan when she instantly lifts her other hand to placate me.

"I have this. Please don't touch me or we may both be aflame. You've eased off so I am fine now. Let's finish this, as we must." Never one to tell a woman what she can't handle, I honor her request and stay still for the next piercing. Serenity's smooth wood gliding in is like a promise, or maybe more of a plea or a prayer. My time will come, but when is anyone's guess. This time I work at a swifter pace, unable to bear the thought of causing Verus discomfort.

"It's done." My whisper is a prayer of relief for the princess. When her breath regulates again and her hand withdraws from my wrist, I relax, knowing that at least this physical pain has ended.

Having the fighting staffs with me again provides a renewed sense of hope. I am armed, with connections to my friends through the feather and the bead. Valant has thankfully made the silver ball even more potent by giving me a boost to counteract the Fae lobotomy. Now, topped with Verus's help, I believe my luck will turn around very soon. These staffs helped me defeat the Demon in Montana, bringing my father back to us again. Oh, how I long to use them on the damn royal bastard in this Fae world. The thought of a couple good cracks at his body parts brings a devilish Cheshire grin to my face.

A tingling sensation starts at my fingertips and toes before beginning to radiate up my arms and legs. My mind becomes fuzzy and my sight is giving in to an encroaching darkness. No! Damn it. I'm losing myself to the drug from that ogre Flea. Shit. I haven't even been able to ask Verus if she knows what her dad wants from me. She'll be back tomorrow—I hope.

"Eila, I am so sorry." She uses my true name, Eila, the earth. It's one spoken by only a few, one of the last being Lestan when he begged me to come with him. Is this where I would've ended up if I had complied, or did he have a plan to save me? I fear he may not have had a way, not with the spell he was under. His father was in command, I am certain of it, and I would be just as doomed as I am now. Or was. Now, with Verus's help, I'll break out of this prison.

There are tears in her eyes as she looks at me.

"I was only able to temporarily stop Flea's potion, but what I have given you will continue to help by slowly eating away at her concoction. This is the last time, I promise. You must fight, but do not let them know. Use the weapons your friends gave you, and soon you will be able to use these as well." Verus's finger touches the hidden spot in my neck and her tears cease. How can she care so much for a stranger? She is so much like her brother. He barely knew me, yet he cared for me in a way no one else has. How did that crazy king create two such amazing beings? They must take after their mom.

"Know that I will be back for you, Eila. You aren't alone in Avalon anymore."

My body has become immobile once again as the drugs burn through the last of whatever Verus used to put its progression on hold.

"Remember who you are, Eila. Lestan loved you. He told me so often. He spoke of your bravery and power, even when the darkness consumed you. You can do it again, you know you can, because you've done it before."

Yes I have, but even then, under Steven's control, I had my mind. Down here, in this dungeon, the king is taking it over and over again, hijacking it for his own gain. I can't let him have what he wants, because after seeing how he treated his own daughter and how he cared less about his own wife and son, I know he will kill me the instant he gets it.

CHAPTER 5

Ryan

by taking my heart
you have imprisoned my mind to think only of you.
by leaving
you have paralyzed and bound me to the despair where I now reside.

✳

"**P**acing like a caged tiger is not going to help anyone, and your nonsense is bringing me to the edge as well, so knock it off, hot shot. You succeeded. She has the ring and it'll help protect her, so take a seat!"

Dana's words seem easy enough to obey, but she doesn't know how overwhelming my unease was. There in the vision where Alex didn't even know who I was. I was almost too late, and that was weeks ago. The next time I may be, which is what scares me. After all that time watching her on the Council's behalf when she didn't even know I existed, to the times we touched, kissed, slept next to each other in Arizona, and then when I lost her when she believed we had no future together, we were finally going to have our chance. Our time. Then she was taken.

Being back within the Council walls isn't making things any better. Someone here was controlling Lex's father, forcing him to murder Healers. I can't even focus on investigating that with Lex missing; it was something we were supposed to be doing together.

There are a lot of things we are supposed to be doing together. Dancing with her, pressing against her body, it made my pulse quicken, though if this had been real and not a vision, I would have been able to bring her home. But instead she slipped away again. Her eyes tear at my soul. Since the first day I met her I wanted to make her mine, and just when we could finally be together, I what, run home and leave her alone? Unprotected? Stupid. Stupid. After all she's been through, I should've known better—been better.

I tried to leave her alone after my feelings for her got in the way and nearly caused a bloody mess when we tracked Greg to the Pacific Ocean. Jealousy after seeing her back with Justin jacked up my judgment. I'd never experienced any emotion that intense until I saw her kissing him outside Rapture. I let that shit get in the way of my duty to her, and we almost died. Stupid. Stupid. When I get her back, I swear on my life that I will never let anything get in the way of her safety again, especially when the cost may be her own. But first, I must get her back to prove it to her.

And how in the hell am I supposed to do that when I can't control all the variables in this fight? Especially Valant. That filthy Demon may be the very reason she's trapped in Avalon. Hitting the wall with my fist wasn't what Dana had in mind when she said I should stop pacing, but it sure kicked some of my frustration away.

"Why does he keep leaving like that?" I shout. "We still have work to do and he just takes off before I can even let him know what happened. He's been gone for weeks, doing what? Pestering Sandra? We need to get back to California. Working on this from here is driving me nuts!"

But I know why. Valant is a Demon. He's not part of a team. He's only ever and will only ever care about himself. I still can't wrap my head around why he's even helping, aside from needing to feed off Lex's chaotic life, siphoning off her emotions like all Demons do. Valant was drawn to her in that basement Greg held her in months ago, just as I was when I first laid eyes on her, but the big difference between us is that he only wants to use her; no Demon cares for anyone but themselves—ever.

Damn it! All I want to do is protect her, touch her, make her happier and stronger, and I'm not going to do that here. The velvety coverings on the couches and benches in this borrowed Council office should be soft and inviting, but they feel hard and cold to me, which may be why my body is refusing to sit. After what happened to Lex's dad, all the offices

48

are getting a thorough search and overhaul for clues. They've been in my office for quite a while, which is making me steel my thoughts in readiness for my next act of betrayal. The Council's actions have been triggering that sort of behavior in me for some time now. It's why I've kept Lex's true abilities hidden from them, even though I was supposed to locate the one who carried both the ability to protect and to heal, the first in countless generations to do so, the one they believe could possibly be more powerful than anyone else alive. They still don't know she's the one they've been searching for, but even if they did, I wonder if they'd be able to get her back?

In the meantime, the terrible distraction at her father and the Healers' expense has bought me some time, though not much. Eyes like magnets hone onto me when I walk the halls. They know I'm keeping something from them, but I don't think they're bothering to blame me when an agent may have been behind the killings. Trust is now even harder to come by.

So far I've found very little on Avalon in the data system. Either they know more and have hidden the information even with the clearance Dana has been able to get us, or the Council isn't all knowing after all. Just fairytales, that's all Sandra said her family ever knew. Tales of ancient people called the Fae, believed to be the first beings after the gods and goddesses built our many worlds. A cocky lot, if you ask me. Well, when I get my hands on any of them, if they've harmed Lex, I'll show them who they can bow down to.

"Ryan, you know that if you could travel this world as Valant does you'd be flitting here and there just as much. However or wherever or whatever his reasons may be, he's been indispensible. Alex became aware in that blasted Fae nightmare and was able to remember. Oh, don't give me that pouty look, beefcake. I'm sure your little bauble and man hands touching her brought about just as much recall, at least at the primal level."

I laugh out loud, which is out of character for me, but this angry regret has me needing a way to keep my head on straight. Not to mention that even though Dana's skill with weapons and potions may be the best there is, it's her ability to add light to dark times that is every now and then even more valuable.

"Feel better?"

Dana is giving me a wary look. She's right to. I don't know the last time I laughed. Not once since Alex left.

"I'll feel better when we have her back. How is Vex? I know that took a lot out of him. Should I visit him or do you still suggest we wait? He's the only one of us who's ever truly been to Avalon, and for all we know he may be the only way we can get her back. We can't risk Sandra trying again; that king's got her in his sights now. If he gets his hands on her, they'll both end up prisoners."

Dana brings the tips of her fingers to her lips and closes her eyes trying to hold on to her patience with me before she responds. "Vex is lucky to be alive. He was nearly destroyed by that Demon inside Alex's father. Thanks to Alex and Terra he survived, but he's a shade of his former self. And Alexander is powerful in his own right, at least doubled by the Demon who merged with him during the Healer deaths."

I roll my shoulders just thinking about Terra. I've dealt with my share of shady characters in my work for the Council, but Terra still manages to scare the shit out of me. She's older than time itself, and I suspect she may be a direct descendent of one of the original goddesses that created the worlds.

"Lex is devastated by what's happened to Vex. You know she's known the fox since she was a child. He's been one of the few constants in her life. Regardless of what we may need from him now in order to help her, don't you think he deserves—she deserves—to have her friend back? Stacy would want that for her daughter, and so would Alexander."

I'm driving ahead now, pushing to sway Dana to agree with my plan. She isn't looking at me like I'm completely incapable, this time, so I don't let up. "We keep waiting for Vex to get better, but his weakness is making it impossible to travel to Avalon. Even Terra hasn't been able to help him get his full strength back. We know Alex's father could help him. He's her own flesh and blood, after all, and passed on his Healer gift to her. We need to tell Stacy that they have to come out of hiding and help us."

Dana looks down at her feet. "We're already in deep, my boy. Being here with the Council is sketchy at best. Soon, I'm sure, they're going to demand the information you're holding back about Alex. She's the one they sent you to find and you haven't given them much in return. Now, what do you suppose they'll do when they realize she's Stacy's daughter? You know they won't fall for some story about Stacy not knowing about her daughter's powers, and then we'll have all three Conners being hunted. On top of all that, they want someone to pay for the dead Healers, and Stacy and Alexander need time to build his case. If you bring them out of hiding now, all pawns are in play and we may all be exposed."

As always, things are a bloody mess.

"She doesn't even know Lex has been taken, does she?"

This time Dana doesn't look down. Instead, her eyes bore into mine as she takes a few steps to close the space between us. She may be much smaller and much older than I am, but there's no denying her power. It seeps from her while she also contains it between us. No one knows who she really is here; she's a talented potions master who's been posing as my mother for days. "If I tell Stacy, you know she won't be able to keep it from Alex's father. No one knows exactly what state he is in. For all we know he can wipe out the entire Fae race with a flick of a finger."

She's being rational, I know that, but my thoughts have been spinning, bordering on irrationally desperate. Desperate enough to have a passing thought of caring less if the Fae race is eradicated, not if it means I get Lex back.

"Why don't we reach out to them, check in and see what's happening. Let me do it. I won't tell them she's gone. It will purely be to assess things. Maybe he's in better shape than we thought. Maybe he can help us get Alex back unawares by healing Vex, or, if nothing else, we can find out what they know about Avalon. We're shackled by limited knowledge. Stacy's a Council agent and she may have intel we need. She knows we're looking for help inside the Council, people we can trust. I'm the one inside, so let me try to get help without them knowing why."

Dana turns away. The fact that she won't look at me causes my muscles to tense. She doesn't trust me.

"Only one point of contact and that's me. We agreed, remember?" Dana's reminder doesn't deter my reasoning.

"Yes, I know, but that was an agreement with Alex. Now that she's gone, I think we need to consider other options. My job is to read and track people. I'm good at what I do. We need them, Dana."

That earned me a swift turn on her heel. This isn't going to be good.

"As I said, Ryan." Damn, she nearly chips a tooth saying my name. "If we open all the lines of contact, teasing to reveal all our cards, someone in the Council is bound to be tipped off sooner or later. What happens if they find out Alex is with the Fae, and a prisoner no less? I can see evil deals being brokered to trade for her, which gives her a new prison here. Or perhaps they'd see her as a liability. The Fae having Earthen Protector and Healer secrets and blood may lead the Council to decide she's better off dead than alive where the Fae can use her. Remember why you've gone rogue, and that the Council doesn't know that little secret of yours and how that's working to our advantage now and for our needs in the future."

My jaw clenches and I feel my eyes narrow. Does she not care what Alex is going through? How can she be so calm?

"Easy there, big boy. We are going to get her back, but we're going to do it the right way. Don't doubt your girl's ability to survive. Plus, you don't know Stacy like I do. There's fragility in that woman. You've mainly seen the hardline professional Earthen Protector, but she's been through hell and she will never forgive herself for what happened to Alex. Alex wouldn't want her mother or her father put in danger, so let's honor her wishes. Inside, you know this is the right thing to do. Your Lex will be grateful for this decision—that I promise you."

"Fine." Taking a deep breath, I shove my rising anger down, knowing my emotions fail to stay in check where Alex is concerned. "I'll agree. For now. But if we don't get her back soon, unharmed, I will bring this up again and I won't be as agreeable. Now let's get out of here. We have what we came for and I need to go hit something."

Dana and I grab the files on what little the Council knows of Avalon, along with data on agents we hope turn out to be trustworthy and those who seemed suspiciously missing or recently reassigned.

After pounding and sweating my anger out in my parents' home gym, I'm in need of a shower and a bed. Sleep has been difficult knowing Alex is out there, alone and being stripped of her memories for a mad king's gain. Lying in my bed, the Arizona air so hot I can only stand to lie naked on top of the covers, I try to run through what happened the night Alex was attacked. Sandra got all of her memories back, and Valant's small pieces here and there revealed that her on-off boyfriend Justin—or Lestan, although it really doesn't matter to me who he was—was trying to take her away against her will. Valant killed him without a second's thought. Would I have done the same if I'd been the one who heard Alex's fear in my mind? Would I have snapped Justin's neck or would I have given him a chance to explain? Alex told Sandra that Justin didn't appear to be in control. Valant won't admit it, but I think he knew that but wasn't taking any chances. Maybe that's one good thing about Demons; they don't usually gamble unless the odds are stacked highly in their favor. The odds against a Fae prince had to be dicey at best, and I don't doubt that I'd know that as well, leaving Justin in the same place he is now—underground.

The reliving of the story begins to push my mind toward sleep. I don't deserve to rest, but Alex needs me at my best and that means I have to get some sleep. Perhaps I'll dream of her or of a way to save her. Either way, I expect any dreams will be filled with angst and worry. Sleeping a couple hours at a time hasn't allowed for much in REM land. Maybe tonight will be different. If I hold a picture of her in my mind, will she come to me? Dream Lex is better than any part of this reality without her.

CHAPTER 6

Dreams

My eyes travel along your body
As tones of my heart titillate your eardrums.
You are my treasure
A fount of endless pleasures.

✳

How did I even get here? Wasn't I just housesitting for Sandra? I can clearly remember her instructions. *Go easy on my closet, Alex. Don't try on everything, Alex. Don't make me replenish the bar again, Alex.* I must be going crazy. Didn't Nic keep calling me asking me where she went and when she was going to be back just a while ago? He was acting like it was some sort of emergency, and when I told him she was back home he acted like he had no earthly idea where that was—the crazy loon. Once I told him she was back in Virginia with Logan and Jax, he practically hung up on me. He's being way more diva-ish than usual.

Then I must have fallen asleep, but then I wake in some pimp penthouse? Seriously, where the hell am I? An alien unknown pushes at my chest. I must be dreaming. I try gathering my hair out of my face; waves and curls are flying in all directions, but I begin to tame them with a hair tie I finally find after fumbling around and knocking over shit on the bedside table. When I smooth my bangs back I feel something in there. Hah! It's a feather with a small bead attached to it, secured like an extension. The soft feather seems to tickle me all the way from my fingertips to my toes before being replaced with a sensation of soft sand and warm water. The saltwater air is cool and invigorating, but there's a humidity to it that is absent on the west coast. A voice slips into my mind, calling my name. A man. Logan? He's saying something else that I cannot make out. Something like losing or lost. Something about a connection, and just like that, the ocean air is gone and the feather goes stagnant and cold. Odd. Yep, this must be a dream, and Logan is floating around in it for some peculiar reason.

My fingers, sliding down my head, touch the bead and a cool liquid smoothness rushes into me, changing to heat and fire as it works its way down my belly and into the warmth between my legs. Holy shit, it's hot in here. Throwing back the covers, I spy the seriously sexy lingerie I have on. Deep cobalt blue bra and panties with plenty of see-through lace slithers sensually against my skin. I'm liking this dream more and more.

A knock at the door freezes me in place. Who can be here when I don't even know where here is? I inch to the door and peek through the eyehole.

"Alex? Alex, are you there? Where are you? I can feel you close. Please, please open the door."

Regardless of whoever that deliciously fine man is at the door, I am not an idiot. Opening that door is in the first scene in the slasher movies from hell and I am not going out like that. I smooth my hair back again before I nervously run my fingers through my ponytail as I inch away. My nail hits the bead again and pictures of that man outside my door rush through my head, of him sitting with me wiping my tears, holding my hand in the ocean waves, and of lying next to me with my hand in his while a ring of never-ending moons, suns, and stars glows in the darkness. And suddenly I'm wide awake. Ryan. My Ryan. I fling open the door.

We don't wait for words. I have no doubt it's the real him. Somehow, with the help of his bead, I've escaped another one of the Fae king's tricks and fallen into our own dream together—a Dreamwalk as Dana and Vex call them. Ryan slams the door, using one hand to lock it behind him while the other wraps around my waist and pulls me to him. He walks me backward, farther into the room. His lips find mine in a ravenous urgency, suddenly taking my breath away. This was how that night Lestan died was supposed to go—Ryan and me, pressed together in ecstasy and passion, and I am not going to lose my chance again, even if it's only a dream.

He turns us around during our passionate progression and my back hits the wall. "Lex, Jesus I want you. I can't stand not having you near me."

He touches my face and his eyes ignite with their silver power. My body is on autopilot, rubbing and moving against him as his hands roam possessively over every inch of me. His soft lips trail kisses along my neck and when they brush the top of my bra I start panting. He groans into my chest while his fingers touch the smooth satin and lace. I can feel my nipples pushing against the fabric, begging for skin-to-skin touch. Hooking a finger down, he frees my right breast and takes it into his mouth. My head falls back, carelessly smacking against the wall.

Even though my hands have been pretty much plastered to his back and hips while he ravishes me, they are now uncontrollably seeking the hem of his shirt because that shit is coming off *right now.* All I want is to touch his taut, trembling stomach. With his shirt off an instant later I am welcomed by smooth, strong muscles. I want to dig my nails in and knead him like a cat in heat. Another situation is begging for my attention, but before I unzip his pants, my hand moves along him, touching the growing need pressing against his jeans. My knees quiver at the thought of him deep inside me, and are those tears of joy springing to my eyes?

My brain suddenly gets hijacked, drugged by the sensations of what his mouth, teeth, and tongue are doing to my breasts. The warmth down low in my body is about to overflow and my fingers fumble as I try to free him from his jeans and boxers. Once the jeans fall to the ground he lifts me so I can wrap my legs around him, crying out when I feel his hot, hard stomach pressing against me and his tight, firm erection pulsing against my wet panties. He lays me down on the bed, and his intoxicating body moves off me. I hate the absence of it, even if it's only for a split second, but then I give myself a mental slap in the face as I realize I'm getting a full-on show of nearly naked Ryan. His body is a fucking temple and I am aching for him to enter me, but not before he fully displays himself, that is, driving me mad now that he's removing his boxers and standing in front of me smiling at the look on my face. I lick my lips, not caring in the least about his *hey, my eyes are up here* look; instead, I'm on autopilot, crawling to the edge of the bed and taking him fully into my mouth.

That must have caught him by surprise because I swear his hand lands on my shoulder for stability while his moan of pleasure teeters on a primitive growl. I think someone wanted first dibs, but what did he expect standing there like that? I love the smooth, hard warmth of him and so I take him deeper and deeper each time, wanting only to please him and show him that I am his. With one hand in my hair, he touches me lightly with the other and watches my mouth devour him over and over again.

With one last growl Ryan lifts me and turns me around, still on my knees, and climbs onto the bed behind me. I obey when he moves me to the headboard, placing my hands on the top before spreading my legs out wide. He moves away again and I hear him shifting around behind me. When his hands touch the inside of my legs I nearly melt. His finger moves my panties aside to let his tongue begin work on my clit. This sexy as hell man is on his back, and having slid underneath me, begins to return the affection and attention I gave him tenfold. He pushes my ass with his hands, grinding me into his mouth more than I was already doing myself. I can hardly handle the way his tongue moves in and out of me, diving deeper and deeper and only stopping to allow his fingers access as well. My goddess, I am going to climax right now, and I could care less because at this rate I'll reach it ten more times with all the things we want to do to each other. No matter what this night is, what this dream is, I know we are making love, even if only in our shared consciousness.

I release my scream of pleasure into the space around us, allowing him to devour me as my body is rocked with delicious spasms. Pleased with himself, his distraction leaves me an opening so I nearly leap backward to straddle him before he can take charge of my body once again. Keeping my position, I slip my panties off so I can hover my hot, wet slit above his hard cock, giving him a flash of lustful desire from my eyes before using my hand to guide him into me.

Pure ecstasy floods through me as soon as we are joined. This man is meant for me, was made for me. It's as if every part of him was molded to be the perfect match, the perfect piece. I lift up and down on him. Hoping to keep him in check for a while, I playfully hold his hands over his head, not letting him touch me, which seems to be driving him a bit mad.

"Lex. Lex, you feel so good. Damn, you're so wet and so fucking sexy. Shit, I'm going to lose it if you don't let me touch you."

I ease off my hold on his hands and he grabs my hips, pushing me up and down with my rhythm. Strong fingers knead into my side and slip to my ass as he lifts and squeezes along with our perfect motion.

My hands have a life of their own, roaming all over his sculpted body. I bend down to kiss him and the heat intensifies. Our lips press together as if they're two magnets demanding their connection while our tongues flick and touch like an erotic dance. Words I thought I would never say to anyone again flood my brain. Do I love this man? I know I trust him— it's taken a while to get there, but I do without a doubt. I can't find the strength to say the words, not yet, and even though this feels real and seems real, I know what the Fae king is capable of and I will not allow him the satisfaction of knowing whom I love. Looking deeply into Ryan's eyes, I can see my own reflected in his dark irises. He reacts to my gaze, lifting strongly with his hips as he thrusts into me over and over again. I am wild with need, pushing and lifting from him. Our thrusts and pulls bring about unstoppable moans from my lips. It's as if he was made to be inside me. I want to savor every second of this. Slowing down, I lift slowly, allowing his cock to gently pull out of me before I push back down again with a force that has me nearly screaming out. Ryan's response is to push up to a sitting position, with his hands gripping my hair while he pushes me up and down on his cock over and over again. His lips touch me like tiny fiery flames, while his tongue adds fuel to our lovemaking, teasing sensitive areas along my jaw and neck.

"You're driving me wild, Lex. I'm going to cum. Cum with me, Lex. I want to feel you release all around me." My goddess, his sexy ass words are going to be the death of me. The buildup is so intense I can hardly sense my own movements any longer. It's as if my mind has left my body and I am in another reality with Ryan, bonding on a level deeper and higher even than this shared vision. Everything we've been through over the time we've spent together has been building to this amazing experience, these moments, and we've reached the peak where the thrill of tearing it all apart is shared equally between us. Twinkling stars spark to life all around me and explode in a beautiful mirage of colors. My mind sinks back into my body where my arms are wrapped around Ryan's in a tight embrace while we ride the wave of unimaginable bliss together. I have never truly experienced an orgasm before, if this is what it is supposed to be like. Or maybe this is what sex is truly like when love is mixed with danger, or is it that he is an Earthen Protector like me and our powers allow us to reach something more?

I snuggle into the crook of his arm and we kiss softly with a whole new level of intimacy. Ever since I first saw him I hadn't even thought or cared about my circumstances, only wanting to be with Ryan no matter how it happened. We've barely spoken, but the words come rushing out of me now.

"I wish we were really here, that all of the shit happening was the dream and this, this right here and now, was the reality."

His soft fingers touch my lips and pull some wild curls behind my ear before answering. "It will be our reality soon. That I promise. If we can be together on this level, it won't be long before we can break into the Fae world and save you. At least you remembered me right away, this time. Let's just say last time I was so worried and pissed off that a wall paid the price." He flexes the fingers on his right hand in front of him and gives a hmm after examining their perfect condition.

"How long has it been since I last saw you?" Please don't say weeks. Months. "It's been a couple of weeks." As hard as this has been on me, it must be torture for him and my friends. I have some good news, now that I have Verus and Misa helping me, but how do I let him know, here in this space where I'm uncertain of whether my words are protected?

"I'm kind of afraid to say much in case we are being eavesdropped on, but maybe you can understand what I'm trying to say. When I first met you, and then found out about what you were, I knew I was no longer on my own in the world. I know that now, in *any* world." I'm trying to tell him about Verus without speaking outright. Ryan searches my eyes, and I think I see recognition within them. He realizes I have help on the inside, and his deep intake of breath helps spread the smile on his face.

"I'm not surprised, Miss Conner. You are . . . a magnet for trouble. Stay safe and be careful. We're coming for you, so if he can hear us I hope he knows that when the roles reverse you're going to kick the bloody hell out of him." He seals his statement of faith in me with a kiss. "Don't forget me. We have a lot a time ahead of us, and I don't think I could bear it if you're hurt in any way." He narrows his eyes, his tough guy persona fighting his emotions, trying to keep them in check as our naked bodies hold each other.

"And if you see that I do . . ." He needs to understand that I'll be playing a part. My acting ability may now mean life or death for both the princess and me. My pause, one that gives Ryan time to see the look I am giving him, begs for him to understand. It registers and I get a quick nod in reply as well as a creasing in his brow. He's worried that I may still forget him and everyone back in our world. Troubled also that if he doesn't act on what may be my play for the king, I may be lost forever. I touch his face delicately, then skim my fingers down his chin, to his neck, and rest them on his defined chest. While his chest moves slowly up and down with his breath, his heartbeat pulses into my fingertips—I am one with him once more.

"Don't worry," I say. "You will know true danger. You always do." Ryan was the one to help me defeat Steven, and again, when I needed to save my father and end the murderous rampage of the Demon inside him, he was at my side in a show of our unity and power. We have each other's backs, and even though we have known each other only a short time, I am more in sync with him than with some people I have known for years. He was the first Earthen Protector to teach me things I was never able to learn from my grandmother.

Having a mother who would rather hide us behind her drug use or abandon me in hopes of keeping me safe didn't allow for a normal childhood, and neither does knowing you have powers and the only other people you know are evil, dead, or gone. Ryan brought some very important things into my life: a sense of belonging, confidence in my powers, and acceptance of who and what I am. Not to mention that intense need to devour him every time I lay eyes on him. Aside from that time in Arizona, we've never gotten anywhere near this close. Now, in this world within our minds, we have made love and I am forever changed.

A sudden wave of exhaustion rolls through me and I can't hold back a yawn. This is super odd since sex usually works on me like a shot of espresso, but hey, we aren't really here and our minds' sexipade must be coming to an end. I'm having a hard time fighting it. For the first time since I saw Ryan, I am terrified. I must have been kidding myself; how could I be so nonchalent about what is and has been happening. Now I am being pulled back into a cell in a dungeon of a Fae castle with no Ryan, no Sandra, no Vex, no anybody who really knows and loves me, and I am afraid. Plus I have a vicious suspicion buzzing around in my head that the king got something he wanted from me. My feather now feels lifeless, and I fear I've lost a very important link outside of the Fae world.

"Ryan. Ryan. Don't leave. Please."

My fear is reflected in his eyes and he knows as well as I do that our time is up. I can control this; I am strong and I have help in Avalon. I need to focus on what is to come—my freedom and Verus's revenge.

"Everything's going to be alright, Lex. This is huge. If we're lucky, the king knows nothing of this and we can still be together, even if it has to be this way for a while. It means I can check on you, and trust me when I say that soon you'll be somewhere safe. I know it. You're not going to be there forever, I promise." Pulling me close, he touches his forehead to mine before his mantra-filled words infuse me with warmth and hope once again. "Lex, I promise. Remember how strong you are. He has no idea who he's messing with."

My lips meet his and we kiss more passionately than ever. Our physical connection in this dream has brought us to a whole new level. We hold each other, falling asleep in this new place within our shared consciousness as it slowly fades away.

Yet one thing hums incessantly around in my mind despite the blissful fold of sleep that encompasses me. It's entirely possible that this sadistic Fae king *does* know exactly whom he's messing with. I fear this isn't a new thing he wants from me, and he just happened to find Lestan's link to me convenient and used it to his advantage. Perhaps it's something he's sought from me since I was a child, back when I had my first dream with Lestan. Maybe the king even created our link to begin with. I flash back to the time Lestan's greenhouse was destroyed, when his father had been terrifyingly mad at him for failing him. I remember Thatcher telling me that my name was spoken within his father's angered words. I can't recall all the guardian of Lestan's greenhouse said, but pins and needles prickle throughout my body followed by an uncontrollable chill. Could it be that this whole time the king's been plotting and planning to get his claws into someone, and that somehow—I am the key?

CHAPTER 7

Sandra

Falling into flowers
Swimming through these rains
Trampling over hillsides
Tumbling down again

Just when I finally had the line in the sand blurred just a little between my brother and Jax versus Valant, Yi tore out of Logan's skin from his tattooed home, screeching and carrying on like crazy for what appeared to be no good reason. That of course led to Logan shouting and freaking out in response.

I swear my life has completely turned upside down in a matter of a month. I know it's all for an excellent reason, meaning both to get Alex back and to have two very important men back in my life, but I can't resist looking longingly at the high heels and tight skirts in my closet, wishing I could put them on and hit the town with Alex.

"What are you doing, Miss Oman? You have some aberrant stuff happening in your house. I mean, you think I'm freakish, but you do know your brother has an eagle that rips out of his skin, right? I mean, I know I told you to get the Nanda-yi, but even a Demon can tell that what's happening in there is against the rules of nature."

I'm ignoring him, of course. When I left after the chaos died down in my living room, it was to try and get some alone time—to clear my head.

My hope now is that Valant will leave and not let the door hit him in his Demon ass, but instead he inches closer, staring into my closet and then back at me with his arms crossed, broad chest stretching the fabric of his pinstriped suit that I admit looks great with his blond ponytail. Looking down at myself, I see I'm still in my velour pants and tank top. I reach out to touch a tiny sequined jumper and sigh.

"Now, I may be a Demon, but I can entirely relate to anyone pining for their love of style. Though I have to say, how do the girls stay locked into this?" Long fingers snatch at a bright red bandage dress and I smack at them absently. "No touching, Valant. If I can't, nobody can." I can't believe myself right now. Alex is in danger and here I am pouting in my closet.

Once Yi and Logan calmed down enough, they told us that the connection to Alex, through the feather Yi managed to sneak to her in our vision, had been destroyed. The king must have found it and a way to nullify its power. Aside from Alex warning me, just as Ryan had, about the king nosing around about me in her dream a couple of weeks ago, I haven't heard from her through our mental connection. She told me she wasn't going to reach out, that it was no longer safe just in case the Fae king could use the connection to get to me. My argument was that if he wanted me, why wouldn't he just take me like he took her? At least then we'd be there together and the two of us would find a way to break out. She wasn't having that. Alex has always been so selfless. It's one of the many things I adore about her. The feather though, it was like a spy's bug left in the world she's trapped inside, a way for us to know when the coast was clear for another rescue attempt. So now I can't mentally speak to her, and the feather can no longer let us know when the Fae aren't around. Great.

"Oh, don't feel bad, my battle Barbie. We all need a break from time to time from our . . . worry about Alex."

Now that got me in his face. "Look, Demon. I'm not sure what your play is, but I know it has nothing to do with you *worrying* about Alex. The only thing you're worried about is feeding off her emotions or getting in good with her mom. Oh ya, V-man, Alex told me about your little obsession. One word for you, Mr. Vampire CEO wannabe. Husband!"

Instead of the annoyed expression and battle of wits I was itching for, the bastard just starts to laugh.

"Oh, bombshell Betty, you are slaying me. Do you not think I can still feed off her should I choose to? I am Valant, Demon of untold and unseen dimensions. If I want something I can have it, and no little mentally damaged husband or Fairy king can stop me. Ah, I do love the beauty of irony. Like now for example." Valant takes a seat on my bed, and I clench my fists and huff. I may not be able to fight like Alex, but I can send Valant's ass to nowheresville if he pushes me too far.

What in the hell is he doing? I have never seen this look of bliss on his face before, and instead of invoking happiness in me, like it would if the expression were on Alex's or Jax's face, Valant's expression is sinister, terrifying, and teetering on what looks like a . . . an orgasm? Yuck! He needs to get off my bed right now. Before I know it he is gone and I hear voices rising in the living room.

"Oh shit," I squeak before tearing out of my room. Is this really happening again? Rushing out there in slippers—yes, fucking slippers instead of high-as-hell heels—I see the three men (well, that's a stretch for one of them) facing each other, all but one with clenched fists.

"Oh, that was just pure deliciousness from dear Ryan. I don't know what those two kittens did in their little mind mingle, but I am stuffed."

I have no idea what in the world he's talking about, and before I can ask his Demoness what in the world he means, he's looking right at Logan with a fake-as-hell pout on his face.

"Sorry gorgeous, guess Virginia isn't for lovers after all, eh?"

I slide between them, putting my hands out to stop the fight that's starting to flare to life once again. Yi's sharp beak twists left and right from where he sits on my bookshelf just behind Logan's shoulder. I swear he's looking for the best way to peck one of Valant's eyes out without losing anything of his own.

"What in the hell, Valant? Haven't we just about had enough drama for today? Tell us what happened right now, and this time without any of your diva Demon shit and snide comments, or I swear to the gods and goddesses that I will remove your ass from this dimension *right now*. It's fucking late and I am tired, so get on with it."

Valant, with his tiny needle-tooth smile, steps back from Logan and Yi while smoothing down his jacket and taking a seat on a high stool at my island.

"It seems the little connection I helped buoy in Ryan's ring allowed him to connect with Alex in a very deep and personal way this evening."

I am going to break skin with the fist clenching I have going on right now, or give myself TMJ with my jaw clamping.

"I forgot to say to also get straight to it without all of your poetic nonsense. Are you saying Ryan got to Alex again? What did she say?" I can see he's trying not to giggle. What in the hell? "Get on with it, Valant! We haven't had contact with her in weeks. Now what happened?

"She didn't say . . . much. It was more of a *doing* kind of Dreamwalk. They were together, but really only in their minds. And when I say *together*, I mean *together*."

Holy shit. Did Alex just literally mindfuck Ryan? With all the crap she's been going through? I give the little naughty cheerleader in my mind a high five. Of course my outward self smiles a little and Logan doesn't miss my reaction in the least. Well shit, I mean, let's get real here. He hasn't even really met her yet, and this crush of his can be seen from space. Alex and Ryan have been doing this tango for months now, and my girl finally got some, or something close to it by the sounds of it.

"So what does that mean? Was it a creation of the Fae or did they find each other purely through his ring link?"

Looking cocky, Valant starts to serve his answer with his usual trademark smugness until I give him the don't-you-fucking-dare eye.

"Eh hem, I believe the ring brought them together during or possibly within a drugged-up Fae dream. It was different this time, which it should be with my ring boost helping her fight off those naughty fairy lies, but something alien was there as well, something actually burning away the amnesia-inducing Fae magic, and it doesn't appear to be from any of us."

Don't get my hopes up. I cannot get my hopes up. But I perk up all the same hardly hiding the wide-eyed, hopeful look upon my face.

"Yes, Blonde-nado, with your dumbfounded optimistic face, I believe our little girl has some help on the inside. We may just get her back yet and possibly in better shape than I originally thought."

Now it's Logan's turn to butt in. "You mean in better shape than you *hope*. Don't tell me a broken Alex isn't more of a treat for a Demon than all-in-one-piece and powerful Alex. You only feed on a person's despair when you aren't creating it yourself. What could you possibly feel or care for in a human—a Healer and Earthen Protector no less—one who can take down your kind in a blink of an eye once she knows everything she is truly capable of. If you were a real Demon you'd want her as your doll or dead, but here you are acting like you lost your puppy."

Logan's muscles flex and he seems to grow in width and height in his anger. My Jax strolls up slowly behind him, having my brother's back but giving off an unconcerned appearance with his gorgeous slack jaw and diverted eyes. Give the boy a long piece of straw and I am all in for riding that cowboy. Oops, losing focus here, Sandra.

"Guys. Come on! We had just recently got to where we all agreed that we need to work together. Valant helped by increasing the power in the ring, and let's not forget—though the neck snapping part was a bit overboard—that he saved Alex from Justin. She was in trouble and he didn't feed off her fear. Instead, he reacted immediately."

Saying that out loud, *again*, gives me pause. Just moments ago I was in his face, accusing him of not giving a rat's ass about Alex. But who can blame me with my history with Demons? The same goes for Logan and Jax. We've all had our share of Demon nastiness, but who are we kidding? No one is all good or all bad, so is it possible that not all Demons are evil? Okay, that's a stretch even for Valant; perhaps I mean that maybe he's not totally incapable of good. The thoughts spinning around in my head start like a verse from a new Dr. Seuss book about a Grinch named Valant.

"Maybe he does care about Alex, in his own Demon heart way. Maybe, just maybe she means a little bit more."

That earns me a straight-up look from Logan. Not a Seuss fan anymore I guess.

"Look, I know she's an investment of sorts for him, but don't tell me the mighty Valant can't find himself another snack bar with a snap of his fingers. So let's all ease back down and work together. That means you too, smartass."

69

Valant begins to give a *who me* finger point with matching look, but my cutting gaze has him deciding to choose the higher, more mature road and he instead gives me a much needed nod of agreement.

"Busting each other's balls isn't going to help us get her back, so it all ends now. Capisce?" I move to Jax and lay a hand on his arm, which earns me one of his sexy smiles. Subdued for now, he saunters over to the couch. Next, I touch Yi's feathered body. He screeches while his swiveling head oscillates from me to Valant. Logan isn't breaking his concentrated gaze on Valant, but I can see his shoulders easing down a tad. "Look," I go on. "This is a win for us and for Alex. She may have some help in Fae-land and with Yi's feather no longer working, and Alex basically cutting me off, we need all the help we can get. I think everyone can agree on that, and we still have to work together to find a way to get her back."

Logan turns away from Valant, opting to head for the cooler where he can grab a couple of beers. After he strokes Yi's head, during which some sort of communication passes between them, the eagle dives back into Logan's flesh and becomes the tattoo on his arm once again. To my surprise, Logan tosses a beer to Valant who catches it with a clink against the many man rings on his fingers.

"Thank you, good sir. If it's any consolation, I like you much more than that beefcake Ryan. You've got that whole Brad Pitt meets Tom Hardy thing going for you. Has anyone ever told you that?"

Oh geez, that's exactly how Alex described my brother when she first got a look at him through our mental connection when I came to get him at Quantico. Why do I have a sneaking suspicion that our conversations were hijacked by an eavesdropping Demon, or are Valant and Alex more alike than I could have ever imagined? Hell, I hope not. Their link is confusing at best, sort of a love-hate type of thing or maybe more ying-yang. I know Alex struggles with some parts deep within her, those pieces of her that are dark and formidable. Valant embodies those things, and maybe Alex has to just accept them in order to accept herself. As for Valant, maybe Alex shows him the good that can come from having the influence they can each wield.

Is it possible Valant wants to be a decent . . . decent what? Decent Demon? Is there such a thing? Where they come from is a mystery, but I suspect they were like us once, but took such a wrong turn that they've been damned to live as Valant does, cursed to live off the emotions, both pain and pleasure, of others, and that isn't usually given freely. So maybe they adapted out of necessity and now take what they need, no matter whom they hurt in the process. Needing from others in that way can twist someone irreparably, like the Demon who wanted the Nanda-yi's power and possessed my grandmother before becoming that poor man killed in the mountains of Virginia. Killed by Logan and I. That Demon had not an ounce of good in him, but Valant doesn't seem like that, not entirely. I shake away the memories; we've recently healed and moved away from that past. We had to in order to have our lives back and with each other.

After opening his beer and downing nearly half of it, Valant moves to the bar and starts to mix a vodka drink.

"Here you go, Marilyn," he says, handing me a glass. I take a nice, long sip. "It's nice and stiff, just the way you like 'em."

And just like that, said sip comes spitting right back out.

"Damn it, Valant!"

CHAPTER 8

Another

Utterly addicted to passionate thoughts, guided dreams, and memories—
an all too brief reality.
I never stopped being a part of you.
I'll never stop looking for you.
Bring me closer to those future days.
When I will be loved and forever embraced.

"Ow! What was that for?"

My eyes blink away some serious sleepytime crust. Damn, I must have been out! Maybe that's the only way Ryan and I were able to be with each other that . . . intimately. I mean seriously, Fleabag must have really given it to me with her potion. Now what or who is messing with me? Looking down at the source of the needling pain I see a familiar feline form, like a slightly smaller version of a panther, scratching and biting at the Fae king's bracelet on my arm. How is it not burning him to a crisp?

"Hold still, Eila. You're going to chip one of my teeth. I need to get a good sample of this thing to help get you out of it. Unless it is removed from your person or neutralized, nothing can be done."

I am so damn excited to have his tiny sharp teeth on me I nearly yell.

"Thatcher! I was so hoping to see you here. If you can get that damn thing off me that would be amazing. Maybe I can even get my own ass out of here. Weren't you the first to tell me what I am, a dimensional traveler?"

His large, midnight-black cat frame freezes, a sharp saber-shaped tooth wedged in the bracelet. He mumbles something to me, but I haven't a rat's ass idea in hell what he's saying with his mouth pried open in such a way.

"What was that? Sorry, Thatch, my man, I can't understand you, which is funny 'cause if we were back in my world I'd be one odd woman actually understanding a cat, no offense."

Freeing his tooth, he hops up onto the bed and gets so close that my eyes cross while looking into his bright, gold-flecked eyes in their long, white-whiskered face. Damn, I miss Pitter. "When I am finally able to free you from this bracelet, Eila, you cannot leave. Not just yet."

The hell I can't. What is this pussycat playing at? I sit up in a blink of an eye, causing him to jump off. I try hard to keep my voice low, but my hands are gesturing wildly.

"Thatcher, come on, you know I can't stay here if you take that off. One, I have a feeling they'll know, and two, I've been a damn prisoner, not some willing BDSM participant, in case you haven't noticed. I need to go home. I want to go home." The great cat's sadness weighs down the room before being reflected in his eyes. "I'm sorry about Lestan. I didn't have time to stop it, let alone register what was happening to me, and to him. He didn't seem fully in control of himself, and I had *no* idea it was him, the entire time, posing as Justin." Something occurs to me. "I honestly wonder if he even knew."

As if he drifts back in time, Thatcher pulls me into his story with just another look into his large panther eyes.

"I have heard many tales and secrets in this kingdom. It helps to be able to alter my form, and I've gained the trust of some truly important people. With their knowledge I can share what I know of Lestan and his demise and even more about his father. The king is extremely powerful, as you have discovered, in both his magics and his manipulation. Even though I knew Lestan was in your world, I don't think Lestan realized it. I was forbidden to see him, and when I snuck in anyhow, he was angry—agitated—and at times didn't even recognize me. He was losing himself to become your Justin. I know part of him agreed to that so he could be with you, but Lestan would have never agreed to abduct you, or force you against your will. Having lived his whole life under someone else's control, he would fight tooth and nail to keep you from that fate."

I hardly notice the tears running down my face until I see them falling like blurry sparkling diamonds onto the cold stone floor.

"The Lestan I knew would never hurt me."

"He would have given his life to keep you safe. That he did, by agreeing to become Justin for his father and hoping he could keep the façade going long enough to keep you protected. He was forbidden to show you his true self, but the king didn't care to trust him and instead slowly poisoned him to inhibit his powers in your world and to make him forget he was Lestan. The powerful magic made him attracted to you and you to him."

So I wasn't imagining things. He was like a drug I couldn't get enough of when we were around each other, but when apart it was like my free will came back to me and I remembered my feelings for Ryan. Ones I couldn't ignore. Ones I still can't.

Thatcher continued. "In the final moments, when the king knew Lestan had failed and that you were instead choosing Ryan as your mate, he took matters into his own hands, turning Justin into a jealous, desperate abductor."

I knew he hadn't been in control, and not just on that night. He was acting out of character before then, the green-eye having come out when we spoke on the phone before I left for Montana. Then there were the dreams about my time in Avalon, and how they began to star Justin instead of Lestan. The drug-like attraction and my altered dreams were why I took Justin's items to Sandra to read. Our life together had been bringing questions to the surface of my mind, along with an intensified feverish lust for him when he was around me, and I wanted to get to the bottom of it. Yet the Fae powers eluded Sandra and even took her over at one point. Now I can only wonder if the dreams were a warning, maybe from the part of Lestan that was still in control of some of his powers, of some of himself.

"I have to be honest, though." Thatcher was striding powerfully around the cell on his muscular black legs, tail twitching back and forth. "Part of Lestan was still there, alive in that shell, and he loved you deeply.

He would never have purposely harmed you. But just knowing you were slipping away again would have caused him great distress. That, mixed with his father's control, would have made him dangerous. Your Demon must have sensed that. He saved your life, and Lestan would have wanted him to, no matter the cost. Maybe even allowed him to."

So I was right. I don't think I can handle this. The boy who saved me from my depression after Steven's abuse is gone, and here, with Thatcher, I am finally able to truly sink into my grief. Things have been so frightening and confusing since that night that I haven't been able to process a single bit of it. Now, with Thatcher here setting the pieces into place, the floodgates are yanked open, torn and ripped away and taking pieces of my heart and soul with them.

Thatcher's paws can be heard padding across the dirty floor, even over the heaving breaths that rattle my ears as years fall away from me faster than I can count. Avalon was a land, a world I thought to be only a dream I could escape into when the real world sucked to oblivion. Now it's become a nightmare of epic proportions and the one person who made it so special for me is dead.

A large furred head rests on my lap while the weight of his body shifts my legs awkwardly. I barely manage to keep from tumbling over. Thatcher allows me time to cry, to mourn, but before I lose myself much further I remember the last thoughts before falling asleep after my intense Dreamwalk with Ryan.

"Thatcher. Do you know what the king wants from me? Or rather, who? He's taking me into these dreams where he's trying to get information from me, but I've either forgotten who he's asking about or he hasn't spoken the name right out yet. I know he asked about Sandra again last night, and I think he got what he wanted because our connection seems to have been altered, maybe even severed. But I don't think he has all that he needs from me yet." I pause, noticing a dreadfully bad taste in my mouth. "I hate that I don't know if there's something else he may have gotten from me. It's a blur really. I mean, wouldn't I be dead by now if he had it all?"

Lifting his head from my legs, Thatcher steps back, cocking his head. "Or he's waiting for you to see the final act when he brings this person here. Remember, Eila, he's demented in that way, though perhaps he was not always." Thatcher tosses his big head as if he's shaking something loose. "No, I don't recall hearing of him being this evil as a boy or a young man. Something changed when he met the woman who would become his wife. She was powerful, you see. More than he, I can honestly say. It was perhaps that difference that sparked his thirst for dominance, a need to become greater than she, than anyone. Corruption comes with such a need and it overtook him easily. The Fae, especially those of royalty, have always had a tendency to believe they were the closest to the gods and goddesses of all time, that any other being is beneath them, but Lestan's mother was different. She wanted to rule differently."

With what I know of the king now; he would disdain such a thing. I wish Lestan could have realized she lived. Or had he perhaps known and he never revealed that truth to Verus?

"Did Lestan ever learn that his mother was alive? It would be a pressure point for his father to use over him. Yes, I know Lestan loved me, but what he allowed himself to become seems to be more than what my existence merits. I mean, Lestan and I had barely seen each other in years. Why now?"

I swear Thatcher appears to smile. His whiskered cheeks pull up to show his sharp white teeth as my mind ticks back and forth, flipping through snapshots of my life with Lestan and then his alter ego, Justin.

"You are ever so clever, Eila. Lestan always knew that. Maybe even counted on it. There are two reasons that ultimately led him to agree to pose as Justin, but he never intended to let his father get his hands on you. The king threatened to use someone else to get to you, someone who didn't love you or care what would become of you. He would ensure, by any means necessary, that the king got what he wanted. Then the king told Lestan his mother was still alive, and he agreed to become Justin for your sake, and because he needed to do it to get a location on his mother, something the king promised him." Thatcher's tail swishes wildly. "I don't know if he ever got it, and even so, he died. Which brings me back to why you cannot leave."

We did leave that topic a while back, didn't we? As well as the one about what the king wants from me. Neither of us means to not listen to or answer the other. I have always regarded Thatcher as a creature true of both word and character. We are alike, he and I. He is a hybrid also; he is a fixer and destroyer of inanimate objects and he was cast out by his kind and taken in by Lestan. I may not have been cast out, but I have been purposely hidden from my kind by my family and am now sought after by the Council for the rarity that I am. Thatcher and I have both lost so much, and now I think I know what he wants from me. His matter being more important than my own, I push my questions about the king's desires aside for now.

"You want me to bring him back, don't you? I offered that to the king, who of course doesn't care, but in all honesty, I have no idea how or even if I could do it. Being a Healer doesn't mean I can bring back the dead, and anyway, who knows where or what is left of him? His body turned into the plants and leaves of his greenhouse, blowing away on a mystic breeze to goddess only knows where. Don't I need some part of him to even start to think of a how?"

An answering feline stretch suggests that Thatcher knows how and where to start, as well as confirming that, yes, this is indeed what he hopes from me in return for helping me gain my freedom, however the hell he plans on doing that!

"I have him," Thatcher says, licking a rather large paw. "Well, the pieces of his soul. They flew back to me where I lay in the greenhouse. Knowing something had occurred, I hurried to capture his essence in a flowerpot, where I covered it in his own soil and hid it from all who might be seeking him. But no one ever came; no one ever cared, and just as so, his plants have started to die as if they are mourning his loss just as I."

My thoughts drift back to when I last saw Thatcher, when we worked together to restore Lestan's greenhouse to its original glory after his father destroyed it in a fit of rage. I healed the plants, and Thatcher used his powers and shapeshifting ability to mend the tables, pots, glass, and metal.

"I can fix that, if I can get out of here and out of this thing," I announce, shaking my arm at him, the bracelet a constant reminder that it will burn me if I try to leave, and that I am pretty much magically castrated. Well, there's a word I never thought I'd ever use for myself.

"I'm happy to fix the greenhouse, but that's a lot easier than raising the dead."

Another cat grin. "He's not dead, Eila. Not entirely. You see, there is a part of his mother in him that neither he nor his father knew about, something alive within him that a mere killing of his body cannot destroy." Seeing my boggled-mind stare, Thatcher waves a paw at me in a very human way. "Let's not worry about those details right now. What we need to do is figure out a way to keep you here while you are also with me. I hope I can make for you as I have done for myself. Here, let me show you." And, just like that, the one Thatcher turns into two. The identical cats turn to look at each other, arching and hissing with teeth showing and muscles flexing. I launch off the bed to wedge myself between them, but my leg brushes right through the new Thatcher.

"Only inanimate objects, Eila, remember? He's a hologram. Good to know you thought him real enough, though. Now I need to make one of you. It will work well enough when they come to bring you food or look in on you, and it will also give us enough time to get you back here should they come to put their hands on you again."

It's an intriguing idea. "But how will you get me out of here? And I haven't even told you yet of my agreement with Verus. The princess needs me as well."

He nods. I have a suspicion he knows about Verus. If Thatcher was Lestan's secret, and if the siblings were as close as they seem to have been, Verus and Thatcher know each other very well. "Yes, of course. Verus let me know you were here. Her love, Misa, and I have a bond for all we have in common. Her artistry and my abilities work well together, as you can see."

Yep, I am now hitting myself in the forehead. Verus told me Misa would make it appear as if I was doing nothing in here while she and I worked on getting my powers back, but she didn't mention Thatcher. Of course, our time had been cut short by Flean's evil medicine.

"Well, peachy. Happy to know we're all one big happy family. How do we hologram me? Don't tell me. You can take a picture with your eyes, send it back to Misa's cool covert lab, and project it back here! Now that would be cool." That earns me a shrug. "Is that seriously how it works? I was totally just kidding." An exuberant lightness overwhelms me in response to a rare laugh I unleash. A bright light has been brought to me in this dank dungeon in the form of two from Avalon, and now I can only hope to soon meet the mysterious Misa as well.

"Something like that. Between us, we will get the bracelet removed and keep the king and his people unaware and then you will keep your word to us as we will to you."

The next hour consists of standing, sitting, walking, sleeping, slumping, and any other pose I can think of to help Misa and Thatcher make a believable illusion of me. After realizing how foul my clothes are after all this time down here, I grab some clothes from the Fae pile and find them surprisingly fitting. Brown leather-like material, smooth as butter, greets my legs while a cream tank top and sheer shirt is like liquid on my chest. Woven long, grey fingerless gloves keep my arms warm, as do soft boots for my feet. My chin lifts as I take in the little kick-ass outfit. Thatcher's eyes pull a smirk from my lips when I see him snarling at my pile of old clothes. I take the hint and toss them into the corner. They may as well be burned at this point.

Thatcher and I work together and eventually Thatcher is able to pry a bit of something off my bracelet, and I help him get it inside a locket attached to a string around his neck. What happens with that next I'm uncertain, but I'm just happy to know it will be gone soon.

It must have been plain luck that breakfast hadn't ever appeared to interrupt and possibly even halt our efforts. Kitty cat hearing allows Thatcher to hear my stomach growl and the large cat vanishes, giving me a heart attack at first, before reemerging with a sack attached to his back. Inside is a feast fit for a queen. I thank him between mouthfuls as we take a break from the prep work in building the hologram. I've never eaten this well in my shit hole cell. The pause brings my previous questions bubbling back to the surface.

"Thatcher, do you know why I'm here? I mean, what does he want from me anyhow?" The cat, who has been gnawing on the meat and bones of his prey, stops mid-crunch to consider my question.

"At this time, we do not know. Somehow the king, even in his madness, has kept this secret from all of us. We suspect it has to do with a time when he left Avalon. Some say he left to find a powerful object, but no one knows for certain. You said he asked you about someone? Maybe that person has what he seeks."

This is a new theory. I was so fixed upon the *she* he was asking for, that I never thought the person might have what he wants, only who she might be. Sandra may very well have something he needs, but he knows where she is and where she's from, and she's not here, is she?

"Would you know if he'd brought anyone else here?"

"It's just you from outside Avalon, Eila. Well, aside from me."

Thank goddess. Okay, so then there's Dana, Carmen, my mom—it could be any of them, aside from Carmen who is truly the only purely human one of us, though I had thought that to be true of Justin once. Great, now my crazy trust issues are taking my mind for a whirl once more. Damn it all, and just when I thought Steven's death helped me bury some of those demons away for good. With Sandra's connection to me severed and the eagle feather lifeless, I can only hope to see Ryan again so I can let him know about this idea. He could maybe pass it on to the gang. Of course, with their minds more intact and less screwed with, unlike my own, perhaps they've already thought of it.

Dana has some seriously powerful objects at her disposal, so she comes to mind as the forerunner in this guessing game. The only thing my mom seems to possess are secrets, which can be powerful, but how so in this realm seems uncertain. Now that it seems the king has been after me for a long-ass time, it could be someone I knew when I was young. That shortens the list. That is, unless the Fae have some reading future app I don't know about. Argh, even with the drugs fading slowly out of my system, the damn king manages to make me fuck with my own mind.

A smile spreads across my face and I cease with the questioning as the memory of fucking Ryan in my mind replaces this psychological torture with one of pleasure.

Thatcher doesn't seem to notice my change in mood, or he chooses not to show his awareness. "Verus will continue looking into what is driving the king. Someone or something has to know. Keeping it all in his head could be one of the reasons he is so far gone. We all leave trails though." My eyes can nearly see the trail of Lestan's life floating away from me again while Thatcher speaks into the cold cell. "Even in death."

CHAPTER 9

Jax's Plan

Follow my eyes—they wander through thickets of fairies and clovers.
I will be watching—snuggled, hidden by the mossy trees.
Paths, you will follow—leading you through this enchanted moment.
I know you want to trust me.

A fter finally getting some sleep and saddling myself with a bit of a hangover from overdoing it in the booze department with my ragtag gang last night, my buzzing phone has me leaning over Jax's sleeping body to grab it. It's Dana. No offense, but she's not my idea of a hangover cure.

"You up yet? Ryan and I are on our way to you. We have some ideas and some files to go over with you all. Perhaps your brother's training with the man will finally come in handy."

Dana's not much of a fan of anything that involves the government or any governing body overseeing the people. She's more of a do whatever the hell she wants type of good gal. I have to agree with her on some points. Even though the Council came through for my loved ones and me in the past, they have proven to be corrupt, and we know almost every government in the world has had its day in that power-hungry sun.

"Yep, we're up." Nudging Jax's passed-out form I add, "Well, some of us. When will you be here?" Trying to find my underwear in the covers is a fool's errand, so I jump out of bed butt naked and grab a new pair along with pants and a shirt. I stopped putting my clothes back on after about round three last night.

"We should be at your house in three hours or so. Bronze Bronson woke me up at the ass crack of dawn this morning. Looks like our girl found a way to get her some help even in lock up. Plus, she's just blown the history of conjugal visits to pieces. I know she's exceptional, but that's gangster."

Hearing this kind of talk from a woman who looks like she bakes cakes for a living is giving me the giggle fits, which causes Jax to finally stir. I spy some scratches on his back and fling a clean shirt at him. He better keep that on around everyone today. I am not in the mood for all the jibes, or Logan's nauseated looks.

Not surprised that Ryan told Dana about his seductive dreamscape with Alex, I chuckle slightly. "Oh yeah, we heard about that from Valant. Seems their little Demon deal still allows him to sense her, um, strong emotions." Something that sounds close to 'vampire scum bucket' falls from her lips before I continue. "Does Ryan know anything about her having help inside? Valant's pretty sure she does, so that's good. I mean it's all good, I mean, I'm sure it was . . . oh, forget it." Stone silence follows, only broken by the sound of a man clearing his voice. "I'm on speaker, aren't I?"

After Ryan confirms my question in a short and matter-of-fact manner, I disconnect. I wonder who is helping Alex? I mean, I suppose a crazy-ass king must have made some enemies, so lucky us.

As I stand alone in the kitchen, downing coffee and mechanically preparing another, Logan walks in with a puzzled look on his face. "I've been thinking. If this was anything at all to do with revenge, which is what we originally thought, then why does everything he's putting Alex through seem more like an interrogation technique?"

"Good morning to you, too, good sir. Starting out with a brain-busting bang I see. Let a girl get her liter of smart juice first, please."

Not listening, or possibly caring less about what I said, the genius twin from hell moves on. "We know he wants Alex to help him find or get someone, and we know it seems to be a her. I've thought that it might be someone to help him bring Lestan back, but Alex told you it's like he doesn't care about his son at all. If that's true, and he's not toying with her, than we're dealing with someone more sinister than I feared."

He's right. If the king doesn't even care about his own flesh and blood, what will he be willing to do to Alex to get what he wants? Time to bring the Oman brains together and do some hashing out.

"Okay, let's say he doesn't want her to pay for what happened to Lestan, or to bring him back, so what does he need this *her* for? I had been thinking that maybe he needs another Healer or necromancer, but I guess you're right, he isn't acting like he cares at all that his son is gone." I tap the side of my mug with a fingernail, but stop talking when I catch sight of Yi's eyes moving around in his tattooed home. Is he thinking along with us as well? We've spent so much time and energy on how to get her back, and barely any at all on what the psycho wants.

"Maybe he wants to control someone with immense power, just as he's trying to do to Alex. I mean, he said that he wanted us for his *collection*. Perhaps he plans on using Alex and this other person for something that requires massive influence. What woman does Alex know with formidable power?"

Logan's question brings a list of people to mind.

"Well, there's Dana, Terra—"

"You," Logan interrupts, leading me to innocently and uncontrollably roll my eyes at him.

"We already agreed he would've shown some cards when he saw us in the vision. It's got to be someone else. Now let it go and let me think." This is both an "I hope" type of response and one to steer him back to us getting to Avalon and getting Alex's ass out of there. This sideline crap is driving me crazy, not my usual MO I might add. "Not to mention," I add more confidently, "we know he sabotaged our connection to Alex through Yi's feather, so he got close to us before we knew what was happening, but we're no worse for wear, right? I mean, I'm not sure how he did it, which honestly freaks me out, but we're still all in one piece, so let's stop worrying about me being a target. He has to fear us a little bit or things would be much worse, right?"

Logan looks concerned. He hates it when I test fate by claiming things are perfectly fine. He's pretty jumpy and superstitious for an agent.

"I have an idea." Jax has strolled in as silent as if he were on cat paws.

"What do you think he wants?"

A sly Jax smile makes parts of me melt. My god, his control over my lust for him just never stops and I'm barely awake!

"Not about what he wants, more about how we might be able to try and get her out of there." Now we're talking. I'm going to tear that damn shirt I told him he had to wear right off him this instant. "In the dream Ryan went into, did he say he saw any of us—you?"

This is an interesting question. I give a finger up, the polite one, to pause the conversation so I can text Dana. I want to make sure of my answer, even though I have a fairly good idea what it may be. A ping tells me that she's responded quickly. "Nope, no one in our group, those of us with any power that is, seemed to be there. I'm guessing he didn't want our presence, even as a shade, to trigger some awareness in her mind. Ryan did see our friend Nic—who was the interrogator, as you so lovingly called it, Logan—and her college buddy Shane. They were in the club that served as the backdrop of the vision." An aching to dance the night away with my best friend drifts in and out like the breeze, invisibly dragging small pieces of the world as we knew it and lived it far away.

"Okay, but the dream didn't fall apart or change when Ryan got there, did it?"

My forehead creases. I don't think so, but I start typing to Dana again just to be sure. I'm starting to think this may soon require a call.

"Ryan says that Nic didn't act aggressively toward him when he was talking to Alex, but that when he was still able to overhear the conversation, it seemed as if Nic could tell something had changed in Alex, and he got angry. After that, Ryan lost the connection to Alex again, and that was due to Vex not being able to hold him there any longer."

I've seen Nic pissy and annoyed, but thinking of him ever speaking or acting viciously to Alex is completely impossible for me to imagine. Wherever Jax is headed with this questioning, I am totally lost right now. My eyes narrow and my man knows I'm about to start tossing him some questions about what in the world he's thinking. Raising both hands, he assures me with calm and cool eyes that he's getting to the point.

"Hear me out, sweetheart. The dreams seem to involve only people without powers, and I'm sure we can agree that the king is doing this because he's trying to make Alex forget about what she can do and anyone like her. So, he only has people in her dreams who are *normal* and who won't serve as possible triggers to make her aware of the lie she's in."

"Okay, I'm with you. So what can we do with that info?" Logan's perking up to this line of thinking. I'm getting there, slowly, but whatever, I bet he slept much more than I did. I feel kind of sorry for him, not.

"What if we can get somebody in there that the dream and any of its spies might expect to see, but that person is somehow given a way to bring her back. Like a potion, spell, or weapon of some sort."

Now I'm awake. "If we can give that someone a way to get that bracelet off her in the dream, maybe it'll work for real and she can get herself out. I mean, if she's aware in there, with this newfound ally we think she has, then she'll know what we're doing and we can bring her home. Oh, Jax, this is genius." I throw my arms around his neck, smiling and pulling him in close to kiss him.

"There's one huge problem, guys." Logan the party pooper makes my desire to press my lips to Jax's disappear. "We cannot risk someone's life, especially someone who may not be able to defend themselves in there. Don't forget that we really aren't supposed to let anyone know about us either, let alone give up Alex's secret without her consent. It's too risky." My super IQ twin is right, again. Though he also seems to be underestimating our little band of misfits.

"I'm positive Dana can create something to help free Alex and keep our volunteer safe. But who would it be? It can't be Nic, not if he appears to be the main character in the dreams working to break Alex. And that's assuming it's always him—what if it moves to Carmen or Shane? Not to mention that I worry those two might be a package deal. I don't think we can ask one of them to keep such a secret from the other. It would most likely have to be both of them or neither, I'm afraid."

This was actually shaping up to be a plan with some potential, but now our options are failing. Oh, wait. "Why don't we get Valant in there? He can take on the shape of anyone."

Of course Logan looks as if he swallowed something sour—no, I take that back, more like something rotten. It'll take more than a few shared beers to ever have him on team Valant, that's for sure.

"Do you seriously trust him with Alex's life, Sandra? He's a wild card and he could get her killed, or worse. I know I'm only one voice, but I say no to Valant spearheading this mission. Jax, what do you say?"

I know what Jax is going to say. Thick as thieves those two, yet I slink my body into a pose meant to create confusion in my man, or at least cause a delay in his team-Logan response.

"I agree with you, Logan my boy. Which is surprising, I know."

Valant has joined the party. This calls for more coffee, hell, maybe with a dash of something stronger too. "Someone as powerful as I will definitely set off alarms and possibly endanger our little magic mini. I do like the idea though. We need to send some dull do-gooder in there that the king won't think twice about. Though worrying about your pet's fate leaves me far less concerned than you three. You should try it sometime, shutting off your feelers. It's liberating."

Demon equals sociopath; now why do I keep forgetting that? Not a problem though, as Valant keeps on reminding me each time I get more comfortable and maybe even trusting of him. Shaking off Valant's less empathic feedback, I try to move us forward. "Let's return to the how we get someone to Avalon if Vex no longer can. I can move someone there and then . . ." I have to stop right there because then *what?* I leave Shane there and return home safe and sound? How would we know what happened or what to do next if one of us isn't there or linked to Alex? Without Yi's spy feather we can't even tell when or if she's asleep. We're flying blind now and it's driving me crazy. Valant's all smiles at the distressed look on my face while my mind ticks through all that could go wrong.

"GI Bronson has his little link still, thanks to me. I'm sure we can figure some other way to use it than the boy getting his jollies off. Maybe he gets all tingly down there when she's in her little wet dream state and then we shove your human there with something to help sever the bracelet or get her alone so you can pop over and take her from her cell while she dreams."

Clever and straight to the point—that's not usually Valant's style, though his extra descriptiveness is per the usual.

"Thank you for the visuals, Valant. That's really made my morning complete. Let's go over everything again to get a clearer picture. We know

Ryan was able to give her the silver ring during the vision, so it makes sense that we could possibly remove the bracelet. But if we can do that, why can't we just take her from the dream? If objects are moving within the dream world, can't she?"

Logan's getting tense, and Jax is moving closer to me, the two of them ready to pounce and stomp out my plan, so I carry on quickly. "If we know she's in the dream, then that removes the possibility of facing off with the flesh-and-blood king. His dream spies may alert him, but it'll be too late and I can get her out of there before the vision can be ripped apart."

"What if you're wrong and taking Alex in that way causes major damage to her psyche? You're talking about taking her from a drug-induced vision when her body is back in the cell."

Logan has a point, but that's just one way to look at it. This may be crazy talk, but what if we've been thinking about this all wrong. What if she isn't in a dream at all?

"But what if it's not? What if she is actually moving herself into that vision, all of her, like when she traveled to Avalon when she was young or to the lake when she saw the Healer die? She said the stones were cold and hard underneath her feet, and her body shivered in the cold air. Maybe that's how the king makes it so real for her. Maybe he's creating an alternate reality. I could take her from it. I could bring her home."

Ya, and this time without the king's crazy glowing ring aiming at Logan and me like the last time. That's assuming my idea is right. I don't think Logan cares either way as he comes at me again.

"If it's an alternate dimension, Sandra, then what will keep the king from going there to get you as well? If he made it—if he sends her there—then he must be able to get there himself, don't you think? Come on, sis. Be smart. He managed to take out Yi's power, so he knows more about us than we think. He could know the instant you're there and then what? You and Alex are both trapped?"

"It's better than sending an unprotected friend of ours to some crazy Fae dimension, and plus, last time I checked I was a grown woman and capable of making up my own mind and my own decisions. I've pussyfooted around your concerns for days now, but I'm over it. She has help there. Ryan is still linked to her in some way." I glance at Valant, whose answering gyrating action is really not helping. "Don't forget, Logan, your little tattoo parlor ritual has you, Jax, Yi, and me connected by more than blood and love. We're inseparable through time and space. You can get me out of there if you need to. I know you will. Everything is lining up for me to get her out of Avalon. I can feel it in my very soul. We have to try. *I* have to try."

Logan moves closer to me, grabbing my hands that have started shaking with the frustration and resolve building within me. I haven't been this person for years, this Seer running with heroes and saving people. Last time things went in this direction we were all much younger, and blood, regret, and love spilled and fell away. Yet I was drawn to Alex, to her caring nature, and obviously to her power as well. We're a team now, like it or not, and things are always going to be dangerous. Tears pool in my eyes as I look at Logan, willing him to understand that I am ready for this, that he doesn't need to protect me by keeping me on the sidelines. What he needs to do is help me get it done.

Logan frowns. "We need to wait for Dana and Ryan to get here. He may be the only way for us to know if she's there or not, and there's something about that bracelet. We saw that with our own eyes. I think we can both agree that you wouldn't be able to take her without removing it, and didn't you just say Dana could help with that? You don't want to pop over there right now and possibly ruin your only chance, do you?"

My brother's depth of insight is annoying as hell sometimes. Of course I want to act now, but I guess he's right. We need to wait.

A couple of hours later and I find myself dressed in slick garb, like I'm a ninja or something. Of course the tight black shirt doesn't keep the girls hidden well, so flattening against a wall will still leave plenty of me to be seen. Alex is more the ninja; I'm usually the blonde in the red dress distraction. With her gone, Yi is lining up for the distraction role. Well, he and maybe Ryan. That's still being hashed out in the living room while I look for sensible sneaking shoes. No one seemed to like my plan of blending into the crowd and dressing like normal Sandra. *You'll stand out too much* they said and the words *easy target* and *obvious* were also tossed around. Of course, Valant's descriptive words nearly started another brawl, but luckily Dana squashed it this time. Playing referee all the time was getting a little old.

"Want to borrow mine?" Dana has been fiddling in my bathroom with who knows what, trying to come up with some sort of spell or tool for me to get that bracelet off, and now she's pointing at one seriously roughed-up pair of boots under her long, heavy cream skirt.

"Um, no, but thank you. Ah, here they are," I answer, grabbing a pair of tall lace-up black boots, and feeling happy with the fact that the heel is a little wider than a stiletto, and looky there, they even have some tread. See, I can be practical. Of course the look on Dana's face isn't vibing with my overeager smile.

"Hey, they're Timberlands!" That should shut her down.

"What, from the rapper's stripper collection?"

I guess not. Ignoring her, I lace them up. Okay, she has to help me a little, but they look killer and I may need them in a pinch for kicking and stomping. Oh, I hope Alex can do most of the kicking and stomping if need be, and that she truly has some aid in Avalon instead of being doped up. If I'm lucky, it won't come to any of that and this will be a quick grab and go. That's what I'm counting on, and crossing my fingers and toes for.

"Do I have to go back out there?"

Dana helped me get away from all the testosterone filling every crevice in my house. It started with Jax and Logan being overly protective of me, but then it grew and grew as Valant messed with everyone, rising tenfold when Ryan showed up and Logan went into this competitive mode of wits versus brawn, which only led to more of Valant's shit. The only one who seemed to not react like a teenage boy was Ryan. He seems focused, subdued even. Man, it must have been some night he and Alex had; I only hope his laid-back attitude doesn't throw him off his game. We kind of need the big guy. Whatever his mood is, he seems to think we'll have no problem knowing when Alex is in the other space. The ring has a constant pull, but there's a change in it when she's moved, although that's all still somewhat of a theory.

Dana and Ryan seem on board with the plan, almost kicking themselves for not thinking of it before. Ryan gave a few shrugs and a few words to explain how he'll know when Alex is there. His stoic stance and decision to move to another room gave the impression that he was not in a sharing mood. So we're just waiting with anticipation here, all of us. Did I mention this is a two-bedroom home in La Jolla? It's not exactly big on space, especially to hold all these egos filling it up, but pretty cute all the same.

Hours go by, as do takeout boxes.

"Ah ha! Eureka. This should do the trick."

Dana comes into the living area where Jax, Ryan, and I are sitting. What looks like smoke is billowing off the back of her head and a squirming black thing is held between her fingers. Ryan circles her, checking that she isn't, or is no longer, on fire. As she gets closer, glossy snapping jaws appear to be working hard to get at her finger.

"This little devil here can cut through anything," she says, pushing on what looks like a beetle's back. The thing stops moving. She presses it again and his jaws go at it once more. "He not only cuts through anything, but also absorbs—or eats, I guess you can say—and takes on what he ingests. Then he stays on Alex's person, and even though the magic won't be put together exactly the same to control her powers, it'll still be there, so if there's a booby trap to signal the king, he'll be none the wiser. Sweet, right?"

Oh, he's sweet all right, when he's off. I'll be turning him on only when he's on Alex's arm. She's the all-loving critter keeper. I draw the line on bugs. Oh, and snakes. And scorpions. Screw those guys!

"Take him, girl. Hide him in your little coat pocket there and try not to turn him on by accident. It won't tickle like your Jaxhammer, I assure you." After a huge smirk, Jax helps me out and we place the little guy gently in a pocket that won't get bumped easily. I give him a shaky smile then look at Ryan who gives me a headshake. No go on his Alex radar, but now I'm armed and far less worried about the trip. The only other thing I'll need is my weapon, which is the Nanda-yi, and when Ryan gives the word, he'll come to me at Logan's command and enter the reality Alex and I are in. I worried at first about keeping a large war eagle with me, but Yi can shrink in size when he chooses; it's part of how he becomes Logan's tattoo.

More hours tick by and we're all getting edgy. What if Ryan's link has gone as well? What will happen then? I don't know about everyone else, but I do know what I am prepared to do.

"I can go to her cell instead. No big deal. If the king or any of his minions are there I'll pop right out and try again later. Easy peasy."

Jax's long drawl comes in extra sultry from where he sits with Logan at the island.

"He knew you were there right away last time, Sand. It's too risky in his castle and you know that. Now we've agreed to this plan of yours already, so just give it some time. It's always been nighttime when Ryan could see her. We knew it might be a wait, so relax, don't be hasty. I bet that's what the king wants us to do. Make sloppy mistakes. For us to get comfortable and feel safe."

I glance at Ryan. He's still calm and cool over there. Maybe I'm mistaken and it's really just confidence. He let emotions get in the way before when it came to Alex and he nearly lost her because of it. He's smart to be the master of Zen. It's what drove Alex nuts about him to begin with, meaning whatever works doesn't need fixing, I suppose.

Just like that, Zen Ryan is alert and ready to pounce. "She's there. You have to get in there now!"

I jump at the sound of his voice, but the little critter in my pocket is a reminder to keep my cool. I like my lady parts, thank you, all of them.

Logan gives me one last worried look. "Are you sure this will work? That you'll be okay?"

"Well, there's only one way to find out. Isn't there." My face feels tight, so I take a deep breath to calm my nerves before giving them a spunky smile. "Yi. Saddle up, big guy. It's time to go."

Yi tears from Logan's right arm, my brother's grimace the only sign that it's never an easy transformation. Instead of growing to his full eagle size, he stays small as a chickadee. Ha, cute, Yi the chickadee. A small peck on my neck has me wondering if he read my mind, or maybe it was in response to the goofy look I gave him when he landed on my shoulder.

"Right then. See you in a blink, Dana. Bye, boys." A wink first and then my eyes close. My winged tattoos blaze to life like a catching fire as the link to my brother, lover, and Yi ignites and I know my boys have my back. Here we go. My brazen attitude is starting to get a little shaky, but there's no turning back now. I think of Alex and where she is now. Wonder where we're going this time? Hopefully it's back in the club with lots of people and not in some sexy hotel where she's waiting for Ryan only to get her cat burglar–looking BFF instead.

A raucous noise hits my ears and my smile spreads, knowing it must be the club. The king knows where to bring her so she'll be most relaxed and wide open, and there's no place better than where she can dance the night away with her friends.

Before the focus begins to sharpen, Yi grips onto me with his tiny sharp claws. "Easy Yi, you'll be fine. Get back into my collar, will ya." He cheeps. He sounds a bit alarmed. Great. If Logan's right and I'm screwed he'll never let me live this down. *If* I live this down. My eyes clear and I see not at all what I was expecting. Waves breaking against a rocky cliff assail my ears and the dark night sky has only its moon to contribute light in the darkness. Where in the hell? Looking around, I see trails spidering off. I'm at the top of one of many hikes Alex and I take to the Pacific Ocean cliffs. But if I'm here, then where is she?

A holler echoes into the night and I turn to see a tall, lithe form running at me full out.

"Sandra, get out of here! You have to get out of here *now!*" Alex? Something hard hits both of my ears, a sound that is deafening and nearly paralyzing as it attacks my mind. It's like an alarm going off, and if its aim is to create confusion it is certainly working. Thankfully I can still hear Alex over the painful noise. "He knows you're here. Get out, *please.* You *have* to get out."

Shit, is this a trap or is something else at play? Another figure approaches to my right, and this time it's not a friendly.

"Miss Oman. How lovely. It was so nice to get into your little eagle's powers, not only to shut it down, but also to set up my little security system. Oh yes, I knew you'd try to come back to save her. I was counting on it."

Shit. Again. I don't have much time. Ignoring the excruciating pain in my head, I turn away from the king in his crazy velvet get-up and instead run for Alex as fast as my booted feet will carry me. Yi begins to change into full eagle size ready to take on the king to the right while I dig into my pocket for Dana's beetle, not caring in the least if I lose a finger in the process. I can do this; I'll be fast enough this time.

"Sandra, no!" Alex's large doll eyes can be seen even in the night surrounding us. The shape in the corner of my vision is moving faster than I thought possible. I'm not going to make it. No!! I have to get her out of here. But if I can't . . .

"Yi, get it to her. You can make it. I'll distract him."

Yi shakes his head at me, screeching and looking at the king. Maybe he's right. He gave the feather to her last time and the king will suspect that, plus, Yi has better battle skills. I nod at Yi, and he lifts off me and goes barreling at the king while I continue running full out to Alex. Lifting my fist to my heart so only she can see, I point to my wrist and then to the little bug. I think she knows I have something for her. I hope she knows. I can't get too close or he'll realize what I'm doing, so I drop the bug to the ground, digging my heel in a line in the dirt right behind his tiny black body so she'll know where to look. Glancing behind me, I can see a dark green glow on the king's hand. Yi attacks, retreats. He's keeping the king busy, but he's also hovering in a dangerous game where he's going to get himself killed or taken. Giving my best friend one last look, I see her eyes pleading with me to leave. She mouths to me *I will be okay.* I have to believe her, trust her, and the hardest thing of all—I have to leave her.

Screaming out into the chorus of the waves breaking against the rocky cliffs, I haul ass away from Alex, yelling to Yi to leave his fight behind so we can get out of here. He lunges once more at the king, perhaps even getting a talon into him before using his powerful wings to fly swiftly toward me. He's nearly to me when I hear the king yell out to me once again. Where Alex once was, she's thankfully gone, and I take a breath to use my Seer skill to move out of this place right now.

"You should have taken my warning, Miss Oman. I thought you'd get the hint when I broke the connection, though I so hoped you wouldn't, and now that you have come back, I must make you pay. I have your histories, your hearts. She may not have given me what I want, yet, but she's given me enough to keep her trapped against your meddling. You

95

will all pay, more than you already are. In more ways than you will ever imagine. I'm there. That's what you keep forgetting. I'm always there and always here. You'll never get her back and she'll never leave. Now get out and never come back, or I'll keep you here as well."

Part of me wants to tell him to fuck off, but he aims his glowing ring my way and an impossibly strong magnetic pull jerks me to him. Swallowing hard, I know it's time to go. I may not be able to fight off the king's magic if I stay any longer. Closing my eyes, I think of Logan and Jax, and my ink wings answer, flaring to life as I think of home.

Once my feet press against the floor of my house again I nearly choke on the sobs that rack me. I've missed her again. I was so close. Jax embraces me in the chaos of voices asking me what happened. I hear Alex's name being repeated over and over again, and I can only allow Jax to hold me for a moment while I try to calm down and remember that she's okay and she's strong. Regaining my composure, I reassure Jax that I'm alright, and I turn to look at the room of faces staring at me.

"It was a trap. He used the magic he removed from Yi's feather to know when I tried to come back." They wait calmly for me to continue even though anxiety is rolling in obvious waves all around the room. "He was talking in riddles about us, about what he knows, histories and things. He said we would pay." My faith and confidence in Alex being able to take care of herself is now starting to break apart as fear settles in at what his words meant and what may be in the cards for us. "I'm so sorry. What have I done? I should have listened to you, Logan. He's going to come after us."

Logan touches my shoulder, looking calmer than I would have expected. One of us has to be. "He may have been scaring you off. Let's not worry just yet. Remember, it's Alex he needs something from, and now that he knows we can't get in without him knowing, he may have been threatening us to seal the deal so we don't try again. I've seen it all before." I do hope Logan is right. Though I fear he isn't.

"We need to use our Sight to check the future. It isn't necessarily personal so we aren't breaking any laws. We can check Alex's or Ryan's and maybe we can see all of ours." I'm walking a thin line. Seers aren't supposed to use their skill for personal reasons, but this situation affects more than just us.

"I'll do it, Yi and I will. Come on, Yi. I'll hear what else happened in there later." Logan moves to the guest room with Yi. I long to go with him, wishing to see what's next together and dreading it all the same.

"Did you see Alex?" Ryan's question, though asked in a very relaxed way, was expected, and this time I can smile.

"Yes, I saw her. We were on one of our trails by the ocean cliffs and she told me to get out. She warned me. I tried to get to her, but he was there in an instant. She begged me to get out of there. I didn't want to, not without her, but she said she was going to be okay. So Yi and I got out, but not before leaving her the critter you gave me, Dana. Perhaps now she can free herself."

Energy vibrates around the room. Dana gives Ryan a smack on his shoulder and the big guy seems to ease down more than he already was. Valant murmurs something about creepy crawlies being useful, you see, and Jax wraps his strong arms around me telling me I've done well. So why does my heart keep fluttering around wildly in my chest?

A phone starts to go off with an unfamiliar chime, and Jax moves his hand away from me slowly. He reaches into his back pocket with the strangest look on his face.

"Who is it?" I can barely ask the question. My mouth has gone dry and I tremble with a newfound chill.

"It's Nora. It's been years. I don't even know where she is."

Same. I've never been able to find my childhood friend, Jax's sister Nora. We were all inseparable, but she was always the freest spirit of us all. Jax answers and we can hear the screaming and madness coming from his phone. His expression changes from curiosity to terror, but before he can tell us a thing Logan comes tearing into the room with Yi screeching behind him.

"It's Nora. There's been an accident. She's hurt. It's bad. She's dying. Others are dead. We have to get to Spain. Now."

The king. He wasn't scaring us off. He was telling me exactly what he was going to do.

CHAPTER 10

Paradise Lost

Who will open these burdened walls?
Our own minds enclosing us
As if a prison.

✳

The surrounding air is suffocating, as though I am stuck beneath quicksand or struggling to break through the water's surface. I can't breathe. Panicking, I wonder if I will make it back and away from the dreamland the king has placed me in once again. Darkness surrounds me, as does the air, which is as chilling cold as night in the Colorado desert. I'm trembling, afraid. Get it together, Alex, this is not how you'll go, not after everything you've already been through. I mean, there is so much more to do, and you're an Earthen Protector, a Healer. Focus. But my focus earns me a painful burn on my wrist. Trying to harness my abilities is of little use with this damn shackle on my arm. Though I'll give it some props right now since the fiery warning seems to trigger an end to my near-asphyxiation and I can breathe normally again. The dank coldness remains though, like I'm floating in a starless space. I've had this weightless experience before. It reminds me of how I traveled to other dimensions trying to find Mom when I was younger. How does the king's dreamland make me feel as though I'm moving to another place? Or is it more than just similar? Could my body actually be moving?

Remembering the odd bug-like object Sandra left for me, I pat around for it in my jacket. I swear it's moving. Ouch. What in the hell? I think it bit me. I touch where the critter is hidden once again and it goes still. Letting the darkness be what it is, I play around with the object some more, realizing I can turn it off and on. Please have this thing be what I need to be able to use my powers again. The sooner I can get the damn bracelet off, the sooner I'll have freedom to leave my cell and work with Thatcher to try bringing back Justin, which will mean one huge step closer to home. The final act is in Verus's hands.

"Eila?"

Looking around in the dark is useless. She's only in my mind and I am—well I have no idea where in the hell I am. What I do know is that her crazy dad saw me with Sandra, and that I was aware, so I have to warn Verus.

"Verus? Oh, it's good to hear your voice, but you have to listen. I think you need to be prepared for your father. My friend tried to save me and your father had set a trap for her. I'm sorry, Verus. He had to have known I wasn't under his influence. He could very well come down here to blame you for that, and everything will be ruined." Verus had sent me away to follow whatever the king had planned for me, but with my full awareness. He wanted me to see Sandra, but why?

"Eila. Don't worry about that. Just focus on my voice and keep talking. It will help bring you back. I'm your anchor. I had to bring you into this dark void where none of his spies could find us. Just hold on. I nearly have you home."

Okay, that should be easy enough. Maybe. I mean, how can I not worry about the king coming for both of us? He has to be furious.

"I may have some good news," I tell her. "My friend gave me something that might help us with this little ball and chain bangle. I'll give it to you, so keep it safe, and maybe you guys can figure out what it does and how to use it."

Not sure the stiff, stony bed against my back will be any better than the nothingness I'm stuck in, especially when I know the king will soon be freaking me out with his anger. Grabbing the critter from its hiding spot and putting it into the palm of my hand, I tell Verus to take it and am relieved when warm fingers wrap around mine. My cell comes into focus and I look at Verus's red hair and Lestan's eyes. How can she not hate me?

"You better get your Glena suit back on. He's coming and he's pissed. What are we going to do?" Is she laughing? Oh my goddess, my way out of this hellhole has made her lose her mind.

"Oh, I'm sorry, Eila. I'm just so excited about what's about to happen. Flean will never know what hit her. Well, I mean she'll know because it may even be the king himself, but she'll have no idea who set her up. Being this good is hard work, you know."

I am seriously confused now, but not at all opposed to a doomed Fleabag. She sucks and I mean with a capital S.

"We've made it look like Flean made a deal with a Demon to trade you to him, and she's going to pay ever so dearly. My father hates Demons more than anyone or anything else in all the worlds, even more than you all. Flean is as good as gone, and guess who is next in line to take her place?"

I point to her, biting my lip and raising an eyebrow. I do hope her sanity is intact, because she's making me a little nervous.

"That's right! Me. I will have complete control over what is done to you, aside from what he does, of course, but if I know my father—and I do know him—he'll be so happy to throw my ascension in Flean's face that he won't even think twice about trusting me. The cad."

I look at her warily and she brushes her hair back from her face, straightening it and giving her head a shake. I wonder if she's rattling loose some crazed thought.

"I may have neglected my sleep to ensure this plan went without a hitch, not to mention the actual Demon trade I had to make, but no matter. Things are looking up for us."

Demon trade. Oh shit. That's something I'm all too familiar with.

"Please stop looking at me like that. I'm fine. I've just used quite a bit of my power, or given rather, and need to rest. I'll be tiptop tomorrow. Now, I need to sedate you so he doesn't come in here and smack you around. You see, it wasn't your fault, and I was the good medic, stepping in, bringing you back, and putting you back under for him. It's delightful."

Why does she sound like a crazed Mary Poppins? Of course I've been where she is right now, having been pushed to the brink of madness when Greg and Valant snatched my sleep and served me with a side of mind-splitting migraine. I trust her though, and Thatcher. Whatever she's done has made it possible for me to get something from Sandra—and right under the king's nose, too—that will be very important in ensuring we all get what we agreed upon. And if she has managed to get rid of Flean as well, we're in an even better position.

I will say for the record that I am sick of being put to sleep. If the king doesn't manage to take my memories, he may take some part of my physiology with all of this Fae drug crap. Verus is confident of his blame on Flean and newfound faith in her Glena impersonation, but what if he just decides to take everything over himself? Verus's smile is still plastered on her face as she roots around in her bag. Stay positive, Alex. This will all be over soon. It has to be.

"This won't last long, I promise. I'm going to get this object to Thatcher as soon as I can, and he'll come to you when I give the all clear. You'll have freedom this time. So go where you're needed, where you want, or to whom you want."

Freedom to go where I want? There's no way she knows about Ryan and me, does she? Funny she uses the word *go*. Go where? To sleep? And didn't she say she brought me back? Before I can question the wording of a sleep-deprived Fae, I hear the cell door open. I look at Verus, who simply says,

"Have a good trip. Don't go too far. I'll bring you back soon."

I hope she isn't giving me magic mushrooms or making me part of some Timothy Leary LSD experiment. Or is she being literal? Are these visions, these Dreamwalks, more than they seem? Is it like I thought? Am I traveling dimensions? Worlds? My eyes flutter, closing under the medical spell injection. Without my power, how can I travel, or is the king's concoction given so he, or Verus, can direct where I go, and if so, how did he create a world like my own? Knowing more now about Misa and Thatcher's powers makes all things possible. Perhaps the king is moving me to his own stage, a world created to be just like mine, one I could lose myself in if I really wanted to, one without the dangers of my reality.

If I'm able to travel, and if I finally have some control, can I go home? Can I see everyone? Oh! Was my time with Ryan truly real? But then how did he get to me without Vex?

The bracelet shifts on my wrist, reminding me that whomever I see, I'm fairly sure I can't stay. It must be a shackle to the Fae dimension, but somehow it allows my powers to work in particular ways, at least to travel to certain places. For goddess's sake, I should have kept the little critter Sandra gave me. But then . . . I would be gone and my promise to Thatcher and Verus would be broken. Can I bear to see my friends only to be yanked back again? Would they try to get this chain off me, unable to understand that I have so much to do before I can truly come home? Sandra would get it; she knows that when I commit to helping someone I won't walk away. Ryan would have to understand as well, wouldn't he? Choosing the strangers in this land over my friends may be hard for any one of them to truly understand, but we are Protectors; our lives are meant to save others from darkness. Even though Avalon isn't our world—my world—part of it lives in me, and part of Lestan remains as well. I can't leave him shattered in pieces under the dirt in his greenhouse, and I can't leave Verus and Misa to the ire of the king.

Thinking of Sandra and Ryan sends a pull from my heart, and my body becomes buoyed, like I'm floating in thick water. I can breathe fine this time, perhaps because I am truly in control. Maybe I'll be able to maintain it and remember every part of this journey. My mind was probably so freaked out by the void Verus brought me to that I terrified myself into a panic attack. All of the other times I have moved into a dreamland, or the king's fake reality, I've only truly awoken back in my cell and without having recalled the actual journey. This time things are different. This time I am the pilot.

Looking around, I see twinkling lights in my dark surroundings. They provide enough brightness to see my hands in front of me as I swim through this thick space. Is this what astronauts experience? I try to kick and move, but walls prevent me, pushing against me on all sides. It's like a tube or tunnel of some sort. Perhaps this is the path in and out of the king's world. Instead of allowing the restricting walls to close in and quicken my breathing, I inhale deeply, rolling my shoulders and letting the trail guide me. I have my wits about me, according to Verus. That is, as long as I am here and away from my cell where I am safe from the king for now. A tiny trickle of worry appears. I certainly hope Verus is right and not just fearlessly, and sleeplessly, confident in the outcome of her framing of Flean. I also can't forget that a Demon is involved. That will surely mean trouble, and if not now, there's sure to be some serious kickback later.

Lost in my thoughts, I mistake a pang of sorrow as my own. But I am not sad, only wary. No, this grief isn't my own. The sadness grows and hits me like a wall of bricks and the sounds of sobbing tear out of a deafening chaos. The sparkling path is taking me toward the sound and images begin to play around me, rushing past like a burst of photos scrolling on a screen. I catch clear glimpses as they fly by; some are flashes and images of Yi flying and attacking, some are Sandra running at someone in the distance, and others are of a glowing green shining into the night. This green is dark and sickly, not like my energy tendrils at all. These images are not from my past, not really; the point of view is off. Yi appears to be attacking me, and wait, is that the real me Sandra is running to? Oh no, not again.

I try to scream out, but stop when my brain catches up with my eyes. I'm watching what has already happened. Sandra stops. I can't see what she is doing before she turns on her heel and runs at me, her eyes going blank while the eagle flies away from its attack, latching his clawed feet onto Sandra's shoulders just before they disappear. Shooting my hands out, I try to stop myself like I did as a child going down a slide. I saw something, but can I go back and see it again? Screams of terror break through my focus, and pelting vibrations of urgency follow. I kick my legs; I just need to see it one more time. As I slide backward, the images rewind, and I stop when Sandra's face is clear and staring right at me. Her expression is defiant and angry, but then changes to one of fear and worry. I hear words—the voice of the king. Dread drips down my spine, one vertebra at a time, and I flinch at each step it takes. Something has happened, and I am seeing what that is from a path that was not my own. No, this is the king's path, and the muscles tightening in my neck signal that there is something at the end causing the terror and sadness that's been creeping into my awareness.

Swallowing hard, and praying to the goddess that this isn't a trap, I find myself on the rocky cliff again. Ocean-driven wind hits my face, while the brush and dirt crunch under my feet and the calls of flying creatures in the night air assault my ears. This has to be real. Still wearing the Fae clothes, I'm happy to have the gloves on in the chill coastal air. Something tells me that the fight is long over, but that whatever happened has been brutal and swift. The sounds of fear have faded away against the angry Pacific background, but even without the noises I can sense the terror. It pulls me to the right, toward where I recall seeing the king standing, his cloak flying behind him and his evil ring glowing toward Yi and Sandra. I concentrate all my attention on the pull, pushing away this stage by the sea and urging my body to the next stop on this path of rage and destruction. Something terrible awaits, but I am not going to let that keep me away—I'm a chaos magnet, remember?

I begin to move through the tunnel of lights and darkness again, but this time the flashes are absent, and only revenge, madness, and hysteria fill the space, causing my teeth and fists to clench. It's suffocating. It feels as if I'm actually in the king's mind. At first I try to pull away from the alien thoughts and emotions but then realize this may be my only chance to get a real peek inside what the freak of nature is thinking—maybe even what he wants from me. Deliberately drifting into the king's mind, I follow his free forming thoughts.

This shit is not pretty.

Revenge is front and foremost, along with a swelling pride that was easily broken by a woman. With that thought, Sandra's image comes to mind. Seeing her makes me—or rather, the king—even angrier and the irrational thoughts cycle on and on about women and how dare they stand against me, turn on me, leave me. Leave me, deny me. I start to move past this tendril of thought to a place far away, somewhere in a blue ocean—an island . . . but I know, I know, I've touched on something important. Focusing, I try to grasp back onto his last thoughts before his travel plans take over.

My mouth moves. Lips, my own, but the voice is not. "How dare they oppose me? Don't they know who I am? What I am? The power I am? They will pay. They will all pay, and once I get my hands on her she will pay for all of them, for leaving me, for denying me."

105

I can't stand it any longer; I shove his terrible words and thoughts away, throwing them from my person and into the darkness. Being within the king's psychotic mind is crazier than cradling a bag of rabid rats. It leaves me queasy. I can't bear the taste his words have left in my mouth, his thirst for power, his hatred for Sandra, for me, for someone else, someone who left him, who denied him. It's that person who riled him up the most, though we all blend in now to him. He hates us, but he needs us—no, he wants *her*. Yet who she is remains a mystery. Perhaps it's his wife? Did he lie to Lestan and Verus? Did she actually choose to leave him, to leave her children? And if it is she, why would he need me to bring her back?

My reeling thoughts are cut short when images begin to fly by once again. One word tears through the darkness. Ibiza. What does the king want with an island in the Mediterranean? I doubt he is dying to club hop in paradise. Shane keeps saying I need to go there with him one year—research he says. Yeah, right. Yet the king's trip isn't about fun and games. Not at all. That man has no idea what fun is. His fun involves pain and torture, which are most definitely not part of the five star highlights one reads about when planning an Ibiza vacay.

Stunningly clear turquoise water, sandy beaches, and glorious hotels mixed with ancient buildings become pictures upon the curved walls of this traveling tunnel. Ibiza is alive with people packing the beaches, dancing along the pools and outdoor bars. Ferries and boats move from shore to shore along a water so inviting I long to dive in and feel its coolness surround my skin. Music and laughter become clearer, and I need to tell myself more than once that I'm not going to club and gorge on delicious food while basking in the sun. No, this is not a social visit, so what is the crazed king up to?

The view changes rapidly, flicking from left to right and back. One name emerges from his ramblings that I can still hear even though I'm no longer immersed in them. Nora. Who in the hell is Nora? He's more determined now, as if he's located his prey. The images focus on a stunning white hotel by the water. A sandy beach connects to a poolside that leads to the hotel and to a smaller building holding a bar and a DJ booth. Throngs of dancing bodies surround the pool's edge, up onto the many balconies of hotel rooms, and atop the open second floor of the bar. There, on the bar's balcony, is a girl. This is who the king was looking for. She twirls and floats around throngs of bodies, smiling as she goes, stopping to dance with someone closely from time to time, then moving on until she reaches what appears to be a group of her friends. They embrace, dance, drink, and laugh in the Mediterranean paradise. Watching this creates a longing for the freedom this blonde beauty appears to have, a freedom I used to enjoy before I stopped ignoring what my life is truly meant for, which is to save people.

Something in me knows she is one of those people. I want to scream out to her, to warn her, but these are images of what has already come to pass. All I can do now is hope I can reach her and help her once I get through this dimensional road and that what I am seeing now wasn't a time long since past.

All at once two things happen. The girl Nora looks right at me—rather, she looks at the king—and her eyes glaze over the way Sandra's do when she slips into her Sight. Nora's a Seer, and by the look on her face she knows what's coming for her, but it's too late. She tries to warn her friends, helplessly trying to push them to an exit while yelling at everyone else to get away, but they are wrapped up in the frenzy of the DJ's beats and the near shaman-like trance she's created. It's too loud; no one is listening to Nora's warnings, and I want to close my eyes to avoid watching whatever is coming. Just as I am so focused and worried about Nora, a wild wind swirls within the tunnel. It's the king's magic. His power pushes and rages, tossing my hair and breaking against my skin as if thorns were scratching and tearing at my flesh. This is new. This is a magnified, multiplied version, and different from when he tore me from Sandra's home. It's nothing like anything I've seen the king unleash before. This is different, and it's driven by the memory of a woman, a woman he thinks I can bring to him.

Small objects smack against the side of my head, scratching my cheeks and raking through my hair. No, he isn't just going for Nora; he's tearing the entire place down. A vacuum-like suction takes my breath and shoots a surging tidal wave of power outward and all around me. The picture doesn't change much, though I can make out a shimmer of sorts surrounding the hotel. I watch as people who were coming off the beach toward the pool just suddenly turn around. What has he done? As I continue to watch, horrified, the king's gleeful mind nearly claps with delight and now I understand that he's trapped everyone inside, and anyone outside has no desire to approach. It appears both groups are unaware of this oddity. No one even tries to leave, and those outside change direction, seemingly forgetting they ever wanted to enter, or perhaps to them the hotel isn't even there.

Why would he do that? The answer comes unbidden in a vicious spit from my mouth. *Now these miserable humans will perish with no chance of escape or assistance. They will all die!* No. No way. What is he doing? No.

A deafening boom escapes from my pathway and the pictures change in an instant, passing me as tears sting my eyes and drive a cold path down my cheeks. Cyclones of earth tear people from the balconies, flinging them into the air where they crash to the ground. Terrorized screaming breaks out but no one tries to leave, no one except Nora who seems to have her wits about her despite the danger. She, and one other person who holds tightly onto her hand, race around the balcony trying to find a way off. I find them easily, she with her creamy skin and red swimsuit running alongside him in stunning contrast with his long dreaded hair and dark skin tone. They are beautiful even in the misery. She catches my eyes from time to time, as does he, and a nudging at my skin must be her friend's attempt to use his abilities to squelch the king's attack. The king's laughter bounces around my dimensional slide in response to the destruction he's wrought. Not holding back, he continues to unleash his magic on the hotel crowd as more bodies are lifted into the air and hurled into the pool or against the walls. There must be nearly a hundred people here; does he plan to kill them all?

Outside the hotel it is just as I feared. No one can hear the screams. No one stops or even looks baffled about what is happening mere feet from them. It's a terrifying scene. The open pool area is only separated from the beach by a low clear wall, so everything should be plainly in view to anyone looking at the hotel, but the king's power has cloaked them, and his vengeance continues to unleash onto the innocent partygoers. I just want it to stop so I can get there—maybe, just maybe I can still save some of these people. Reality smacks me hard across the face. *Okay Alex, how? How are you going to save them?* Looking at my wrist I see the power cock-blocking bracelet still there. Damn it. Stay calm; I just need to get there first and then deal with this. What am I thinking? I'm not a doctor. Shit. I'm nothing without my powers, nothing that can fix this.

I watch in horror as the building itself begins to tear apart. Pieces of rock, cement, and metal rip through the air, some pieces flying into people, knocking them to the ground, pinning them beneath a bone-crushing weight. Then it truly hits me; in some way this has to be my fault. Whatever is happening here is somehow directly related to what happened moments ago with Sandra, which means none of this would have happened if the king didn't need me and if my friends hadn't tried to save me. Why won't the king just ask me for what he wants? Why can't he just reason with me, or with this person he wants? A small voice in my mind says, *he has.* Shit, if he's asked me and I've fought him, refused him and then he made me forget, then there's no reasoning to be done. All I can hope for now is to fix this. But how?

The final scene along the tunnel is of Nora trying to flee with her friend, both of them trying to climb down the roof, but to no avail. They look at each other then peek over the railing to where the pool lies below. Backing up, they run full force, side by side, and jump from the balcony into the water. It's a small win, and I send up a fist pump hoping that maybe they can escape. Yet the king doesn't miss a beat. Instead, he tears a piece of the building away and viciously flings it after them. It sinks and I can only watch and pray. The man's head breaks the surface, but a pool of blood surrounds him; he's hurt. Not caring, he dives back under the water, bubbles break the surface, and thrashing moves the pool water in waves. His dark head reappears and he gasps for air before diving down again. Nora must be trapped. Damn it, can this path move any faster, because I have seen enough! I smile and fist punch the air once again when I see his head, and then hers. He has Nora. But my celebration ends quickly when he reaches the wall, pleading for someone to help him get her out of the water. Anytime someone tries to help they are torn away by the king's ferocious wind. Whoever these two are, the mad king has deemed them fit to torture. After finally dragging himself through the water, Nora's friend makes it to the shallow end and pulls her from the pool, laying her crushed body upon the edge. I can hardly look at her mangled form and the amount of blood she's losing. Instantly, her friend starts trying to resuscitate her; his breaths and pulses on her chest are focused at first, but as time goes on he becomes frantic. Finally he straddles her still form, pounding on her chest, trying to jumpstart her heart as their blood mixes around them in a pool of death and carnage.

Success flashes across the portal. The king is pleased with himself and his bloodlust is sated and lessening—for now. He turns from the place of his destruction, and a spectral feeling passes through my body. Coldness seeps into my bones and I hold my breath. Becoming very still, I hope he won't see me. I also hope I'm overreacting, since his departure must have happened before I even left my cell. Who can blame me though? I've been close to him before and this reflection or memory loop of the path he took to Ibiza is frighteningly close to the real thing. Time is of the essence, so I calm myself, knowing he must have already returned to his kingdom where he's been dealing with Flean and hopefully praising Verus. Now that his memories end, the images stop, followed by my own fear I won't get a chance to help the injured and dying. Will the portal close before I can step into the chaos of the Ibiza hotel? And even if I still can, what is my plan?

Before I can think of anything that makes sense in my current state of powerlessness, warmth spreads through my mind, giving me a moment of happiness before the soothing rays of sunlight are followed by the sounds of panic. A smell assaults my nose, bringing me back to the cellar of Greg's house. Blood. Human blood and death.

My eyes slowly focus, but I shield them when smoke and dirt swirl all around me. Screams ring out and people are running everywhere. The words are unclear at first and I think it's my hearing, but then I realize people are shouting and screaming in different languages. English and Spanish mainly, but Ibiza draws people from all over the world, and everyone here right now is frightened beyond belief. I must be at the hotel, right in the middle of it. Scanning the area, I realize I'm on the pool deck. All around me, every inch is littered with bricks and debris. It looks like a bomb went off. Close to it. The king of Avalon unleashed his explosives of earth, air, and magic, and still, no one outside this hotel appears to be aware. The damaging blows have stopped, though pieces of debris still fall from the building and swirl through the air. Bodies, bloodied and covered in dirt and soot are all around me; some people are helping others, and some are just sitting crying out into the sky or huddling over a still form as their bodies shake with grief.

I have to do something. First, I seek out the king's target. I need to try and help her if I still can. As I move nearer to them I hear the man. He's fallen upon Nora in his sorrow and his own blood loss, and he appears to be talking to someone. I'm nearly beside him and I hear the name Jax followed by one word over and over again—*sorry*. Jax? Sandra's Jax? Getting a clear view now, though it's hard to see with all the blood and dirt on Nora's face, I try to make out who she is. I know she's a Seer and she must be someone close to them, or why else would the king target her in this way? I kneel beside her friend, and his body barely reacts, only releasing a small quake when I touch him lightly with my fingertips.

"Let me help you. I'm a friend. Is this Nora?" The man's head nods, but his eyes stay downcast, looking at her and weeping. A voice calls out from the phone that is now resting on the deck in the man's weak grasp.

"Troy! Troy, who is that? Troy, are you there? Sandra and Logan are coming. They're able to get to you through Sandra's vision. They're coming for you, right now. Stay with me. Troy?"

I reach slowly for the phone, soothing Troy with my words and using my other hand to touch Nora's wrist, praying I'll find a pulse. Lifting the phone to my ear, I try to remain calm, but what is in any way calming about what has happened here? I can only hope I can get someone here in time to help. But who? I need a Healer, and the two I know are both too weak and out of reach.

"Hello, Jax? This is Sandra's Jax, right?"

Silence answers me while a discouraging stillness meets my fingers while I hunt for any semblance of Nora's pulse. I may not have trained as a doctor or a medic in the traditional sense, but my grandmother taught me many things that would help hide my healing powers when I worked on someone or something. Now if only I had those healing abilities to mask.

"Who is this? Did you have something to do with this? If she's dead, if my sister is dead, I swear to god I will kill you myself."

My chest convulses. Nora is Jax's sister, Sandra's best friend growing up. The king's gone after the jugular while tearing apart their hearts.

"Jax, Jax, it's Alex."

A bellowing holler answers me. "*Alex?!?* But how?"

"Jax, I don't have time to fully explain. I followed the king's path here. He did this. He worked a spell to stop anyone leaving. No one outside the hotel knows that this even happened. He attacked the entire hotel. We're in Ibiza. People are dead, dying, and terribly injured. We need a Healer here now." And I stop there. What I don't say is what rages around in my head. I can't do it, I can't save her . . . I can't save any of them. My fingers tremble on the pulseless wrist of the girl beside me, and I shudder. Grief comes through the phone as well, and I try to compose myself.

"Stay on the line while I try to help them. Troy is hurt pretty bad as well, so keep talking to him and tell me when Sandra and Logan are here."

I speak softly to Troy, encouraging him to move off Nora. I hand him the phone and ask him if he knows where he's injured. Hands shaking, he lifts his shirt, wincing. There's a huge gushing gash on his stomach. I crawl to grab a couple of towels, wrapping one around him tightly and telling him to apply pressure to it. Then I move back to Nora and try to assess her injuries without moving her much. Though she's bleeding, that's not why she isn't breathing. She drowned at the hands of the king. I search again for a pulse and finally sense something so faint and small, but enough to hold on to hope.

Yanking off my gloves in the hot sun, I begin CPR, just as Troy has done already, but I'm not going to give up. His injuries may take his life as well, so the least I can do is try when he no longer can. Pulses then breathe, pulses then breathe—nothing. "Damn it!" My scream tears from me. I need help. I need this bracelet gone, and when I look up I know I need more than that. Nora is one of many, and though I see others helping the wounded, there are also many trying as I am to bring someone back. I can't lose focus, just do what I can, one person at a time. Sandra and Logan can travel fast with Yi so I mustn't lose hope. While continuing to try and revive Nora, I also begin to cry out from my mind, pleading to Verus for help. She was able to talk to me in the last path I was on, but here I am on someone else's path, as well as somewhere defined and real. Can she even hear me? If so, what could she possibly do? Verus can't travel as I can. I'm alone. Worse yet, what if someone else can hear me as well? Someone less inclined to assist? And then a name floats to my awareness. Thatcher. The massive cat can travel, and if I'm lucky enough, he will have figured out a way to get this damn bracelet off me so I can be of use among this carnage. I might be able to save some people.

Not giving up on Nora, I focus on Thatcher, on his fur, voice, face, and whiskers, all of him, and I send my thoughts his way. Memories flood from my mind into the space around me, and I look over at where I first appeared here. I see a movement, like a breeze shifting an invisible curtain, and a pull follows. It's the opening to the path. I don't want to stop trying to help Nora, but if I can get a word to Thatcher, perhaps I can truly save her and others. I push off her and make a run for the path, Troy hollering after me with some of the last of his energy. Once I reach the opening I scream inside, all of my heart, my passion, my fears, my love, all of me that I have both cherished and hated are in my voice as I scream his name. A rumble answers me from the path, the path back to Avalon, and I tense at the thought of the king returning. But then I hear him, the large cat.

"Eila? Is that you? Where in the worlds are you? I was just . . ."

Before he can finish, his large black paw appears from the invisible path, followed by another and then the rest of his great feline form. I throw my arms around him as his head moves from side to side and his muscles flex for a fight. Before he can ask, I tell him what I saw and he calms his fight reaction.

"The king must have left in such haste that he forgot to cover his tracks and close his path. We must work quickly and close it behind us before he realizes. Then we'll have to hope he doesn't come back for a peek at his handiwork."

I'm so happy to see him, but the huge undertaking around us has me falling back into despair.

"I can't do anything without my powers. I'm trying to . . ."

I look over my shoulder and see Troy has slumped over in a pool of blood, while Nora lies there, still as stone, with her fingers touching his. I run back and take up my position again, counting, pulsing, and breathing.

"She's his target; she's important to my friends. I can't let her die, but I can't save her, not with this holding back my power."

Before I can even hold up my wrist to help state the obvious, Thatcher's mouth moves to my arm and that black beetle from Sandra crawls along it, the insect's large jaws opening just before they hammer closed on the king's bracelet. I'm not sure what I am seeing, aside from magic at work that makes me think of Dana, clever lady that she is. The beetle keeps moving along the bracelet, ingesting it, a glow emanating from its shiny black body. I wince, hoping he doesn't catch on fire or blow to pieces. I glance at Thatcher who's watching intently as well.

It's mere seconds before the entire bracelet disappears in the beetle's jaws and then he begins to stretch. Well shit, this is it, he's going to burst and I need to prepare for the mere seconds I may have to heal these people before the king knows his magic has failed and I am free. But he doesn't blow to bits. He instead circles my wrist with his body, becoming the bracelet once again, but this time he leaves my connection to Gaia open, and without a second thought I yank on her power with a force that may even rival the king's. Emerald-green vines grow and twine around my arms and fingers; their pulsing shines and glows intensely after having been pent up for so long. Powerful Earthen energy fills my core and I place my hands on Nora, willing her body to heal, her lungs to push out the water, and her heart to beat.

"Beat, damn it! Beat! Beat!"

Nora's body lurches with a sputtering gush of pool water and a wrenching gasp for breath. *She's alive!* I don't celebrate long, sensing that Troy is close to death. Holding Nora, I send tendrils of magic over to Troy, focusing on his wound, staunching the blood, healing the torn muscles, and sealing the gash before working on his blood loss. I catch Thatcher's eye and he gives me one of his human-like nods.

"You take care of them and I'll work on the building rubble."

Ugh, the carnage is horrifying and I try to glance, process, and just work out a way to fix—I cannot dwell or cry—I just have to be a machine. A healing machine. This is like nothing I've ever seen or dealt with before. Medicine was never really for me, not when something as ghastly as what's just happened here was possible and with how much of an Empath I was born to be. But now I have no choice. It's only me, and Thatcher. He knows I'm in deep and snaps me out of it.

"Eila, let her power guide you. Gaia will take your burden and I'll let you know when I see anyone you need to help immediately. We can do this—together."

CHAPTER 11

The Fixers

What language of dauntless beauty,
grasping at the fingertips of our minds.
The song, the whisper, how many notes untold?
Who is learning? Who is watching?
We believe.
Only they know.

And so it begins. Thatcher stays intent on repairing the inanimate parts of this disaster while I mend the biological damage. Before we begin, I run a quick sweep over everyone, calming each of them to avoid full-on hysteria breaking out when they take in the weight of their situation and the others around them, the ones lying there lifeless, lacking limbs, or spilling an abhorrent amount of blood. Not to mention, there's a massive black cat roaming around using powerful magic to fix the building. Yeah, that's real normal. By getting a handle on their panicked emotions, I hope to limit the stress and terror; a nice Alex Xanax is what we all need right now. I watch Thatcher for a fleeting second, transfixed by the way the building materials obey his wishes by spinning into the air, binding, and returning to their original state. Yeah, if I hadn't given the crowd a chill pill we would have lost some to pure shock and disbelief at the Thatcher theatre.

As we move around the pool area of the hotel, which is where most of the damage is, I glance at Troy and Nora from time to time, waiting for her to wake long enough for us to talk. I've kept in contact with Jax and learned that Sandra and Logan can't get very close to the hotel. The king seems to have taken extra care to keep the twins far from Nora. At least they can take comfort in knowing she's okay. Perhaps Thatcher and I can rip apart his spell somehow. After relaying this idea to Jax, he replies quickly.

"When Sandra lost her memories, she and Yi broke through many of the king's spells trying to locate you. We need to guide them to you so they can get you all out of there. They have Yi, and together they can tear the wall down."

I agree. Troy and Nora need to get out of here, but what I don't say is that I am not leaving with them, not today. I am using most of my energy working on the carnage left by a madman, and Thatcher has a ton of work ahead of him as we try to save more people while stopping the building from collapsing any more than it already has. What we haven't thought of is, what's next?

"Thatcher, at least five people are dead. As I heal more, they may be able to see what I'm doing, not to mention that you've been shapeshifting from cat to eagle to caribou. We definitely have to make this go away. The memory of you and me will need to disappear, but some people are still going to be dead. How will we explain their deaths?"

"We'll figure it out. I've been in worse stitches than this. Just keep doing what you're doing. We need to work fast and close the path."

I can barely contain my despair when I abandon the lifeless victims frozen in their senseless deaths to concentrate on those I may still have a chance of saving. My curative power forces muscles to stitch together and bones to regrow the marrow to make them whole again. Wounds seal, tightly closing away the barbarity that had ripped the flesh apart. The victims' minds are gently willed to forget the trauma and also the two of us who are giving our all to undo this disaster.

"Alex?"

Nora's voice breaks into my concentration. Turning my head at the greeting, I see Troy and Nora hobbling toward me just as I finish caring for a young German woman. My patient has finally stopped crying and berating herself for nearly dying on what she repeatedly called a frivolous holiday away from her family. "Will I ever see my daughter again?" she pleaded. "So selfish, I'm so selfish needing a break from her to come here and now I'll die in this, and never see her again." Her fingers helplessly pointed at her barely-there bikini. I poured my empathy into her in waves.

"You'll be okay, Tila, and you will see her again. I promise." What I didn't tell her was that we all need a break and she shouldn't beat herself up. I let my power heal the psychological punishment she's given herself. Talking wouldn't do the trick. She'd still never have forgiven herself, no matter what I said today.

"Nora. Troy. How are you feeling?" Despite their haggard appearances they still complement each other beautifully, fingers interlaced as they nod simultaneously before taking a seat on the ground next to me.

"I want to help. This happened because of me and my family, so please, let me." Nora's grief can only be topped by my own, so what I don't say is that this is truly the full fault of *my* fucked-up life, but what good would that do? I push the self-deprecation aside and focus on how she and Troy can help, which is all they want to do—help make things right.

"Nora, you're a Seer like Jax, right?" She nods. "We need to find a way to bring Sandra and Logan here. They can't get past a spell surrounding the building. It's why no one has come to our aid. No one else has any idea what's happening here."

"No one except my friends and my brother," she answers. "We managed to get through to them somehow, even though no one else here is able to call out, and Jax told Troy that Logan saw the attack in his vision."

I nod. The king's brutal plan would allow Nora's family to hear the anguish from Troy, but he'd keep their loved ones from getting to them quickly enough to do much but take the bodies home to bury.

"So if Logan could see what was going to happen to you, and if Troy could call out, then you two may be the only ones who can reach outside his trap. I need you to figure out a way to guide them here. Use Sandra and Yi–Yi's another story, but he can help—to break down the spell and clear the way."

The king must have assumed it would happen eventually—counted on it even. Knowing the world he despises would soon see the chaos and death he created would be one of the main icings on his terror cake. Nora begins to look a little better; perhaps knowing she can be of some use is helping her recover more with each passing moment.

"I'm sure that between the two of us we can figure something out. Troy's an Earthen Protector." By the look they share I can tell he is more than that. I gaze at him differently, knowing we share the same power.

"As am I, Troy. A Protector and a Healer." Troy's eyes grow wide before narrowing, making me feel slightly self-conscious as he investigates every inch of me. Troy's face changes soon after, taking on a look of steeled resolve. "Do what you can," I go on, "and try to bring our friends here so we can figure out the next step together." Nora's smile brightens the dark cloud hanging over us all. She holds Troy's hand in hers, speaking one last time before they leave.

"We'll bring them here and help you fix this. All of this. Together."

The minutes drag, kicking and screaming like hours, although Thatcher and I move quickly. His tasks go at a faster pace than mine, and when I glance up from my work I see the hotel nearly entirely repaired. Not many souls were inside; most were at the pool or exploring the island. Those in the main body of the hotel are employees, and they endured much less than those outside. Seems the king focused most of his efforts on the area around Nora.

I look at the dead as they lie there with loved ones crying over them, cradling their bodies, or sobbing quietly above their broken, battered forms. I've managed to maintain the calm just enough so only whimpers and silent tears are apparent. After having repaired the most life-threatening injuries, and though I would think exhaustion should have set in by now, I'm not as spent as I expected to be. Adrenaline, mixed with the surge of my force that's been dormant for so long, carries me through the disaster, yet my eyes continue to slide to the ones whose injuries took their lives. At least I can find some peace knowing it must have been quick.

"We might as well try."

Silent as ever on his panther paws, Thatcher's wide orbs blink at mine while I work to repair a small wound on a man's head. Ignoring his implication, I prattle on about the work in front of me. Nothing to see here, just a grown woman rambling to a large cat, that's all.

"I had to put him to sleep more than once. He kept freaking out about the world ending and why did he decide to take that second double-decker pill. Drawing the drugs out of him was quite the process. If this hadn't happened he might've died from an overdose, so in a way, the king saved him." The words coming out of my mouth may have Thatcher thinking I've partaken in some of this dude's drugs as well.

"If you're worried about what the goddess will think of you using her power to bring back life, I assure you she will view these deaths as unjust by the one who abused the powers left to the worlds. She will not look down upon you. She will help you."

All I can think of is the time I saved Bear. He lay dying after some psycho lady poisoned him with a coolant cocktail. I used an intense amount of power that night. Even Vex's bushy ass was alerted to my anguish and demands on Gaia to help me both heal my dog and find the bitch that hurt him. Though I was angry and vengeful then, a lot has changed. I have changed. This would be a *just* cause, not that Bear's wasn't, but it was guided by revenge while this would be guided purely by love.

Just. Justin and Lestan the Prince. The Just Prince. Would he be the same boy I knew? Would he hate me? Such a play on words. Was the name the king's idea or Lestan's? My mind is drifting, the carnage starting to overwhelm me as I continue working to repair the horror around me, but I can't stop thinking of how I couldn't save Lestan from Valant. This is my chance to see if I can make amends for that error, a chance to prove to myself that I can fix things with Lestan. That I can bring him back. Will Gaia find she wants to support me in that as well?

I rise to my feet, and move away from party boy whose sliced cranium is mending nicely, then slowly make my way to the closest fallen soul. I touch a girl's arm as she hovers above her friend, sending my power into her and murmuring to let me see the girl lying there for just a minute. "Move over there for just a second. Let me see her. I won't be long. You're okay. I mean her no harm." She moves away on command, holding herself in a convulsing hug. Watching her grieve, I flashback to a memory of my own small sobbing frame when my grandmother passed. Death. So senseless, and this one so terribly wrong and completely and entirely my fault.

Looking down at the dead girl, I brush dirt off a face surrounded by pixie-short red hair, a face that was intact before this attack, before her delightful time in the sun turned into terror. The friend I sent away repeats the name Cinda over and over again so that must be who is lying before me. Her hair is covered in glass and other debris. I start picking it out mechanically and accidentally puncture myself by foolishly picking it out in an unaware manner. I avoid the large piece sticking out of her head, the one that must have ended her life.

"I can do that, Eila. You need to focus on what took her life and work backwards."

Eyes rolling, I lash out. "I know that, Thatcher."

Crap, I just snapped at a sharp-toothed and sharp-clawed shapeshifter who may be as old as Terra herself. But could anyone blame me? I have to move into this warily. What I'm about to do is going to tap into the deepest parts of me, places I don't venture very often. This isn't a routine fix; it's not even as intense as the time I had to heal Shane after Greg's attack and sickly curse that kept him from healing. No, this is something deeper and more spiritual than anything I've done since I was a child . . . since Steven.

"I broke when I sent someone to what I thought was his death. I know this isn't the same thing, but I know where I'd need to go in order to even attempt to make this work. It's going to take me some place close to darkness, close to what's considered evil, isn't it?" I see the concern in Thatcher's eyes, followed by a look of conceding that exact truth. His face appears almost human. I continue, despite the pull his face triggers inside me. "You don't want to see if I can do this before we help Lestan, because you already think I can. What you need me to do is believe it and to know how, don't you? I'm sure this would be easier than Lestan's rise from the depths—at least these bodies are whole." Moving a piece of a hand and part of her jaw closer to where it should be on the ginger beauty, I keep my nausea down. "Well, at least mostly whole."

"Yes, this in an unexpected opportunity for us." My aghast look of *a what?* has Thatcher raising a paw in the air. "Maybe opportunity is an inappropriate choice of word. My apologies." This salutation of regret is directed at the lifeless, grime-covered girl in front of us. He looks back at me. "Don't you want to know your true powers? All that you are capable of? Because once you do, and we bring these people back, you will know Lestan can come back to us as well."

Pet Cemetery is invading my mind with all this talk of raising the dead. I don't want a scalpel disguised as posies stabbed into my back by any of these innocent people, or worse yet, by Lestan. Though maybe I'd deserve it.

"Will they truly be whole again? I don't want to bring someone back if there's a chance they may be different, changed horribly and irreversibly in some way."

Sitting next to me now, so closely my skin tingles as if I'm sitting alongside a furry sparkler on the fourth of July, Thatcher answers calmly.

"You are not an Absolute Protector. You are not bringing them back for your own gain. This is a pure reversal of evil magic, as will be Lestan's resurrection. Take the evil away from them, repair their bodies and their minds, and they will be whole again—bodies and souls."

My next question should be *how do you know so much*, but I've learned some poignant things from talking animals, so why question it now?

"Okay." I take a deep breath. "First I'm going to pull any traces of the king's magic out of her and then I need that glass out of her head. Slowly, please, so I can mend along the way. I'll let you know when I'm ready." Looking at the vicious piece of glass in Cinda's skull, I wonder if I ever will be.

"You can do this. Don't forget who and what you are in countless worlds. You are full of pure goddess light and love. You've been touched, and there may be no bounds to your abilities once you look within."

Putting on my fiercest face with my eyes focused and lips pinched, I look Whiskers in his wide cat eyes.

"Well shit, Thatcher. That might have been the most motivating speech I've ever heard. Let's do this."

I take another deep breath, exhale, and get to work. I start scanning Cinda's body for any leftover charges of the crazy king's energy in her lifeless body. I sense his wicked signature power right away. It may have traces of Lestan's unbridled energy, but it is nothing like the pure and kind nature that makes up the whole of his son. No, this is harsh. Pinpricks of it pierce along, and inside, my skin. I pull the lingering evil out, thorny bits at a time, and meticulously form them into a ball before I envelop the writhing dark energy in my green vine glow and dig down deep, willing my force to destroy the evil's very existence.

Stifling a yell at my use of power, which instead comes out as an unladylike grunt, I feel sweat breaking out in places that haven't already been saturated by our work. Places I didn't even think could sweat. Then I reattach the portion of her hand that was ripped away, then her jaw, and then all the other bruising and internal bleeding. And then I move to her head.

"Okay, Thatcher. That bastard the king is out of there. How are you going to approach this? Your ability or tooth and nail?" My voice is slightly high-pitched. Hell yes, I'm nervous. I'm not sure if either his cat form or his control over objects is the best approach to this delicate task. "Maybe some hands would be useful?"

And just like that, Thatcher shifts into a large, and very cute I might add, chimpanzee. Brilliant. Moving to Cinda's head, he delicately wraps his rough primate fingers around the shard of glass then looks to me for the green light that I provide him with both a swift nod and the green power swirling within my eyes.

"Easy does it, Thatcher. Good, keep going, there you go. I think we're almost there." Repairing brain matter is tricky; not only does the tissue need repairing, but all the parts must be exactly right so as to not change her personality in any way. Neurological pathways are repaired, chemicals are replenished, and finally I piece her skull back together, reforming skin and hair as Thatcher extracts the last bit of the glass. "Now I'm going to try jump-starting her system. Heart first, then lungs, and then we'll see if I'm truly as capable as you say I am."

My hands on her chest serve as defibrillators, and I send a huge burst of Earthen energy into her body, willing her heart to beat just as I had Nora's. The difference is, Cinda's pulse disappeared a long time ago. Nora was never truly dead.

Nothing changes aside from my powerful jolt making Cinda's body arch upward. "It's not working," I say desperately. "I can't do it."

Thatcher's warm, leathery hand touches my shoulder before he leans in to me, hugging me with his long hairy arms. It's a small act of kindness, but more than that, it's love. This creature and I bonded a long time ago over a work of compassion for a boy we loved, and now, even more so over the loss of that very same person. Thatcher's simple gesture moves me to the point of tears, not of sorrow, but rather joy at knowing that despite all the evil in the world, love will always exist, and that it is the most powerful force of all.

I glance at her friend who is in the corner, staring at me wide eyed. She moves closer, placing her hand on Cinda's shoulder and speaking to her through her falling tears.

"Cinda, I love you. We all love you. Come back to us. Come back to me. You're my sister, my friend. Please. Come back."

The three of us together seem to weave a whole new form of magic within my core. My green vines envelop us, and I reach deep to pull my grandmother's dandelion seeds and my father's brightly glowing golden sun. I fire them into Cinda's heart and her body responds by lurching into the air once more, her chest arcing for the sky. This time her head rises as well from the sheer force of my power. Her eyes fly open while her lips part to take in a sharp, heaving inhale of the fresh saltwater air. Before her body slams back to the ground, Thatcher releases his grip on me and catches her, breaking her fall. After easing her back down, he moves to allow her friend to comfort her as Cinda speaks with gargled breath. No one said coming back to life was going to be easy.

"Aimee? Oh god, Aimee? Am I back? I was so scared."

Who knows where the king's kills went. Would it be a heaven or something else entirely? My lips spread into a smile. I've done something extraordinary, but then I sigh with exhaustion as my power wanes. And there are still four more souls to bring back.

Moving away from Cinda and Aimee, I stumble a bit as I make my way to the other side of the pool where victim number two lies within a circle of his mourning friends. Troy heads over and I glance around, getting eyes on Nora just to make sure she's doing okay. Jax's sister sits cross-legged a few feet away, most likely continuing to work with Sandra, Logan, and Yi in a vision to get them here.

"Nora and the others have things under control. She's helping them find their way here. Sandra and Yi are tearing apart the king's blocks and will be here soon. Seeing what you've been up against has me realizing that you may need my help. What can I do for you?" Troy's wide eyes shifting from Cinda to the still body of my next task hold the real question, which is what in the world am I doing. I'm sure he's had a ton of Protector training and education on our ways and rules, much more than I, but from his look I can tell that the Council doesn't hold necromancy in high regard. I am certain of that much; any abuse of power that borders on wickedness or selfishness is a big fat no-no.

I try to reassure him. "I'm undoing the work of someone who is pure evil. Gaia is still flowing easily in and through me, guiding me. We are doing just work today, and I have four more to bring back to this world. I could use all the help I can get." I'm not certain what Troy can do as a Protector, but I'm not going to turn down anything. I can feel Earthen energy surging through me sporadically.

"I'm a battery," he unveils. "Meaning I can hold immense amounts of Earthen energy inside me. I can also tell when someone is weak. Maybe I can help you make it through this, even if it means giving you all I have within me." Troy's broad smile and mellow voice fill me with the sense that he is pure of heart. Luckily, he is also just the battery charger I need.

Coming alongside me, he takes my left hand in his own and I jerk at the rush of energy forcing its way into me. I squirm at first, not having experienced another's power in such a way before, but then I let go of my fears and barriers and allow his boost to replenish my tired body. Hand in hand, we walk to the group surrounding their fallen loved one. Troy uses other tools in his Earthen Protector bag to influence the others to move aside calmly, and we begin working on the next soul. This time Thatcher doesn't need to embrace me; his presence is reassurance enough as he holds the young man's head while I remove the king's wickedness and repair the broken bones and crushed lungs. Jump-starting him takes time, but with Troy's extra boost I finally succeed. This time I walk away with a spring in my step and sly smile on my face. I'm ready for the next one. And the next.

"We did it!" Hugging Troy and then giving Thatcher an ear scratch after he's turned into his panther form once again, I can't stop the gleeful smile spreading across my face. If I've experienced a greater level of joy in my life before, at this moment I cannot recall it, which seals the deal for me that this is what I am truly meant to do in this world, and that love is stronger than hate, no matter the odds. Being trapped in a cell, on a boat, in a cellar, or by Steven seems lifetimes ago.

Fixing these people is fixing me too.

We walk over to Nora who stands up from her meditative state. She also has a smile on her face. "They're almost here," she says. "They've broken a path through to us, but they won't let anyone else follow yet, not until we make sure all is well here. So, what's our plan?"

Still on my high, I nearly scream out my response. "Group amnesia and putting everything back the way it was, that's the plan. First, I need to get to the DJ booth and a microphone. We need to get the party back up and running before I send my power out to make them all forget. It'll be the end of my usefulness, I'm sure, but I hope it'll be the last act needed from me. Sandra and the others can bring down the king's wall surrounding the hotel. And after that we can leave."

My false smile hides the truth. Once I'm done here, I am done here. Thatcher and I need to close the path to Avalon behind us. Sandra won't like it, but I'm sure she'll understand. She has to.

Troy has to catch me more than once as I make my way to the DJ booth. Even his own power boost has been dampened, and he stumbles once or twice himself. Grabbing the mic, I enlist my party-starting powers and get everyone to their feet once again. Thatcher did well. The hotel looks untouched, and everyone is cleaned up and looking good again. No blood remains, though looking at my hands I see we missed a spot—several actually. My microphone wavers in my hands at the sight, and Troy moves closer to catch me in case I fall. The DJ slides up next to me, getting the music going again, and I hear chatter break out as my amnesia-laced powers fly around, hitting everyone within the king's invisible wall. Nothing happened here, no one died, no one was injured, and the building wasn't torn to bits. It all becomes a distant memory, perhaps just images from a movie they once saw. Any fleeting aftershock, shivers, or stomach clenching were fabricated by a Hollywood mirage, not their own.

The festivities start back up again, and I stand there for a moment, taking it all in, longing to stay in paradise. I can see Thatcher's large orbs glowing down below where he's hidden within the king's pathway, one only we can see. Wishing I could stay, I sadly drop the mic and Troy and I move downstairs where I automatically head to the bar, grabbing a stool as I wait for Sandra. Not caring what I look like at first, some bemused glances from the crowd help me decide I should probably use a little of my ability for my own good. No need to scare everyone when they are finally back to having a good time. Willing my power to heal some small scratches, dispatch the blood and grime, and make me at least presentable, I add in a dash of lip gloss, but even that doesn't do much to lift my spirits.

Looking out at the crowd, I pout while my hand rests under my chin. Am I perhaps giving off a vibe of longing, and yes, maybe a touch of jealousy? Well, who can blame me? My life has been hijacked by a Fae freak while the world keeps spinning, laughing, and dancing. Many of these people may still be partying when the sun rises again. Ibiza never sleeps, so I hear. I force my lips out of their ridiculous pout and blow air at a curling strand of hair as it plays around in the salt breeze. Some day, Alex, one day you'll be back here, and it won't be like an episode of *MASH*.

Thatcher had agreed to the few minutes I asked for to see Sandra and to ensure the king's wall falls. Despite the circumstances, I can hardly wait to see her again. I miss my friend. Fingers touch my back as she slides next to me onto her own stool, ordering two vodka sodas with orange slices.

"This isn't the Ibiza trip I dreamed of. Especially not looking like this." Checking out Sandra—I mean really looking at her with her cat-woman get up and slicked-back hair—makes me nearly fall off the stool laughing.

"Are you robbing a bank after this?"

Her answering swat leads to an embrace that neither of us wants to leave. I can hear the greetings and words of love and good wishes from the others in the background. Our drinks come to us, cold and delicious. Seeing where she's taken a toll, I touch her hand, sending her a little burst of healing. It couldn't have been easy getting here, but, being Sandra, she selflessly focuses on me.

"Are you okay? Nora told us everything you and your new creature friend did. It must have taken a lot out of you, even with Troy helping." Sipping and smiling, my only answer is a nod. "We need to drop this wall and get you out of here. Ryan is freaking out that he hasn't spoken to you yet. I told him you've been a little busy, but he keeps insisting that we should be back by now. By the way, what the hell did you do to him in your little sex dream? He's been a little off ever since."

I'm not going to sugarcoat this, mainly because I don't have the time, but also because that's how Sandra and I are—real and to the point with each other.

"I won't be leaving with you. I have to go back."

Instead of answering me she takes a huge gulp of her drink, not caring about the damn straw, which she tosses behind the bar.

"Well, I'm sure there's a good reason. Spill it."

Mimicking her ladylike sip, I tell her quickly. "I've made two promises that I have to—no, I want—to keep. One to Lestan and Thatcher, who's the creature you spoke of, and one to Lestan's sister, Verus."

Giving me a wary look, she takes another sip. "Are you going to try and bring Lestan back?"

"Yes."

"And do you think all will be well after? That he'll be well and you'll be able to leave? He was working with the king to try to take you, maybe even kill you, or don't you remember, because I know none of us have forgotten. None of us."

See what I mean? Straight to the point. Ryan is going to be pissed when he finds out I'm going to do this, and without him as added muscle if things go wrong, without any of them, really. I hope I know what in the hell I'm doing.

"Yep. Fully aware, and honestly, I'm not one hundred percent sure how he'll be, but I have to try to bring him back. You never knew him as Lestan. As Lestan he would never have hurt me. Maybe, once the king is out of the way, any influence he had over Lestan will be destroyed for good. Oh ya, killing the king is part of the plan as well. The princess's plan. Good times."

"Talk about daddy issues." We both laugh and finish our drinks. "I'm not going to try and stop you. I know Justin's—Lestan's—death wasn't something you wanted, and I hope you're right and that he's cured of whatever sent him after you in the first place. Do what you need to do and get back home. Is there anything we can do for you? How can we help?"

Something impossible, I'm sure. She'll listen, but she can't control anyone else in our powerful company. Small as we may be in number, we're mighty!

I look at her intently. "Please just make sure nobody tries to save me again. It's making the king even more unstable than he already is, as you can see, and I don't want anyone else to get hurt. Promise me you won't come back. Any of you."

Turning around on my stool, I look at the others full on for the first time. Logan stands there shirtless, looking a little battleworn with his tanned, chiseled chest and a massive eagle tattoo on his right arm. My wide-eyed gawk and the curl of my lips as I take him in can't be helped, which is a truly odd mind fuck with all the thoughts of Lestan and Ryan swirling around in my mind as well. So many hot boys and so little time. Not to mention only one little ole me.

"Thank you." I manage to say while looking into his gorgeous, liquid-brown eyes. "Thank you for helping keep Sandra and my friends safe." Reaching out with my right hand, I touch the bird's head on his arm, which makes Yi move underneath my fingertips. "You too, big guy." Yi's mouth opens, unleashing a soundless screech while Logan takes my hand in his own.

"Can't you leave with us now? Then we can find a way to help the others in Avalon, together. What if the king knows what you did here? He'll make you pay."

His hand is soft and warm, but the pressure is also strong and protective. My best friend's brother, the man with a strong jaw, slightly odd but beautiful nose, and full lips with a faint scar that hides a story I want to hear, gazes at me with eyes wide enough to feign innocence, but laced with a haunting and a need that I've seen before. My life is so confusing. Not to mention my sudden worry that I must have some ooze or bodily fluid on me still, and shit, did I even mess with my hair during my pity party a moment ago? *Really, Alex? Who gives a shit? You just brought some people back from death, and I seriously doubt he cares what you look like, just like you shouldn't care whether he cares what you look like. Shut up, self, and speak. Logan's eyebrow is starting to rise. Speak, Alex. You look like a moron.*

"I'll be okay," I eventually get out. "Thatcher knows the king is unaware, but I need to go now before he finds out. I also have help, lots of it actually, especially now that I can use my powers." Holding up my wrist, I show them Dana's handiwork. "This is just another mission now and I'm an Earthen Protector and Healer. This is what I was made for, what I'm meant to do. Though His Dumbness doesn't realize it, I'm no longer his prisoner, and he's the one who needs to watch his back."

Troy and Nora must have been filled in because they look surprisingly . . . unsurprised by the words that come out of my mouth. I squeeze Logan's hand and touch his arm one last time, which I really didn't need to do, but damn, and send my flowing healing power into him, which makes me a little weak in the knees and by the expression on his face, him too. I have got to get out of here before I ask the manager for a comped room. I'd say we deserve it, though he or she would not understand why, darn amnesia lifesaving nonsense.

I turn to Sandra, my eyes seductively low. She shakes her head and looks to the sky. "If you say a thing about Tom or Brad I am going to grab that vodka bottle and chug it before your last syllable."

"I was not going . . ." With her gorgeous lips pulled together and left eyebrow lifted, I can almost hear the *ya right* inside her mind. Wait, did I? Sandra's head falls backward as she chuckles. Looks like our connection's still there for now, but I'm not willing to risk using it in Avalon. I give her a hug and kiss on the cheek. Damn it, I miss the hell out of her, and I only hope that what lies ahead brings me back to San Diego and my family and friends sooner rather than later.

"I'll be back soon, and tell Ryan our link is still there so he'll know everything is okay. Oh, and tell him to take a chill pill."

When I turn around I can see that speaking about Ryan made Logan a little uneasy, so I give him a wry smile before hugging Nora and Troy. "One more for the road?" Troy knows his cue and fills me one last time from his super-size store of energy. I feel a little guilty though when his eyes begin to droop once I'm recharged.

"Thank you, Alex. For all of this." Nora's sweet smile causes my eyes to find the ground while my stomach drops soon after. Thank you for what? Fixing the damage my life caused? If it weren't for me, none of this would have happened. Maybe sensing where I went, Logan speaks up.

"No one is to blame here. Let's focus on the good that's been done, and for Alex to succeed in whatever's next so she can come home."

Okay, I've got to go before I kiss this boy right on the mouth. Out of the corner of my eye I can see Sandra shaking her head again. She knows me all too well. Her drink done, Sandra prepares to lead one final act before heading home.

"We have work to do as well. Logan, we need Yi. Let's break down this wall!" My gawking at her brother just won't stop as we all huddle around him while the eagle rips from his tattooed home. "Don't worry," Logan murmurs to me. "He's invisible to everyone else." Logan's pet is the coolest. Sorry, Vex. Oh, and Pitter. Not that Vex is my pet. I mean, he wishes.

After watching the acrobatic raptor of my dreams slice apart different areas around the hotel, the wall falls around us. Of course Sandra's brother has a living kick-ass eagle that lives in a tattoo on his arm. One day we'll talk about my history studying birds of prey, just one more link I have to my best friend's incredibly hot brother.

We all give our final goodbyes. Turning from them, I move to the path's opening, slip on my long fingerless gloves to give one last wave, and step inside as the crowd carries on none the wiser.

Though my heart longs to join them, it doesn't follow suit.

CHAPTER 12

Running Out Of Time

I'll gladly embrace
The day that rids his memory of its resting place

Thatcher and I move through the king's pathway. The cat gives me a moment, which shows his kindness and sensitivity. I need some time and a little space, having just left behind my life and people I love to keep my promises to those I barely know in a world that is not my own. After the space he provides shrinks instead to a need for words, he speaks up.

"Eila, I promise my life to a person who keeps her word as honorably as you do. You could have easily left today, and Verus, Misa, and I would have to fend for ourselves, knowing Lestan would never have a chance at life again."

Perhaps it's due to how I was raised, forced to be on my own for most of my life, that I'm used to fumbling blindly through the dark all alone—even leaving people behind if need be. At least in Avalon I have others—some who have proven themselves to be allies, and one a man I've loved that I owe a debt against death—and I will not turn my back on them because I know all too well what that feels like.

"You're my friend, as is Lestan, and I'd never be able to live with myself if I left Verus and Misa to the king's mercies. Also, never underestimate a person's motivation for a little payback. The king has earned that and then some." A chuffing sound answers me and I know we are on the same page.

"Do not use your power while we head home." Thatcher glances at me to make sure I'm paying attention. "I am going to tear this path apart, but just in case he finds remnants of it should he choose to return, we cannot have him sensing you. We'll be lucky to get away with any of this as it is." Nodding once, I touch my new beetle bracelet, praying to the goddess that it does all Dana hypothesizes that it will. "Not to worry, Eila. Worry more about what awaits us on the other end of this path." Oh, that's so much better. Sharp metallic nails protrude from Thatcher's paws and he shreds the path behind us as we make our way backward along the king's bloody trail.

After popping out at the San Diego cliffs, Thatcher guides me to the place where I ran at Sandra from the path created just for me. "Time to go back to the cell. The king's path is gone, so we are taking your old path back this time. Are you ready?"

"Let's do this. Whatever awaits us, at least I'm no longer defenseless."

Wicked sharp teeth glint at me in answer as we move into my old trail, muscles tensed and eyes shifting. This pathway feels completely different from the king's, but still foreign. Thatcher seems to sense my unease. "It's not going to feel entirely like your own path until you are no longer influenced to travel by the king's magic. You'll make your own way, as you have before, and it will feel like a second skin created by what is pure inside of you." Yeah, that's not what this is, but it's less angry king–made and more sterile. Everything feels normal as we move along it, no screams or scary pictures along the tunnel-like wall, and glimmering lights lead the way, but I know better than to take in false comfort.

"Alex?" It's Verus. Her wavering voice sounds more even than shaky, which I take as a good sign. "He's coming back again, so be ready. Act like you don't know a thing. That's what he expects and I leave it to you to play the part. You know he'll try to break you." My laugh carries through the path and an answering smack by a rather strong tail stops my little *I don't give a fuck* moment of insanity. Having tasted my power, I want to unleash it on the bastard, but I can't risk those who still need me. Plus, I'm on his turf and in his dungeon. Working toward an element of surprise plan is a much better idea.

It's dark again, the glimmering lights start to dull, and I can barely make out Thatcher's glowing eyes. "Time for some new skin. Don't worry. I'm still here with you, even if you can't see me." Bouncing orbs disappear into the blackness and I squint, looking for the new Thatcher even as a tickle cruises along the back of my neck. I raise my right hand to itch but stop before my nails dig in, thinking better of it now that Thatcher has most likely taken on a very small, tickly form.

"Thatcher?" Another prickle answers me. Yep, that's him. "I nearly swatted you. Next time let a girl know when you go into pesky bug mode! A smushed Thatcher is no bueno." That earns me a couple of wing smacks. "You better hope I'm not allergic to you, T-man."

"Will you two keep it down? You're almost back, so shush." Verus is right, of course. I'm all amped up on Earthen energy. Shit, will the king notice? Worried, I quickly store the goddess's life force that's pulsing through my body inside a tiny hidden corner within my mind. I swiftly layer it with memories and secret places; time is limited and I'm nearly back to my cell and whatever awaits.

"Ms. Conner. I hope you had a pleasant rest. My master will be here soon to check on our progress. I believe he got more than he had hoped. He'll have what he wants from you soon, and then you won't be alone any longer." A tight smile appears on my face while teeth greet my tongue. Resisting at first, I soon realize talking shit to the king's lackey is exactly what I should be doing. A better show for the boss man who may be here any minute now sounds like a fantastic idea to me, not to mention I need to give someone a piece of my mind, and a warm up before unleashing on his highness is music to my ears. Even if it is to my disguised comrade-in-arms.

"Listen, Dr. Evil. I think I prefer your buddy Fleabag over your wannabe ass. Bring the real doc down here so you can go back and play with your test tubes or whatever freaky Fae science gear you fondle day and night, 'cause I know no person or Fae wants a piece of all . . ."

A deadly smile crosses Verus's Glena-form lips. Damn, I am so happy she's on my side. The door that leads to the stairs down to my cell opens, and I know the royal jackass is on his way down. Time to pump it up a tad so he knows Glena's been doing her job. Nope, no friendships forming down here.

"Okay, okay. No need to get pointy with me again. I'll be a good little prisoner. I'm just a little hungry, you see. How'd you like to miss your meals stuck alone in a fairy land? I'm starving!"

Footfalls come closer, tangled in a mixture of hyena-like laughter. Oh, it's him all right, and he's mighty full of himself right now. Knowing his glee stems mostly from the carnage in Ibiza, I curl my fingers around the rounded metal edges of my bed, my hold tight enough to bruise. We'll have our day, Verus and I both.

Once he comes into view I notice he looks a little worn and harried. Darkness, nearly bruising, sits under his eyes while his crownless dull orange hair looks fried and in need of a deep conditioning mask. He wears his dark green cloak that matches the power glow from his tractor-beam ring. The rest of him is wrinkled, tired; he hasn't had a moment to care for himself, meaning that coming after my friends and me is taking a toll on the king. Color me tickled.

"As feisty as always, I see. Well, nice to know Glena hasn't turned you into a mindless vegetable yet. Though I may have little need of you soon." Serenity and Chaos tingle in the back of my neck, and my breathing halts. This isn't the time to take him on, not yet. His majesty continues without a hitch, and I exhale, avoiding Verus's eyes in order to glare fully in his direction as he continues. "While you've played around in my designer worlds I've slowly chipped away the information I need. Now my plan is in place and your would-be champions have learned their deadly lesson. For good this time. You're alone, and no one will dare cross me again. Now come here, Ms. Conner. You have something I need."

I will not let the trembles I feel deep inside break the surface, so I force the vicious gnats in my stomach to still. At worst, he knows about the bracelet; at the least it's the feather, and I give myself a kick in the ass for not removing the bead and hiding it some other way. Now I may lose my link to Ryan along with the now useless feather.

"She may still be a little woozy, sir. Is there something I can assist you with or would you like to come in here with us?" The king's face cringes, causing his nose to wrinkle and his mouth to curl. Oh, I'm the gross one. At least I don't kill people in cold blood, the freak. Nodding to Verus, the king takes his doctor's suggestion. "I'm sure you can take care of her for me, Glena. She's hiding something that served as a connection to her disgusting human friends. Take it from her! I'm taking no chances when even those serving under me have tried to give her to the highest bidder." He is undoubtedly speaking of Flean. Verus moves to me with a snarl on her face while she removes an s-shaped object from her pocket.

"Don't try anything, human." The vicious two-sided projections gleam my way in a deadly fashion, and don't think I miss the spark in the king's eyes. He hopes I'll put up a fight. How many sociopaths does a girl have to meet in her life? I must have reached a quota by now.

As she moves toward me, sharp weapon raised, Verus is a vision of power and confidence. She's really good at playing the part of Glena—maybe too good? One of the ends brushes my neck and warmth follows. Did she just cut me? It's all part of the show, I reassure myself. Pushing away the worry that I'm a trusting fool, I lift my chin and stare into her eyes unblinking. "Bet you're a wicked shave on your girlie parts. Maybe you can help the king next time and give him more than this pretty, pussy nick you've given me. What do you say?"

Verus's hands grab me by the back of my head, twisting my knotted curls in her hand while holding the deadly object to my neck. I don't move, feeling her working on the feather in my hair under the guise of treating me like her bitch.

"Oh, you want a kiss, Doc? Sorry Glena, I don't play for both teams." One last yank and the knife lifts away from my neck to give a swift small slice at where my hair held the feather. When her hand comes into view I see Yi's feather, beadless, resting atop her open palm. I don't dare look around for where the bead may be. A kissy sound made in my direction is icing on the cake just before Verus turns her back on me, prize in hand, heading back to the king with her find.

"This must be how they were helping her. It may look like a normal eagle feather, but it was once engrained with a deep level of ancient power. Maybe even as old as our own."

The lines on the king's forehead indent severely. That pesky power trip of his doesn't like to be topped by anything, let alone a feather.

"Study it when you return to the lab and then destroy it." In other words, if it's more powerful then Mr. Royal, then it must not be allowed to exist. I only hope he doesn't make it a mission to go after Logan and Yi to try to harness their strength and make them captives as well. "Are you certain there is nothing else, nothing hidden elsewhere?"

"I've done my scan, but please, do one as well, my king." Gulp. She is sure certain of herself, isn't she? Something invisible and prodding moves all around me while the king stares in my direction. Please tell me Thatcher has the bead and has left this place. Oh, and there's the beetle posing as the king's handiwork. Let it be the best mimicry in history.

"It must have been something else that lead to the last, shall I say, slip up. No matter. I've cleaned up the trash for good this time." Did he just call mass murder a slip up and my friends and innocent people trash? "Isn't it just spectacular, Glena?" He stares at me, mad eyes glinting. "Stripped of your power, and your friends' little tool is mine and has no chance of ever being used again. Oh, and those you care so much about? They are bathing in the blood of their loved ones. They won't help you any longer. I've ensured that you've now cost them much more than you're worth, Ms. Conner. No one deserves more than that. No one."

The man has never loved, if he can even be called a true man. Keeping my smile well hidden, I allow my lips to tremble and tears to pool within my eyes.

"What have you done, you monster?"

His fingers come together in a peak before he presses the tips against his sinister smile. "More than you could dream in your sickest nightmares, my dear. Something that is all because of you and your . . . ah, I digress. I must keep this next act a surprise. All I have taken from you to get what I want has been purposefully removed from your puny brain so that I may spring the final act upon you soon."

I start to take deep breaths while I glare at him. I need to know his plan before it's too late. Whoever he's got his sights on needs to be warned and hidden from his crazy. I've been thinking about helping those here, mistakenly overconfident that he hasn't yet got what he needs from me. Boy, have I been a fool. So how do I handle this knowledge? With my usual spunk and an attitude, of course.

"I wouldn't get too cocky, your majesty. If you're bringing anyone I know to this hellhole you call home—and for how much of a hard-on you've had about her, she must be powerful—then you're going to have to face off against the two of us soon. That is, as soon as you stop being a pussy and take this thing off me."

The king's eyebrows draw together as he pulls his head backward. "That's the second time with that word. What does being a cat have to do with anything, you wretched bottom feeder?" Good ole earth slang doesn't translate so well in Avalon, it seems. "You still fight for the weak and for those doing worse than I. Your world is dying at the hands of Earthen humans even lesser than you, and you don't take action. Why you, with all of your power, fight on the wrong side is beyond me, but I truly care not for your world anyhow. Only one last thing from that *place* concerns me. Well, maybe two." He cuts his eyes to the feather in Glena's hands, and I swallow hard, fearing he may not be done with my friends after all. Please don't harm that gorgeous face or skin on Logan. He's too pretty.

"One day it'll be you and me, your loopiness, and when that day comes I'll be the last thing you see in those batshit-crazy eyes of yours." Another crinkle in his forehead makes him look all the wearier. I'm not getting anywhere with my animal-based shit talking. Plus, he's either super sapped because of his crazed freak-out in Ibiza or something else is going on with him. He's kind of a hot mess, but I'm carrying on as if none the wiser, hoping he's unaware or uncaring, which will lead to a major slip up on his end. "Just know I'm not going to let this end well for you, okay, buddy? You may have me in this cell for now with your little fire shackle, but I'm not going down like this, never in a million years."

His answering fake-ass yawn raises my hackles. He thinks he's going to win. I angrily shake my head to clear the doubt his madness always finds a way to leak into my thoughts.

"Well it's been fun, child, but we adults have things to do and a guest to prepare for. Get some rest now. I may have one last use for you yet. Glena, prep her again. I don't want to take any chances this time. I thought the link was destroyed before, yet somehow they got to her again." Yeah, thanks to Flean's Demon trade, so he thinks, but he's keeping that little bit of info from me. Doesn't want lowly ole me to think he isn't in control now, does he, the prick. "Put her deeper, I don't care if she comes back intact or not. I've grown tired of her whining and pathetic attempts to rile me."

He curls his lips at me once more. Jeez, he makes my skin crawl, and I can't stop my fear making me turn away from him, from another person who hates me enough to have me destroyed. "Of course, she will be needed to make my deal, so don't vacate her brain completely like we've done so many others. Just make her more . . . more docile, shall we?" Dick. God, does Verus know what Glena has done to people under her father's orders? I can't get high and mighty though; who knows what the king does to get someone's absolute devotion or perhaps enslavement. I'm not here to judge.

"Yes, your highness. I'll make it so." Satisfied, the king moves away from my cell toward the stairway. "Oh Glena, maybe you can let her in on our little plan and then take it away from her again. I so long to watch her face when she realizes what will soon be mine, and that she is to blame. Send word to me when you get there, but feel free to play with her first. You know, kill off some friends, and take a limb or two. Whatever you like. Make it fun, well, for us at least. It won't be fun for you, Ms. Connor. Not in the least. It's just an illusion really. But still, excruciatingly painful when you have no idea it isn't real. It's a beautiful thing really. Masterful."

I hate this guy.

"You'll get yours one day, King of the Fae. You can't be as powerful as you think you are. Everyone has a weakness."

"Yes I am, and no I don't."

The king's visit comes to an end, and Verus and I sit in silence as she makes busy with chemicals and Fae medical equipment of all sorts. The quiet is killing me, but I don't want to risk a thing. Pulling a string from her bag with a pendant of some sort swinging from it, she wraps it around my neck. She then yanks me off the bed and motions for me to push the charm. I obey. Once I press it I hear a click like a button followed by a vision of me appearing on the bed. It shimmers at first but then turns into a 3D, nearly solid image that moves and begins to speak as I do. Amazing. I'm looking at a copy of myself and she looks incredibly lifelike.

Verus ignores the real me in the corner and goes to the creation Misa and Thatcher must have engineered. Pretending to stick the form on the table with a needle, she then says some choice and not-so-nice words about my existence. The Alex double closes her eyes. Verus gathers her belongings and exits the cell, just as a flutter of tiny legs tickling hits the back of my neck again.

"Hold tight, Eila. Time to go." Thatcher's voice, though strained, has me at the ready. A whoosh hits my ears followed by rustling wind flying through my hair and into my lungs. The force fills them without effort, leaving me to choke on mere air. Is this how dogs feel when they stick their heads out of the window of a fast-moving car? I mean, whoa. It's not as enjoyable as they make it look.

For the second time today I am carried through time and space, but this time we ride Thatcher's path. Each time I've traveled, the path has had a different feel, like a signature of sorts for the creator. While the king's was laced with wickedness and vileness, Thatcher's is wild—untamed—and yet the focus is on love for the good and the peaceful. Colorful swirls of light float around us like glow stick trails. Some merely twirl around like cursive writing, while others burst and flower, building my awe and wonder in the darkness.

Not caring where he's taking me, I ride along with him, enjoying the peace and quiet, the tranquility after the insanity we broke away from not more than an hour ago. Though, time is odd as we travel and move through the space between dimensions, worlds, miles. My mistake was to think about time; the confusion makes my stomach churn, and what first felt soothing and exotic now has me aching to put my feet on solid ground.

I dare say I should also take a look at myself. Who knows the state I'm truly in after the mess we just cleaned up. Though Sandra would have told me if I was a hot mess, wouldn't she? Well, her brother had no objections—so there. *Alex. You need to stop arguing with yourself.* Actually, maybe I should be more apprehensive if I wasn't being the same ole Alex. I'm allowed to still care about girlie things, to pine for a life I don't have in this world apart from my own, and don't get me started on the food.

The growling in my stomach reminds me of the deliciousness I had in Thatcher's presence the last time. I don't suppose he can make me a chai latte next. No, I'm certain he had some help, and I wouldn't be surprised if we find Misa where we are headed.

Bright light swiftly moves about us, though I still can't see Thatcher, which leads me to wonder if he is able to change form as he travels, not to mention wondering what small body he hid himself within in the king's cell. I step out into the light, shielding my eyes when I am once again bathed in soothing warmth that's been so absent from the dungeon.

Looking around for Thatcher, I spot a small moth flying amongst the plants, blooms, and foliage in the small, steamy glass house I remember so well from my childhood. A clenching in my chest nearly takes me to my knees. I healed in this place. I gave my heart and soul to repairing it to help a boy I loved and trusted, and now here I am, knowing the pieces of him are nearby and that today I will try to bring him back.

CHAPTER 13

The Just Prince

Feeling now . . . lost as if in someone else's world.
Tears . . . stream as if feeding every part of this dehydrated existence.
Missing . . . as if a child running from her flesh.
And waiting . . . as if speaking to my own Mother Earth.
"Believe" they say . . . those voices in the garden of my mind.
Hold on, only please bind my heart as it wishes to go blind.
Journey into the unknown only to view a future loss.
Loving . . . it has been too long, too much worry.
I am lost.

Thatcher flies so close to me, my eyes cross. He flaps his wings frantically and oddly and dips from side to side.

"What are you doing? Can't you change?" A soft, dusty wing slap has me thinking that he obviously cannot. Scooping him up, I spot a twinkle around his neck—Ryan's bead. "You saved it, that's great!" Ah, 'great' may not be the right word. He isn't speaking any longer, and the last time he did, his voice was strangled at best. "Can't you get it off? It isn't alive and you've broken through tougher stuff than this before."

His moth body is spectacularly beautiful. He stays a soft green, though his spots begin to mimic my skin tone. Feet tickling my palm, he moves around slowly, allowing me to touch his fluttering wings and smile at his softness, but I second-guess that move when his antennas fly around his head wildly.

"Hold on, you can only manipulate objects that aren't alive, so does that mean Ryan's ring, the bead, is a living thing? That would make sense, actually. It does seem to have a mind of its own. I couldn't even get rid of the damn thing when . . ." Did he just give me an 'oh no you didn't' moth head shake? "You're right, not important. Okay, let me have a go." Thinking of how I used my power to shape a pendant into the bead, I focus on it, begging it to stretch and change back into its true form—the silver ring that Ryan says chose me, that belongs to me. Thankfully, it obeys, and I catch it when Thatcher takes flight and it drops from his body. A mere two feet away, he shifts into his mini-panther form, his head shaking and fur twitching after his ordeal.

Slipping the cool silver onto my right hand, I move to him, bending down as he paces, reaching out to slowly stroke his fur while my vines move around him till he calms. We both exhale deeply and sit on the greenhouse floor. Thatcher's front paws slip till he's on his belly, and I lie down next to him, partly on him, petting him and enjoying our freedom from death, chaos, prisons, and life for a few pure and meditative moments.

"Are you okay?" The big cat chuffs and stretches massively beneath where I lie partly on his warm furred body. "I'm sorry I didn't realize sooner. What can I get you? Food? Water?"

A small kick of a tiny pebble, just that tiny sound, alerts me and I spring to life, harnessing the powers of all earths within my being. The only thing that stops me from lashing out in the direction of the sound is another one. Thatcher's purring. He is feeling well enough to at least growl a warning should he need to. Turning around slowly, I see a beautiful vision that makes my throat go suddenly dry from great thirst and my stomach yearn for what is atop a platter stocked with a variety of meats, fruits, drink, and breads.

"That won't be necessary, Eila. I think I have everything the two of you need right here." Misa stands before us, her perfect lips softly curled. The heat in my cheeks startles me. Apparently Verus's gift has some unexpected aftereffects. Good goddess, I need to get a hold of myself. She's both a woman and Verus's love, and despite the experimental time I had way back when, I know where my attraction lies. So why can't I stop looking at her? Verus is going to get some shit for this.

"Hi! I'm Alex, well, Eila to you all, either one is fine, really." *Shut up. Shut up.* This will pass. It has to, right? Misa doesn't appear to notice my agitation, and she turns and slides the large tray onto a tall wooden farm table before moving closer to us. The angles of her sharply slanting shiny black hair swing back and forth like a pendulum on her shoulder as she kneels next to me, close enough to touch. Her nails scratch Thatcher's belly and the great cat gives off loving growls.

"He'll be fine. He's just hungry. When he uses a great deal of power this big boy has to eat. Don't worry, Thatcher. I had some luck in my hunt. There's a nice buck outside for you, still warm, and with plenty of meat for you to tear into." Her almond-shaped eyes crinkle as she smiles and I notice that though they looked black to me before, they are truly a deep violet. I've never seen anyone like her, and I'm sure it felt like love at first sight when she and Verus met.

Not waiting for another cuddle, Thatcher takes off out of the glasshouse and sounds of snapping bones and tearing flesh follow. Happy as I am for his bounty, I have no interest in seeing any more blood and gore today. Misa glances at me, then moves quickly to muffle some of the sounds by closing the door. Thankful for the reprieve, I lift off the floor and head for the food. Not looking at Misa, I try to bring pictures to mind of Ryan, both dressed in all black and in nothing at all, in hopes of channeling Verus's feelings out of my mind. Okay, that seems to be working. Verus comes back toward me, and I force my thoughts to jump to the touch of Logan under my fingertips and the scar on his lip that I long to bite. A popping sensation in my ear makes me jump, and just like that the spell is broken. My smile at Verus may hold even a touch of apology, but she doesn't appear to notice, or perhaps she's simply being gracious.

"It's nice to meet you. I can't thank you enough for agreeing to help us, all of us, mere strangers to you as we are. All but Thatcher, I hear." We both look at the door and smile. "He's faithful to those deserving, so you leave no question in my mind of your honesty and your heart, so thank you." She waves her hand at the food. I take the cue and dig in while she pours me some water and finds us two stools. We sit in silence for a while as she allows me the time necessary to refuel the basic needs that even Troy the Energizer Bunny couldn't provide. Have filled my stomach to the brim, I feel like a million bucks, and Thatcher's swagger as he shimmies open the greenhouse door echoes my sentiments exactly.

After updating Misa on Verus and what happened in the war zone that was Ibiza, we find ourselves finally speaking of the next stage in the plan, the one that's going to bring Lestan back.

"I fear we don't have much time, don't you agree, Thatcher? You heard what the king said. He'll soon have succeeded in getting whomever it is he brought me here for, so he thinks, and when that happens who knows what he'll do to me. Plus, we'll have another person to save, and how we'll get to her will be an added snag. Not to mention the mind games that are bound to follow her arrival, whoever she is. Do either of you know anything yet? Someone must know."

"We are still searching. Verus and Thatcher have spies scouring his private notes daily, but it has taken some time since they can only get access at odd moments. He has to have left a clue somewhere, and we will find it. Or perhaps *he* may know."

She means Lestan, this is clear, but my sharp exhale doesn't hide my unease that he could have hidden anything like this from me. Who am I kidding? I'm just some girl from another dimension who visited him from time to time. What did he owe me, if he even knew, or even knew he knew? Shaking my head quickly, I try to release my tangled, dark thoughts. Lestan has a good soul, and if goodness is, as I believe, stronger than evil, then it must still be within him. My hope is that with Lestan starting nearly from scratch, and with the powerful pieces of his mother intact, he will return to who he was and be free of his father's sway for good.

Wide eyes watch me carefully, judging my position before taking in the shift of my lips from tight to curved into a confident smile. An answering wicked curl of the corner of Misa's mouth reveals a glint shining off her teeth while she speaks. "Yes, Verus says we need to bring Lestan back first, and then we will kill the king. He can't hold anyone else prisoner or use them against you if he's dead, now can he?"

Nodding and shrugging, I can't think of any reason to argue that line of thinking. "Let's get cracking then. I've got my power boost, but who knows how long it'll last after the work we just put in."

My eyes dance around our surroundings, glancing at various pots and wondering which one Lestan is buried within. Thatcher turns his big body around, and it suddenly feels like I'm swallowing an entire peach pit, its scratchy surface raking down my throat, blocking my air and my ability to force it downward. My palms are slick and warm, yet I feel so incredibly cold inside.

"Don't be scared." Misa touches my hand. "We will be here to help you, and no one blames you for what happened, least of all Lestan. Thatcher believes he knew this was a possibility, but it was worth the risk for both you and his mother. Once he's back, completely freed of his father's control, Avalon will know of the king's many horrors and beg for his destruction."

I frown at the pure vindictiveness in her voice, but I can't judge her too hastily. This is a different world from my own; however, calling for blood with such venom and dark joy worries me a tad. Though her hands are trembling and her eyes are blinking just a little too frequently. She's scared. Scared of his highness, of this failing, and of what may happen if our plan doesn't succeed. I've seen firsthand what the king's wrath looks like, and I will not leave them to that fate.

"Over here." Thatcher tilts his big head at a large pot. "You might want to bring those stools with you. This may take longer than even all those souls on your island."

Ya think? Lestan doesn't even have a body. As I lean over to push my stool, my world dips to the side and I stumble. Misa's pale hand grasps my elbow, steadying me, while her wide eyes seek mine.

"Jet lag?" I quip.

That earns me a pleasant laugh, like a wind chime tinkling on a back porch.

"With the amount of traveling you've been doing, it's a given. Also, Fae drugs are strong, and one has controlled you for so long that your body must need to reset."

Great, I'm having withdraws, something unpleasantly lived through as an observer of my mother's self-inflicted disease. I wipe my hand across my forehead and feel the beads of sweat. Misa hands me a cup of water just before she eases me down safely onto a tabletop before taking both of our stools over to Thatcher.

Get it together, Alex. You're finally doing the one thing you've wanted to do since Lestan drifted out of the window. Now get it done.

The water is cooling on my throat and I drink way too much. How I haven't yet learned that I cannot slam a drink to save my life is beyond me, well unless it's in shot form. The overflow fills my nose with a pressurized pain. Clumsy as ever. Guess that'll never change, even with power over life and death at my disposal.

Pushing off the table, I take a few cautious steps and, feeling happy with my balance, I walk over to Thatcher and Misa, cracking my knuckles and neck as I focus on the task ahead. Thatcher sits on his haunches next to a large copper pot, nearly as tall as he, filled with a diverse selection of small ferns, mosses, flowering clovers, and rich soil. They sparkle, not from freshly fallen dew, but from within—magic come to life in the living organisms covering what remains of a man I loved.

My vines of power move toward the pot without waiting for my will to make it so. The gift within me is seeking him out, so I follow its lead, knowing Gaia's life force is driven for the sake of the just and the virtuous. Thatcher and Misa move to the side as I stride to the pot and kneel down before it, my bright emerald vines diving into the soil, tugging, spinning, and pulling. The weight of what I'm lifting from the pot has me back up on my booted feet once again. Swirling my hands, I will all within the container to gather together, preparing to place it on the nearly empty table to my right. Misa gathers the odds and ends already on the table, moving them out of the way and sweeping anything that remains onto the floor. The mass of swirling organic matter stays within the confines of my glowing green force that is sprinkled with my grandmother's bright dandelion seeds. I'll tap into my father's boost at just the right moment, though I am relying on my gut, or is it Gaia herself, to give me a sign as to when exactly that moment is. I've found my father's power enhancement to be nearly a one and done, so best to save it for the precise time.

Thatcher backs away as I carefully move Lestan's captive earthy remains to the large table, placing it down gently and pulling my force back for a moment. Using my bare hands, I simply sift through the earth and plant material, spreading it out to cover the whole of the table, feeling that it is all needed to complete his body's return. Tears fall silently, dropping to the tabletop and darkening whatever it touches for merely a moment before they are quickly absorbed.

I call to Gaia. "Please, help me heal your prince, Lestan. Please. Bring him back to us." It's a soft request, nothing like the demands I thrust into her being when I found Bear near death. Tears continue to fall, sadness welling from deep inside my heart, from the memories of my time with him, both as Lestan and Justin. The sorrow shifts, transforming into happiness as the memories move into the warmer places in my belly that tickled when we laughed and when he touched me with his goodness and light. I've been with this man spiritually and physically, this man who is merely pieces of what seems impossible as the last remnants of such a force of nature. Yet, as I spool the energy within my chest before pushing it outward to mend him back into some semblance of what he was before, I begin to sense his presence, or something close to it, part of him and yet more feminine and powerful—his mother. The part of her that lay hidden from both Lestan and the king has kept a spark within him alive and safe from the death Valant inflicted on his Justin form.

"I feel her. His mother. You were right, Thatcher. She's kept him, part of him, alive in some way. Transforming what's here into an entire person is something I've never dreamed of doing, but all I can do is try. I have to try." I glance at Misa and Thatcher. Misa's eyes are wide and her mouth is slightly open, while Thatcher's keen eyes and broad chest give me the boost in confidence I need. Latching on to his mother's hidden gift, I move it around with my power, roving over the table and seeking out parts to form into his cells, bones, muscles, and tendons. I was never very good at sculpting, so I can only hope as the cells multiply that they combine the way they once did within his mother's body. She helped him then, as she is helping him now, creating the man with the wild black hair, the brown eyes like polished stones, and his scent of untamed earth, plants, and the sea. I smell and see all of it, all of him. With my eyes closed, I will the pictures to come, those of the boy I visited. Oh, how much has changed.

"Come back to us," I whisper. The joy in my memories brings different tears to my eyes. They fall, taking with them my plea that his body be rebuilt, to be full of breath and life. My eyes open just as a tear falls from the top eyelashes of my left eye. I watch it plummet down, a tiny sun flaming to life within the small drop of liquid, landing on the spark from his mother, their union igniting something raw and primitive, like the first form of life within the darkness of the universe within my being. My body fills entirely with a deep, long intake of breath, fills with the will of Gaia. Something beyond what I have ever felt before overcomes me. I am stronger than the oceans, than the air, older than the earth, and more deadly than the burning fire. Right here, right now, I am the goddesses of old, the makers of life, and by my will alone I bring this man, this creation of mine back to my worlds. Back to me, for he is mine.

I can feel two living creatures backing away from me. Pheromones of fear reach my nose, but they are of no danger to me as I continue to focus on my work, allowing love and raw power to engulf the table where it creates a dazzling cocoon of bright green vines that hold the swirling matter on the table. Now I tend to the replication of cells, rebuilding the Fae prince's body, squashing the small oozing evil touches from his father between my fingers and snarling at their presence in my thing of beauty. His father will be dealt with later. Cells multiply, creating the parts within him that will be his organs, tissue, bones, hair, and everything he was before his life was taken by the Demon. I spit at the word, but they are also my creation. Our curse that took a turn I never expected.

Within the cocoon movement begins. Fingers press against the walls, reaching for me, a head—nose, cheekbone—presses against the top.

Hello, Alex. Get a hold of yourself. It's going a little dark side in here.

What? I look around but see only the other two I sensed earlier. No, this voice is within me, within this body. Where am I? My hands look foreign to my eyes, yet I know who I am. One of the first goddesses—Gaia, the creator of Earth, Avalon, and countless other worlds, and I am a part of this body. She is me.

"Eila, Alex, you need to gain control. The goddess energy has come alive in you, has taken you over. You must not surrender to it. Use it, but you cannot become it." The cat in the corner begins to walk toward me, but the smell of fear has been replaced by compassion, understanding, and strength. I gaze back at the table, where the cocoon has taken on the full shape of a man's body. Lestan is nearly complete. My just prince. He needs me. All of this power is the only way he can return, even more powerful and beautiful than he was before. Placing my hands upon his body, I prepare to fill him with one more wave of power.

Aching hits my ears and my mind. That voice again. *What am I doing? I can't do that to him. He was perfect just the way he was.* The control of this body and mind starts to change as a presence pushes against me, gathering me into her and pushing me to the side, smothering my intensity and dampening the raging fire. I'm not supposed to be here; this is her body and her life to lead. Don't let me turn her to the darkness as I did to so many others. Let the young woman be, before I destroy her.

The shape beneath my hands begins to vibrate, breaking apart beneath my fingertips. I can't hold on, my hands freeze, and I lose control over my body, falling to the floor and cracking my hip, elbow, and head against it.

"Holy shit! What in the hell was that?"

My shout sends feet pounding in my direction. Thatcher looks down at me, his long legs on either side of my body as his large cat eyes stare into mine. "Is that you, Eila, the real you?"

I moan while trying to touch my head but all I feel is a furred leg, long and strong like a pillar, trapping my limbs to my sides. "Yes, yes it's me. Wow, I went somewhere unreal for a moment there, didn't I? I mean, the power . . . I felt . . . it felt . . . it felt like I could create moons, but at the same time destroy them with a blink of an eye. That's bad, right? Oh goddess, did I hurt anyone? Where's Misa?"

Thatcher's wet nose touches me, changing from cool to warm as it moves over my face, his whiskers tickling me as he gives me a thorough check up.

"You smell like you again. You will be fine, but the pure goddess came through you—Gaia—and she nearly took you over, which would have either torn you apart or changed you into someone unrecognizable. That much power could bring you closer to evil than good, and who knows what the future would have been for you, or for anyone." What I don't tell Thatcher is how freaking good it felt. How even though I understand the danger I was in, I long to have her back with me, to engulf her power and feel the rush of unlimited control. Man, that taste was addicting.

"I can't do any more. If I do I might not want to fight it off again."

The big cat's paws shift backward, and I sit up. Misa's hand comes into view and helps lift me. The cocoon lies shrunken on the table. Lestan was here. I know he was, he was almost back to us and I couldn't go through with it. What Gaia almost had me do was going to be wrong, changing him into something else when he was perfect just the way he had been before. But it's agony.

"I'm sorry. I failed."

Pushing off his back legs, Thatcher balances his front paws on the table and uses a sharp nail to cut into the deflated shell. "There's nothing left, but how? Why?" Petting his head, I tear the opening fully, but he's gone. Lestan has gone. For good.

"Perhaps it wasn't meant to be, and what he truly wanted was to be at peace."

Misa's soft voice makes me want to cry. I just can't wrap my head around that possibility. "Was all this really just so he could finally be at rest? But Gaia wanted him back. Every part of her wanted to make him whole again, just as I did. I felt it. He was nearly home, but I stopped it." My gaze drops to the stone under our feet and my hand slips from Thatcher's soft head. He leans into my legs and stares at the empty table above.

"He wouldn't have wanted to be brought back that way. You did what was right. Plus, we are out of time." I follow his gaze to Misa's wrist where her bracelet glows a bright blue. "It's Verus's signal. You need to get back."

Chest aching, and my feet feeling as if they've been trapped within the thickest form of cement, I force myself to move away from the table. Giving one last look into the pot that once held what was left of the just prince, I spy a single white blossom. Despite losing myself to the choking sobs that wrack my body, I pull out the evening primrose Justin gave me months ago.

"We were so close to bringing him back. So close."

152

CHAPTER 14

Dreaming You

Darkness paints nothing for those who fear the missing light.
Thoughts swirl for me though
In glorious colors from blue to red to your forest of green.
Love me even in the sunless walls and I will come to you.

The king didn't come, only sending a minion who threw my food at me through the door. If the king only knew what is coming for him, that my raging sorrow is churning and filling every part of me with a force I will unleash upon him soon. Playing this game may lock me within this prison for longer than I wish, but it will all be worth it when we execute our new plan.

Lestan isn't ever coming back, and Verus took the news as stoically as expected. Her frozen expression didn't reveal a single inhale or exhale of breath. If she was crying, her tears were invisible.

"I'm so sorry." My voice trembled as I tried to contain the grief once again. Thatcher remained posted on a wall in shadow, staying away from the moment—perhaps sinking within it again as well. That, I'll never know.

The king ordered a hold on my Fae drug therapy, based on faux-Glena's recommendation. Verus knew I was weary, and we can't afford a louse up when we are so close, so she told him I could use a break. According to Verus he was quick to comply. Tonight I can relax and not travel anywhere I might be sent or decide to go. I will be able to close my eyes out of pure exhaustion. The downside to this is the knowledge gnawing at the back of my skull—he has what he needs from me. If that's the case, then someone I know, and most likely care about, is falling into his trap. Though I hope to rest in my weariness and torment, I'll try to reach Ryan. His ring, now turned back into the bead and woven into a braid in my hair, pulses against my skull with a life of its own. As long as I think of him, call to him, we should be able to communicate. He needs to be warned—they all do.

What I didn't count on was immediately falling into a deep sleep. My dreams toss me into a maddening vision of being taken over by Gaia once again. My surroundings are a wild emerald forest, close to where I've traveled to see Terra, but different and somewhere familiar. Something like the forest I always came to before following the path to Lestan's greenhouse years before Avalon became a nightmare.

Looking into a reflective pool of dark water, I see my eyes begin to glow a nearly translucent green, like the icy heat of a crackling fire—like my mother's eyes, though hers are blue when she releases her power. Shaking my head sharply at the reflection, my hair's coiling curls grow and wind around my legs as I lean closer to the water. Soon my hair becomes roots and I'm transformed into a tree, rooted into the ground, stretching to the sky as my hair and arms become branches. I have become just as Terra is, a tree goddess, lost to the wild of the land that has consumed me.

Gaia's voice fills my mind as I flail against the unwanted change, only wishing to feel my own body once again. "Don't struggle, child. I have given you a great gift. You are safe, and you have more power than you could ever want. Stay. Stay with me." I struggle against the grip of the bark that has become my skin, screaming into the surrounding forest for my freedom to choose my life, no matter the pain or the loss of control, I choose it, as I have every time.

"You can be stronger than any of my other children. Know that I am with you, always, but if this is not your wish, so be it." My tree self shrinks back to my normal size and the roots and bark slide away from me along the ground before reforming into a tall woman with hair like my own, but which stays as roots cascading down her back. The bark of her skin transforms into a fiery green, and her eyes are as dark as the nearby pool. Her presence is dominating, but the look upon her face is tender, with a soft smile and a curious tilt. She doesn't look older than I, yet ancient energy rolls off her in tidal waves.

"Gaia?" My voice cracks in awe as I look upon her. "I have yearned to see you my entire life, and here you are. Am I really here?"

A broader smile brings high cheekbones popping from her narrow face, and she pulls an answering smile from me in return. "Yes, my child. You are the strongest of my soldiers. No one has been able to contain me and survive my domains, not in hundreds of years. As you wish, you have your freedom—your body—and now I will give you two gifts before I leave. One, a name you seek, and two, a place."

My feet propel me toward her and I take her hand. Jerking at the shock of pure energy, I nearly let go as Gaia throws her head back in a singsong-y laugh I never expected.

"First, the queen you seek is not where the king told Lestan or Verus she would be. Seek out the tree goddess when you are free and you will find the mother they lost. But be warned. She may not leave the gift as easily as you."

My nose quivers as I fight to hold back the tears in my eyes. What will I tell the mother of the loss of her son? "Thank you, Gaia. That is a truly exceptional gift." Taking my other hand, Gaia holds me softly and this time I brace for the power that races through us like a loop.

"Second, the name. One that will help you solve the puzzle of who the king seeks. You will remember in time, perhaps not right away as our time is short, but soon enough I hope. Tristan. Think back, my child, and you will know why it is and whom he seeks." Riddles, ugh, why can't she just tell me? "We cannot know who may be listening, as his spies are tuned to hear the name of the one he cannot find alone." Spies everywhere; the idea makes my skin crawl. "You must go now, my Eila. I am proud to have a part in creating a creature as strong as you. Now go. You must hurry. Something is coming and I can stay no longer in this form, but know that I will always be here." She touches my chest with her bark-covered hand, and I feel a flitter in my heart. "Always." She slowly fades away, her hands in mine once again are the last parts of her that I feel and see, reminding me of the time I saw my grandmother in Arizona, visiting me just as Gaia has, bringing me a gift as well, and then leaving once again.

Recalling my grief at losing my grandmother has me wandering through the woods. I come across a fallen log surrounded by thick green moss hanging on needled branches and blanketing tree trunks. I sit at first and then let myself sink back on the mossy log. Lying there, my eyes grow heavier. There is one name in my mind. Tristan. I know the name, but my dreamy mind struggles to grasp it. I'll tell Verus when I wake up and we will figure it out together. Now I need some real sleep. No visitors please. I would rather not even dream, if that's what this is. I'm so tired that even the hard bed and cold walls of my cell seem inviting. My body falls, like the cradle from the treetop, but then I jolt awake with a strong sensation that I am not alone. A vibrant red color catches my widening eyes. A stunning strapless red dress spills from where it hugs my waist into a pool of red tulle, the length nearly unending in its path away from where I still lie on the fallen tree. Now I've been both a tree and a guest at a ball tonight. Not exactly my idea of a full night's rest.

Okay, brain, take me back, and now. I close my eyes and feel something like a feather tickling my chest. Yi? I open my eyes to nothing except the fading sunlight that barely breaks through the thickness of the surrounding trees. This isn't real; I'm exhausted and stuck in Gaia's vision. Trying to will myself asleep I again feel the feathery touch as it trails down my neck, on to my chest, and across the tops of my breasts. I lift up on my elbows this time, scanning the area and finding again that no one is there, let alone a magical feather floating around in a tantalizing fashion. Just when I'm lowering my body once again I spot an outline of a figure in the distance, hidden in the forest of green a good twenty feet away.

"Hello? Who's there?"

Of course, I'm wearing this incredibly beautiful but not-at-all practical dress, which keeps me from leaping to my feet as the person in the distance approaches. I can make out dark brown pants, a tight dark green shirt—no, a thin sweater—that hugs what appears to be a man's muscular chest. He strides forward, his wild hair moving in the breeze. My heart thumps madly as I stare at him. I know that I tend to push my out-of-control mind through the reality door and into my fantasies quite a bit in my dreams, but this Adonis can stay. As if hearing my thoughts, his lips stretch into a smile and his eyes light up, showing their polished brown glow.

Lestan.

He reaches for me, a gentle smile on his face and his head tilting to look at me. His fingers touch my cheek with a feathery lightness, just like the one I felt a moment ago, but are they one and the same? I return his smile and, holding his hand to my cheek, my feathery questions drift away to make way for new ones. "Lestan? Is it really you? I thought I'd failed, that I'd lost you forever."

Without a word he leans down, his lips pressing lightly to my own. I feel my cheeks flush with warmth. Soft fingers touch my chin, holding it as he pulls away to allow his thumb to outline my wetted lips. Leaning my head back, I taste him in my mouth, sweet honeysuckle and fiery spice. His soft touch trails down my neck, following a path from my collarbone down my arm, stopping to entwine our fingers. A trail of shimmering dust follows as his hand seduces me and I reach for it, bringing the luminescence to my face and smelling the same sweet and spicy aroma. My Lestan, bringing with him a tantalizing deliciousness to scatter on my skin by fingers I could easily mistake for the softest of feathers. I must still be dreaming.

He watches me as I taste the shimmering powder, as I delight in the intoxicating sexiness of this moment. When my eyes close with lust, he dips down to kiss my clavicle, then my shoulder, and I feel him take a seat alongside me. I shift position; it's surprisingly easy and slightly erotic when the fabric of my dress glides as smoothly and warmly as liquid wax over my legs. A tingle of need trickles down my stomach to a building warmth between my thighs, and I try to gain some sort of control.

"What are you doing to me, Lestan? What is this?" Do I want him to stop? I *should* want him to stop, but in this magical place, a man who began as a boy I grew to love has returned to me by my own hands. Well, with the help of Gaia herself, that is. His velvety kisses have stopped, but he takes hold of my right hand, caressing the top with his thumb. Our hands are together, but nothing is familiar about it. We held hands as kids, but we were just friends. I don't recall a moment like this when he was Justin, and he feels and looks nothing like the man who died at my feet.

"I'm sorry for what happened. For what Valant did to you."

The warmth of his body radiates all around me when our arms brush, his buttery green fabric smooth against my bare skin. "I am the one who should be sorry, Eila. Sorry for everything my father has done to you and your friends, and for what I agreed to do. The Demon was right to stop me. If he hadn't done it quickly, I may have hurt you, may even have killed you with the amount of my father's will scheming within my mind. You should hate me for all I've been a part of, but instead, you gave everything to bring me back."

I knew it wasn't him attacking me that night, not entirely. There's no way he would have hurt me so viciously. Something hadn't been going as planned in the king's eyes, so he took matters into his own hands, commanding Lestan's mind be hidden behind the Justin disguise.

"Thatcher told me that you became Justin to keep me safe and to find your mother. You did what you thought was best and it was decided out of love. I'll never hate you for that. We can make things right for you in Avalon now. For you and your sister. Your mother can return once we . . ." How do I say this? Does he want his father dead? I mean, I would assume so, but . . . Maybe he has another plan, one to try to kill the insanity, but not the only father he'll ever have.

"Kill my father. Yes, it must be done. Otherwise, his terror over my world, and yours, will never come to an end. He is too far gone into the darkness for there ever to be forgiveness for his sins. I know what you had to do on the Spanish isle; I saw it all when you brought me back to life. Your power is beyond what my father realizes, greater than even his own. He won't know what's coming." I lean heavily into him, taking a moment for touch, to allow someone to care for all I've done, for me. "For now, you must leave your cell. He'll send his people scrambling to find you, which will leave him exposed, vulnerable. Meet us at the greenhouse and we will go into the castle together." Unlacing our fingers, he touches the back of my neck, sparking Serenity and Chaos in their hiding spot. "You'll need these. Don't hold back, but don't kill him, not just yet. My sister and I deserve to be at the hilt of his final knife."

His face, his lips so close to mine, are even harder to resist with the protective fury held within his eyes and carried in his jaw. Reaching up, I play my fingers through his dark unruly hair; it's as long as it was when we were kids, the thick curls falling around and below his ears. I pull him into an embrace and breathe him in. Wet earth, forest air, and wild magic dance around my senses while the spiced honeysuckle teases me once again. He's intoxicating, spinning my emotions into a tizzy. We are from different worlds though, and with his father gone, will he rule here? My thoughts tangle. I love him, yet there is the weight of worlds between us and Ryan is waiting for me back in mine.

Ryan's bead warms at my thoughts. I haven't spoken to him yet; I only hope Sandra has and that he listened. Lestan's fingers touch my hair and graze the bead, pausing for less than a second before moving down my back. "He is good for you, your Ryan. But if he should ever hurt you, I will not be kind. Even though I love you, Eila, even though you are my only, I will not interfere. All I ever wanted was for you to be happy, and if he makes you happy, that is enough." Sadness fleets across his face, quickly replaced by an expression of tempered passion. Does he know what he's doing to me? Stepping aside for my happiness? It's one of the sexiest things anyone's ever done for me—another sacrifice.

"Lestan, did you let Valant kill you, knowing what might happen to me?" Leaning into me, taking my waist in his hands, he pulls me close, our lips a breath apart in the forest's new moonlight.

"I'd die for you over and over again."

My body reacts in a blink of an eye, and I'm straddling him, taking his face in my hands. I stare into his eyes. Glancing at his neck, I glimpse parts of the tree tattoo that adorned both he and his Justin form. Feeling him beneath me makes me squirm. I know I've been with his mind before, but not yet his true body. Something in his eyes stills me though, something familiar yet foreign. He's royalty; this is his world and who am I to confuse him after all we've been through? He deserves to find someone in his own world. I would just be dragging him along, and I can't allow myself to do that to someone who was and will always be there for me.

"You're still the boy I've always known, but you're different now. You will lead Avalon, and though I can't help but wonder if I could be by your side, I know it's not right. For either of us. I belong in my world and you belong here, in yours."

He moves beneath me, his eyes not revealing if he is doing it on purpose or if he is merely shifting. Regardless, I moan a little and his grip on my waist tightens. One kiss, one last kiss won't hurt, right? Just one to say goodbye and thank you.

I lean in slowly, gently at first and then crush into him as my body moves on autopilot against the tight hardness beneath me. Breathless, I pull away, moving to my feet in a flash while a hot fire strikes my hair. Ryan's bead flares to life and I look around for him, feeling he's watching, and here I am doing something to him that would break my heart if the roles were reversed. With fingers against my betraying lips, I scan the area again, seeing nothing except eyes of burning brown fire as Lestan joins my search for an intruder.

"What's wrong? Who's here?" And then, looking at my hair, his worry melts away as he nods with a soft smile on his face. "I'll always love you, Eila. Once this is over you must return to him. He's a strong protector and I have seen the depth of your feelings. Once we take over my father, go home to Ryan. I'll always be here if you need me. Always." He gently pushes me back down onto the log. "Now back to sleep, my love. Our time is over and now you must break out of your cell. Show them who you truly are."

A kiss seals our history, locking away my intense feelings for him. But just before I close my eyes I remember what only he may know.

"Lestan, who does your father want? Who is Tristan?"

"Tristan is an ancient Fae name. It means the clever one, but he never did tell me who or what he wants from you. He didn't trust me enough. He was right not to, of course. Return and let us work quickly, then we'll never have to find out his true devious plan. Greenhouse. Be swift, Eila. But keep him alive. My sister and I deserve our revenge."

As I close my eyes, I feel the strength of Ryan within my mind, but when I call to him he doesn't answer and his silver bead has grown cold. Did he see me with Lestan? Is he furious or will he somehow understand? Would I?

CHAPTER 15

Names

Will we begin to live for ourselves and not the "other"?
I will suffer and I will break down until my true self is revealed
And then, I will start all over again.

The frigid, metallic air signals to me that I am becoming aware once again inside my cell. What I don't expect, though I sense it fast enough, is that I'm not alone and that whoever is here is not a friendly. Before my eyes even open, I feel clammy fingers wrap around my neck, lifting me from my bed and then angrily tossing me across the stone floor. The king stands facing me in his green garb and heavy bejeweled robe. He has a maniacally tight smile spread wickedly across his face.

"Any minute now she'll be here, do you know that? All this time you've been caring about little you and how to get out of here, while I've been taking everything I need from you and your pathetic earthbound friends."

Still groggy from my sleep travels, the smack against the back of my head isn't doing my mind any favors as I try to make sense of what's happening. Managing to get enough of my wits about me, I scoot backward, blinking my lids awake and quietly staring at the king's wild eyes. I don't know what he's blathering on about, but I just want to keep him talking. The more I know before I get out of here the better, especially if we have someone else to save—someone from my world this time.

"Do you think I don't know what you've been up to? Of all your little *meetings* when you thought you were alone? How else do you think I planted my seed in him? You wouldn't give her up, which was at first impressive. I thought you were showing your bravery and determination, but after many attempts to trick you I found that you couldn't tell me because you didn't truly know."

I do *not* like where this is going. He does have what he needs. I can't leave, not when someone I know and care about is being brought into these terrible circumstances. The king continues, pacing around the cell as I cower in a corner.

"But you did tell me who else decided where and how she would hide, and it was easy to know who I could influence the most easily through your imprisonment, so I focused on the foolish boy in love with you. Does he not know how twisted and evil you can become? Oh, he soon will once I'm done with you. He's strong, I'll give him that, but who knew you'd bring back the one weapon who could seduce you right in front of him, bringing his jealousy to the breaking point? Hah! I used that as the fuel for my seed to blossom and grow inside his mind. Jealousy will make a man in love do anything to get rid of the competition. Oh yes, he will get her here, no matter the cost. Seeing you with my son and finally knowing my earthbound name—so cleverly given to you by the goddess—is all he needed to get her running back to me."

My head is spinning. Have I been deceived? By Lestan? By Gaia herself? What of Thatcher and Verus then? I am such a fool. He can only be speaking of Ryan. What has he done?

"Don't look so sad, baby Conner. Gaia did not want to help me, but she carries guilt within her for she created me, and though fools may find me cruel, she is responsible for what I have become. She can't refuse me entirely. In a way I think she honestly believed she could still help you defeat me, but she loves me as well."

Tears of anger burn my eyes. I had a chance to get out of here, to leave Avalon with my friends, but I chose to stay to help strangers and to bring back someone I thought loved me and didn't mean to hurt me. But here it is. All of it laid out and tossed in my face. I've brought Lestan back only for him to betray me, and I fell for his seductive Fae charm all over again. *Damn it.* His father being so flippant about his death was all part of the show. He knew I would do it, would want to even more, knowing how little he cared. The Fae king knew the whole time. In fact, he counted on it.

"You knew I'd try to bring him back, didn't you? You bastard. Where is he, your sweet little boy? Hiding behind those ridiculous drapes you wear, cowering like the traitor he is?" I slowly push myself up, my long gloves snagging against the rough grey wall. The king's face is nearly pulsing and deep red, though as I've seen it so often like this, I wonder if it's perpetually so, maybe a side effect of his crazy.

Keeping one eye on him, I look around, trying to see if anyone else is outside my cell, hiding in the darkness to join the big reveal. The king vibrates with devious glee.

"Oh, get on with it!" My words fly out in an angry and fearful rage. I don't know how much longer I can keep up my charade and not tear him to shreds with the proverbial knife in my back.

"Thanks to Gaia, you and your man-in-waiting have my name, and with this one last act he'll lose his mind because he knows I am going to destroy yours, any memory of who you are, and who any of your friends may be. You'll never leave here and you'll be mine forever."

Though he's across the cell his speed takes me by surprise and he gets his hand on my hair, grabbing me and yanking me nearer to him. Ryan's bead warms and my eyes sting with warm salty tears when I hear his voice calling my name.

I'm sorry Ryan, I'm so sorry!

The king's fingers close around my last link to my friends and he tears it from me, taking a chunk of my hair with it. Do I fight for it? I mean, he must know I have command of my power now—or does he? How else would I have brought his son back? Unless he thinks he let me, all part of his plan. I can only pray I have somewhat of an upper hand, but I need to play my cards right. From what the king—Tristan—is saying, I think I know what he's done, but I need to be certain. Though there's only one person in hiding that both Ryan and I know of, so I scramble away from the king, holding my head where he tore my link to Ryan from me. A part of me crumbles as he crushes it between his fingers, the bead igniting in a small starburst before silver shining flecks fall to the ground and fade away.

I can almost hear Ryan's scream across the dimensions. He would know in a heartbeat that his ring in bead form has been destroyed, and what will he do then? Demand that someone come get me. That is, if he hasn't already after what the king claims to have done to him, and after all he saw between me and that turncoat Lestan. Perhaps he could tell I was being deceived when my dumb ass could not. If Sandra comes, which is a near certainty after what they must know from King Tristan's and Lestan's set-up, I must prepare to fight and to get out of here. I've been conned and I'm not letting my friends suffer anymore at the hands of the Fae.

"Now, they will try this first. Your friends chose to not learn their lesson from the last time. As expected."

Just outside my cell a projection of sorts shows Logan, Sandra, and Yi, their mouths moving and shouting silently just before a wall of green power shoots at them with an astonishing, thunderous sound of collision. The force tosses my friends backward and the muted sound seems to be cranked up just in time for me to hear their terrified screams and the crunching of broken bodies and bones as they disappear, having been tossed away from here—away from me. A trembling anger takes over my entire body as it prepares to take on the king and fight for my freedom, for my friends, and to mark the end of his reign. I can't bear to think of what may have happened to those I love. The destroyer king's power reverberated deep within the surrounding stone, so who knows what it may have done to each of them. They'll need help healing from what this atrocious Fae has done to them. I need to stop what's going to happen next; I need to warn them all.

"And now it'll be mere minutes before she comes for you. She's different now, isn't she? She won't abandon you like she has so many times before. No, she'll come for you, without doubt. It may take a while for them to agree to seek her help, but your Ryan will not be denied. The days it may take for her to mobilize and get here will be measly moments to us in Avalon. Oh yes, I expect her any second now." His eyes focus on me for a heartbeat, his lips curling into a sneer as he takes in my fury. "Such a sweet disaster you are, aren't you? Just like your mother!"

It all falls into place now. The man my mother spoke of when she saved us on the boat in Mexico: Tristan. He was the only other person she admitted to having loved when my dad was supposedly dead. A Seer, or so she thought, one who specialized in dreams. She sought him out when she suspected my dad might not be dead after all. They fell in love, but when the dreams came to my mother, teasing at the possibility that my father was alive, she of course wanted to find him. Tristan scared her and he grew furious when she tried to locate my father. She left him, having been fearful enough to take on a new identity in order to hide from the man she once loved. The timing works out from when I first met Lestan. This whole time King Tristan used Lestan and me to find my mom and to bring her back to him. In Avalon, where he can trap her just as he did me. Well, not anymore.

Putting my hands, one at a time, behind my head, I feign sorrow. "No! What do you want from her? She's done nothing to you. Take me instead." Serenity and Chaos greet my fingers and I call to them, willing them to prepare to fight. They're small, hidden between my fingers as I cover my eyes in mock sobs, but in a blink of an eye that will all change.

"Oh, Eila. It's nothing personal. For you, that is. She's my only, my true love. The only woman who can make me even more powerful than I already am. But she left me, and that cannot stand. Nobody leaves me of their own will. Nobody!"

Laughter flies from my lips and heaves my chest. "Love? What do you know of love? A father who twists his son to be just as evil and wicked as he does not know love. A man who rips a woman's only daughter from her world to trick her into coming to him is not love." Holding some of my cards close, I tear into him once more. "And what of your first wife, Tristan? What really happened to her? I bet you killed her, didn't you? You pathetic, ridiculous king of the Fae. You're nothing but a jealous, controlling murderer and my mother will *never* love you!"

Spitting at him with my venomous words, I forget what the treacherous Lestan asked of me and instead focus on how I will destroy the man before me. Willing Serenity and Chaos into their twin fighting staffs, I demand their deadly power to kick in, forcing a sharp lethal metal to protrude from their carved wood before I launch myself at the king. His look of surprise is all I need to carry me through my attack. He's caught off guard, so he doesn't know everything, and possibly not of everyone. Perhaps I do have someone on my side still, but whom can I trust?

My feet propel me to him quickly and I stab both of his arms, using my Earthen power to help pin him against the side of the cell. I pull out the sharp metal of Chaos from his left shoulder, making his muscles and bone grate, then I shove my right elbow into his nose before pulling Serenity free as well, slicing them both down and across his belly. The metal tears into his velvety clothes easily, the cocky bastard not even thinking to wear protection when coming down here to taunt his helpless prisoner. Holding his face and stomach, groans escape him as blood drips down his hands before splashing onto the floor. There will be no mercy today. This imprisonment has taken me away from my life and now dares to threaten my mother? Oh, he will pay.

Using his bloody distractions to my advantage, I reach behind his neck and toss him to the ground. He's a good bit taller than I, but the bigger they are the harder they fall. Once he's on the ground I continue to batter him with my staffs, but something doesn't seem right. Is he *laughing*? Backing away, I allow him to roll up to sitting while blood continues to gush from his face and belly as well as from the side of his head where I've bludgeoned him more than once.

"What's so funny? I wouldn't be laughing if someone was kicking the shit out of me in my own home."

His sickly merriment continues. Does he love the pain and the blood that much? Of course he would, the sick bastard.

"Who has aided you in my home? Tell me! Tell me at once and I may spare your life." Is he high? I will never. "Yes, your mother may be angry with me if I were to kill you, but in time that would not matter. She'll forget all about you, so this is a one-time offer. Tell me who has been helping you and I'll let you live."

Either he's a fabulous actor or he really doesn't know about Verus and Thatcher. Maybe I'm not completely alone and Lestan has fooled us all. But if that is true, then they are all in great danger. I need to get to them, and fast.

"Help from where? Here? From who, Tristan? You've made everyone in Avalon hate those of us from my world, or any other world. You think so much of yourselves that I am nothing. Perhaps you have failed yourself. So cocky that you forgot how powerful I really am. I brought back your son, something I'm certain you couldn't do yourself, or you would have. Am I right? So maybe *I* should rule Avalon, for I am stronger than you. Always have been and always will be, so get up and fight, you con of a king. Fight me!" Calling him by the name my mom knew him as, ignoring his official title, is not making the king happy—my bad.

Not waiting for him to rise, I launch at him, my staffs blazing with the bright green color of my vines lighting up the cresting waves and the little Vexs carved into Dana's enchanted wood. He's on his feet when I reach him and manages to block my swings at his face, but I dip low and crack both of his knees in succession before I leap backward, kicking him right in the gut where his blood continues to eke from his body.

A terrible growl releases from his chest and he tosses his robes from his body, showing how much of the kingly padding went with it. He's still bulkier than I, but I don't shy from him as he lurches toward me. He may be king of the mental battle, but I am kicking his ass here in my very own terror dome. Fat fists swing at me but I dodge them, moving around the cell sprightly compared to his heavy footfalls. I leap over my bed before shoving it at him, knocking the wind out of the cumbersome king. With him bent over gasping for breath, I catapult on the bed, driving my leg at his chest and using the staffs to get a good crack at his face. When he attempts to take out my legs with both arms, I cartwheel off his back, landing behind him and jabbing the sharp metal into both of his calf muscles. My answering battle cry echoes through the dungeon and I wince, worrying that I've brought awareness to what's happening down here. King Tristan has not called out for help. I'm guessing he feels he has this under control, although I'm not sure how he possibly could when I am whipping his ass.

"Enough of this!" He thrusts his fist in my direction and the dark green glow from his ring catapults at my squinting eyes. I answer him with my own, shooting my powerful vines at him fearlessly. They don't clash; instead, they pass by each other allowing us to get a hold on the other. His power oozes around my body like a thick cloud, squeezing me until I struggle for breath. "Now who's the cocky one?" But he starts to gasp once my vines wrap around his thick neck. "Is this your plan? To have us both die here? What a waste, you stupid girl."

No, this isn't my plan. What *is* my plan? His power has my arms pinned so I can't even use my staffs to break it apart. Digging into my being, I search out my grandmother's power along with my father's, bringing them to awareness and sending them after the king's oozing green darkness that's squeezing the life out of me. Dandelions dance around me, burning away the king's hold just before my father's little sunburst drills deep inside the green mass and explodes it into nothingness.

Getting my breath back, I storm at him where he's now slipping to the ground, his back sliding against the cell bars as his red face begins to turn blue. I demand my vines to tighten around his neck while his legs thrash, scrambling for footing on the dirty cell floor. Am I going to kill this man? I hear the sounds of hollering panic and frantic footsteps above. The dungeon door will crash open soon. I need to get out of here, but I do have a bit of time, time to end him right now.

Frustration pools into my mind, followed by a wave of intense anger. "You've held me prisoner, you've attacked my friends, and killed countless others. Your torment lasted over decades for me. I should end you!"

His strangled answer has me loosening the bind I have on him.

"Do it! Do it and you will be just like me, giving me more than I ever hoped for. You'll bring me back, just like you did my boy because you and I will be one and you'll need me to feel whole, as do I with your mother. Gaia's most feared and powerful creations who will do anything with their supremacy. Even kill. Do it and join me. We will rule the worlds together—your mother, Lestan, you, and I. *Do it!*"

Before I can answer, before I can yell in his face that I am nothing like him, not even close, I feel a pull at my back. Keeping a hold on my prey, I look over my shoulder to see a shimmer in the cell and Thatcher's glowing eye. Still gripping the king, I back toward the cat, wary but curious to know what he has to say.

Quietly, so only I can hear, he speaks to me from the hidden pathway. "Eila, no. This is not who you are. If you take his life in this way, in your fury, Gaia will not forgive. She will turn away. Do not travel down this dark path."

I send my energy to seal the king's ears and eyes so I can talk freely without exposing Thatcher's existence. "But Gaia still helps him. She did what he asked even though he is wicked. She is why I am this thing that I am. Gaia has made me into a terrible creature. This is what she wants. It's what I want."

But is it? Looking into Thatcher's large cat orbs, I remember how together we healed those innocent souls in Ibiza, how we saved people from death and rebuilt their world to the way it was, the way it should be. I do not have to stay in this destructive chaos, no matter what the king and others have done to me. This is my choice. He made his decision to turn toward the darkness, but that won't be mine.

Thatcher speaks again. "Even the goddess has made mistakes, but you don't have to follow her, or Tristan. Come with me, Eila. Come with me now and we will deal with him together. You have a choice."

Being an Earthen Protector and Healer wasn't really an option; it was something I was born into. But standing here, threatening to kill a king in another world fills me with an intense and incredible might that is intoxicating, though it isn't what I want, not what I'm meant for.

Thatcher is right, this time I get a choice. I can choose to be good, better than the Fae king. My determination to kill Tristan starts to chip away just as his guards come tearing down the steps and to my cell, yelling orders at me to stand down or they will destroy me. I ignore them just as I ignore the king's spitting at my weakness. Instead, I walk to Thatcher, releasing the king just before stepping into the great cat's path and letting it carry me away.

As the distance grows I can still hear the fury in the castle behind me, and the sounds of another voice, a familiar one calling out and echoing into our dark pathway to the greenhouse.

"Tristan! What have you done?"

"Stacy," the king answers. "Welcome home."

CHAPTER 16

Trust

I was just going to sleep. I was just going to close my eyes.
Oh how I've been a beauty . . . how I've been a slithering snake.
I have no rules to my game and only one suggestion to make . . .
Watch your back, because I am not ever, ever behind you.

"I have to go back! Thatcher, you need to turn around." I've attempted to back down the path leading to my cell and it's like hitting a wall each time.

"We cannot go back, not yet, but we will and everything will work out. Trust me."

My sarcastic laugh stops him in his tracks, and his head swings my way with a tilt. "Trust you? Do you know what you had me do?" His answering chuff tells me to go on. "I've brought back a traitor! He helped his father and now they have my mom. You've either been betrayed as well or you've been in on this all along. Now, I'm inclined to think the former, or else why am I here with you, but you have to admit we're pretty screwed. Lestan is not on our side, and what about his sister and Misa? Where do they stand?"

His whiskers shift around while deep exhales sound like a brewing storm. "You must be mistaken. Or the king has tricked you. Lestan would never help him after what he did to you, to him, to his sister and mother. He would never." The king could be lying, but why doesn't Thatcher seem surprised to know his friend has returned?

171

"Thatcher? Who's waiting for us at the greenhouse?" He paces around in his path, which is barely a pace really, more of a circling in our small space. "Lestan? Are we going to him right now? Am I right?"

He stops to look at me where I stand with hands on my hips in his glowing trail. "Yes, he is waiting for us. He said you would need an exit route and he sent me to you, but I know nothing about what you speak. I am sure he will clear everything up when we get there. Try not to jump to judgment. He has been used just as much as you have, and this is a time to celebrate his return . . ." He pauses, looking deeply at my eyes. "And of course to plan. We will get your mother back, Eila. Do not worry."

But he's the one who looks worried. Of course, I nearly killed someone right before his eyes, so yeah, there's that. Speaking of killing someone, I still hold my fighting staffs in a death grip on my hips, I will them to shrink and then weave them carefully into my hair. Lestan had to know I'd find out about his betrayal and my mom; why else would he keep asking me not to kill his father? Save him so he and Verus can dispense with him on their own? My ass, he's working with his dad and now I'm being led straight into the turncoat's clutches.

Prince Bullshitter used me to stir Ryan up through our connection, one the king knew about the whole time and has been exploiting to his advantage. He used Ryan and me to bring my mother to Avalon, something I couldn't do for him on my own, not knowing where she was anyhow and not ever willing to tell him even if I did. Dana was the only one who knew where my parents were, but even she wouldn't deny seeking their assistance with how adamant Ryan would have been. Topped off with a mad king's influence, he wouldn't have taken no for an answer. Once my mom was made aware of Tristan's name she would have come for me, knowing that her past was the reason I was trapped, but now she's out of hiding and where does that leave my father? How did she even get to Avalon? With Sandra and the others blocked, she must have found another way.

"Thatcher, one of us has been misled. Are you prepared to risk that being you? Do not take us to the greenhouse. Take us somewhere else. We need to regroup, figure out what's happening. Plus, my mom is now a player in the king's game and I am not going to risk her life trusting in someone who's gone evil before. Or don't you remember what happened?" My finger slides across my throat and I stick out my tongue. Yes, Lestan died in his Justin suit and all due to him helping his father. And to think I felt guilty enough to bring him back, believing he had been influenced and controlled by his father's will and not his own. I'm an idiot. Kicking at the dark surroundings, my eyes widen when the path makes a surprising bell sound.

"Don't hit her. She's delicate."

"Oh, sorry, so the pathways are alive as well, eh? Okay, you and I are having a dimensional travel one-o-one lecture when this is all said and done, do you hear me, Whiskers?" Wringing my hands, I begin to pace just as Thatcher had. He watches me closely. "We can't go there. You have to move us. Can you move us?" I didn't think of that. He took the path to me so it's set to go back, but if "she's" organic, can't he politely tell her to move her ass? That is, if he wishes to. I can tell he doesn't want to believe Lestan is a liar, but he is at least showing concern that perhaps even he has been led astray. But his answer isn't the good news I hope for.

"This isn't my path. Lestan and Misa agreed on a new one in case we got found out. I alone can't change it without possible consequences."

Throwing my hands in the air, I stomp toward him. "Oh yeah, like what?" His paw rises and slices across his throat. "Really, you're serious. Well just fucking fantastic! What are we going to do? This could be a trap and then what, we're both done for when I could have taken care of one major issue for us right back there." Pointing at nothing is only irritating the crap out of me further. "Well, you know what I mean. If I weren't such a scaredy cat—no offense—the king—Tristan—would be dead by now. And will the two names ever quit? That's it. I'm starting with me. I'm Alex, Thatcher, AL-EX. No more cutesy goddess names allowed. No more Eila. No one ever called me that except Lestan and it ends now. It's like he has some spell over me with that name. That goes for you as well. No more Eila. It's Alex. Got it? Oh, don't look at me like that. I'm fine."

But I'm not fine. I almost killed the father and now the son is waiting on the other side of this portal. Thatcher leans his heavy warmth against my leg and I reach down to touch his strong head. He's on my side, literally, and his growling purr signals that he's ready to face what's ahead, and that no matter his history with Lestan, he isn't taking any chances.

"In my heart, *Alex,* I do not think Lestan has sided with his father. There must be a reason, but in case I am mistaken and the damage to him prior to his death was so deep that we've lost the goodness inside the boy he was, we should be at the ready. Shall I lead us out and assess things?" He seems to think his is the better choice versus my guns blazing mental state he's obviously picked up on now that Serenity and Chaos have come to life in my hands. When did that happen?

"Yes, you're right. I'll hang back at first, and if I don't need them I'll put them away, okay?" That's right, not too fast on stashing weapons if I'm not aiming to keep them hidden, and he's heading out first anyhow. Armed and ready in the pathway is the best plan while we are both in the dark about the real truth. "We're close. I can tell from when we did this before. Be ready, big cat. You don't know what may be on the other side." I bend down to take his large head in both hands. "Thanks for having my back. You know I have yours." He nuzzles me and gives me a tiny tooth bump on my cheek, then walks ahead of me. I move in the opposite direction until I feel a wall against my back, sealing off the path so we can't be followed. A flick of his tail is the only signal I get before he disappears into the world beyond. I inch up behind his exit, staying out of sight, as if I'm behind a curtain leading to the greenhouse.

"Thatcher! Where is she? What happened?" Lestan's strong voice carries and I flash back to him touching me in the emerald forest, but instead of arousing me like before, it merely sets my insides aflame and my staffs to the ready. Thatcher's gravely growl answers and I listen close inside the pathway. "There was a fight. Alex nearly killed your father and then she refused to come with me. She said you set her up and now her mother's in danger. No matter what I said, she would not follow me."

An answering roar isn't from the mini-panther, but rather from Lestan himself. "I need to talk to her. I couldn't tell her everything when I saw her because my father was listening. Of course she goes jumping to conclusions when she has to know how I feel about her, but I should have known my father wouldn't be able to resist throwing it in her face, no matter how I warned him it would lead to unnecessary wrath on her part. Damn it, Thatcher, you need to go back and get her and I need to get back to the castle before he wonders where I am. The plan is balanced delicately on all of these pieces falling into place." I can hear booted feet walking across the greenhouse floor, but not the sliding footfalls signaling Thatcher's unease. He's staying cool, and I release some of the stress building in my chest.

"It may have been a better idea if you had filled me in on the full plan so I could have placated her. She doesn't trust me now. Why didn't you share this with me?" A thump and the clatter of objects suggests a fist just hit a table.

"I couldn't risk telling anyone the full plan because of this very thing. I wanted us to work it out together and now that's gone to hell. You need to go back and get Alex." He's being aggressive, but do I sense any fear or worry? I'm not certain as I can't see Lestan's eyes. The eyes don't lie. What do I do? Do I go in there, guns a-blazing? Nonchalantly? Or do I stay hidden and see what else might play out? I consider what I may be walking into. If Lestan has turned on me, again, perhaps it's more my fault than I thought. Did I kill him with my secrets and lies as I tried to hide my real life back in my world? He would have known the entire time that I was deceiving him, and how did that hurt him? I played with his emotions, never letting him get too close, finding something with Ryan that was finally exposed, or had it been all along? Perhaps he knew everything I was trying to conceal, poorly at that, and it chipped away at him over time. His own breaking heart may have been the key that allowed his father's madness to overtake him, challenging the rest of his body to turn against itself—accepting death so that my grief and guilt could bring him back to life. And now, what have I brought back? Since I first laid eyes on him he knew exactly what I was, all I was hiding and all I can do. I wasn't the broken girl he loved, I was a black widow, a scam, and I tore his heart to shreds. Now, in his newfound life, he may be exacting his revenge on the woman who lied, cheated, and ultimately let him die—and I am dearly paying the price.

As they continue to argue about who didn't tell whom what, I find myself debating the same point. Why didn't he just tell me? I could have helped him and we could have taken his father on together.

"To hell with that, Thatcher. She's the only thing that matters, so go get her before I kill us all by going back there myself. If her mother's there, what's to keep him from killing Alex as soon as she's trapped? He'll have what he wants and soon he'll have Stacy forgetting who she is, bound to him by a promise she can't break."

The answer lies within his words. He'd do anything for me because he loves me. Something in him hoped I would love him, maybe even return here with him, and if he risks exposing himself we would probably both die. The cruelty of the king continues to assault my mind. Why did he have to use Lestan against me, against himself. Can I blame the prince for hating me and setting me up? The king is his father after all, and I am just a girl. Lestan can have anyone he wants.

Scuffling noises have me leaning back, plastering myself to the wall. Lestan has decided to take matters into his own hands. I need to do something. Maybe he's telling the truth after all, but there's only one way to be sure. Taking a deep breath, I slice my staffs behind me, initializing the absolute breakdown of our path. Once it starts to fall away, I shrink the staffs into the palms of my hands, hiding them between my fingers. No need to get Lestan into attack mode right away, especially when I'm not even one hundred percent certain of the power he holds. If Verus and his father are any indicators, it could be immeasurable.

One last calming breath and I step out of the last thin thread of the path and into the growing light of the greenhouse. "What's the problem, boys? Can't decide who's going to screw me over next?" I flick my hand slightly to the left so only Thatcher can see while I move to my right. We need to surround Lestan in case he tries to bolt. If he's working with his father, he may be useful to us as a trading piece.

"Eila, you came. Please, let me explain. My . . ."

Taking one of my typical pissy-ass stances, I cock my right hip out and cross my arms over my chest. "It's Alex, okay Lestan? Alex. Your father made it perfectly clear what *happened* during our reunion. You are the reason, the only reason, why my mother is here now and she's the only person I care about now that I don't know who in the hell to trust."

Hands rising in the air, Lestan takes a step closer to me, which triggers my stored Earthen energy to react, unwinding in the pit of my stomach and blossoming in my chest. The prince freezes, obviously sensing the shift within me and probably not wanting to trigger a full-scale brawl. He also takes a moment to look me over, and a pained look falls over his face. Yeah, I'm sure I'm a hot mess, blood splatter, dirt, missing hair and all, but I don't care for his pity.

"Stop looking at me like that, like you care. You lost the right to feel that way when you threw my mother under the bus, and for what? Payback? Well maybe if I'd known all along you were impersonating some Justin guy to what, keep me safe? Find your mother? Get in my pants? Any of it, I could have helped you. Maybe we would have had something real if all the lies were no more, but instead here we are, two deceivers who've just about had enough of each other."

Lestan looks at the ground and I barely hear his whisper over the raging blood pulsing in my ears. "I'll never be over you. Even in death I will come back to you. Will you just let me explain? We don't have much time."

"We? You mean my mother, don't you? She doesn't have much time so make it snappy before something happens, and it won't make you look any prettier than I'm looking, believe me." A glint in his eye throws me off. Is he laughing? Is he longing for a fight? But as quick as I see it, it's gone. I should just beat his ass into the ground right now, but I'll wait for him to show his cards, both in the retelling of his story and to see what he's packing.

"I needed my father to trust me. It is the only way I can get back there and convince him to send everyone he can in search of you. He needs you still, to win your mother. Though he can use his power on her, she has come on her own, as he wanted. He's twisted in thinking she'll choose to stay, but that will certainly never be the case unless she sees that you're safe. And he knows it. If I didn't play the role he wanted of me, he'll never trust me enough to leave himself virtually unprotected as everyone else hunts for you."

Don't be a fool, Alex, but it does make a sort of sense. Still, he could have let someone know. "Why couldn't you warn us, or at least warn Thatcher so he could tell me?" Frustrated, he grabs at his hair and turns away. I feel a little bad. He's only just come back to life, after all, but damn it there's a lot at stake right now.

"We were gambling as it is, sending Thatcher in there. What if he were captured? Who knows what my father can get out of him." Thatcher's growl makes me vibrate, and Lestan moves away slightly. "I couldn't risk it. I'm sorry. I can't risk anyone giving me away. It has to be real, believable. It's the only way to get him alone, to get close to him so we can take him down. He'll listen to me now, for I've tricked you and done the one thing he wanted. I brought your mother here, but I promise you that she will be fine. You'll leave together and he will pay for everything. That, I wasn't feigning."

Something feels off. I stride toward him. He doesn't flinch as I approach, but his eyes widen a little. He's scared of me, even if it's just a bit. Good. "But you and I talked about our plan. In the forest. He knows we aim to kill him, to bring your mother back and fix things for you and your sister. That has to be in his mind. He won't fall for this as easily as you think he will, Lestan. Just as I'm not falling for it either." I'm in his face now. It feels so strange to see him this close at this moment in time. The face of the prince I loved, who healed me at my lowest. Now I'm glaring at him, wanting him to say something to change my mind, but not letting my guard down as my staffs long to be used again.

"You did speak of our plan, didn't you?"

Oh no he didn't!

"Oh, throw it back on me. Real chivalrous, Prince Lestan." But he's right, damn it. I didn't even speak of Verus to Ryan. I didn't think. That's basically it. I didn't think of it and I may have exposed us. Well, at least I didn't say anything about Misa, about Verus being Glena, or of Thatcher, and I'm still not going to say a word. Who knows all of what Lestan has been made aware.

"I'm not worried, not really. I only sensed him eavesdropping when Ryan's link to you was activated. He was so gleeful about the part I agreed to play that he didn't care to know about anything else. He appears off, weak. You must have made him work hard to get anything he needed from you. With Stacy here he'll only be concerned with meeting all her needs to keep her here."

Taking a step backward, I feel colder. I hadn't noticed the heat between us, only what was building inside of me. Not turning my back on him, I take a few more steps until I'm a good ten feet away.

"Are you still planning on using those on me?" The prince eyes my hands and I curl my lips. Willing the staffs to their full twin sizes, I spin them in my palms, allowing him a glimpse of the sharp metal tips covered in his father's gore.

"They've already tasted your father's blood. Do you think you'll bleed as he did?" My eyebrow arches sharply. "Are you evil, Lestan? I know you weren't when we were young, but perhaps your father has twisted you just enough. Is that the case, Lestan? Or should we trust you?" Pushing my energy into the staffs I let them flare to life. But instead of the fear I was expecting to see, I see lust pooling within his eyes. He's never seen me this way, and knowing I was keeping it hidden must have driven him crazy.

"You're magnificent. Truly. I wish I could go back and change things, to not be what my father sculpted me into and to not have been so blinded by my love for you and my hope to see my mother again, but I can't. I've made some terrible mistakes. Risked everything. I thought my death would keep you safe from my father, but it all happened anyway." Looking believably grief-stricken, Lestan's obvious sorrow has me easing the power off my staffs. "I didn't want to hurt you, so I took the death that came for me—from your Demon. I thought my death would stop my father going after the Conners, but it didn't. He knew what would happen, but I can use that against him. If you let me."

He didn't know I'd be able to bring him back. How could he have known his mother would keep him alive? Lestan died for me, and the least I can do is give him my faith.

"You need to go," he says. Moving nearer, with a pleading crinkling his eyes, Lestan sways me to shrink my weapons. Twirling my hair and placing the hairpins just so.

"If your plan is going to work, we need to make a move now before something happens to my mother. Unless of course she kills him herself." Chances of that are slim when I know guards rushed the dungeon as I left. I can only hope Tristan's insane smittenness will keep her safe till we can return to the castle.

"If I'm right, he has Glena, or Verus rather, keeping your mother on her best behavior." Ah, so he does know about his sister. "I doubt he'll drug her unless she turns on him. I'd think she'd hold her cards until she knows where you are, and if I know my father, he'll want everything to appear under control. That means he'll try to make her believe you're in the castle somewhere. I'll go there now, convince him to send everyone to look for you, and have Verus signal to Misa for you all to come. Misa will take on the appearance of one of the guards who found you and will bring you to the king directly, which will be his orders. Thatcher can come within the castle walls easily since there are plenty of resident dogs and cats, so he'll shift to blend in." Thatcher's movements have been subtle, but he's now lowered his guard a bit to stand between us.

"And since your father wants everything to appear like he's still in control, he won't want a bunch of soldiers bringing me in and making a ruckus about finding me, so we should have him virtually alone. Am I reading this right?" A bright smile shows me that Lestan thinks this is fun, even though tricky and more than a bit dangerous. This soothes my worry about his loyalty a tad, but does make me wonder a bit more about his state of mind.

"Yes, and then we will all be there together, and he'll be none the wiser. Any stragglers can be dealt with. We aren't the only ones who wish him dead, and Verus says we have friends in the castle who will ensure we're left alone. He'll never know what hit him."

Unless he does.

"This could be a trap we're walking into. You've thought of that, right?"

"My father's mind is not stable, and with your mother just getting here and you vanishing this is the best time to strike. He's weak. You've done that."

Moving to a table, he pulls a leathery object with straps off the top. Wrapping it around his waist, he secures it with a buckle. It's a belt with a scabbard holding a large sword. Other loops hold small knives tightly strapped to him. It dawns on me again that he is a real prince, a royal member of a Fae family. Not only does he hold magic within him in some way I've yet to see, but apparently he's also well versed in the use of some very pointy objects. It's hard for me to not see him as one sexy-ass prince right now. Lestan lifts his head and looks at me, perhaps sensing the pheromones his appearance is kicking off. He closes the distance between us, but not without some glances at where my hairpins are concealed.

Letting him off the hook, I give him a sweet smile and nod. While he rubs the sides of my arms, his charming smile reflects feelings of his honesty and love. I allow my power to wrap around him at the lowest of levels; not a single twitch or pupil dilation gives away that he senses what I'm doing. I feel not treachery, but a dark door I cannot get through. Pain lies behind it, but not evil. We all hold our broken parts hidden, don't we?

Easing back, I store my energy and touch the side of his face. "You make one hell of a prince, has anyone ever told you that? I mean, swords and all." I believe him and in his plan, our plan. I touch the hilt of his large sword and lean up and in to kiss his cheek.

"I promise I'll set you free. You and your mother. This will be over soon."

I step back and fix my eyes on Lestan and Thatcher then plaster a huge grin on my face.

"We're all going to be free."

CHAPTER 17

Daddy Dearest

Thrusting mere flesh upwards.
Driving burdened knees into the ground.
Tears, seem unending
feverish cries . . .
sorrowful moans echo through this night.
I only wish for a blessing . . .
a pure light upon my soul.
Allow me to breathe the sweet air of happiness
fulfillment, purpose, and love.

Misa and I wait outside the castle walls. It truly is a sight to behold, with light brown stonework and twin spires, much of it encased in trees and moss so the building takes on the look of a castle within an emerald fairyland. How can a place so haunting, brutal, and cold to me for so long look this beautiful to me now? It's confusing. I long to go home, but standing here also makes me want to stay and explore Avalon. That is, once the king is dispatched from his throne. First things first. We need to knock King Tristan down a few pegs.

Hidden within Misa's magical artistry, she and I stand at the base of the hill on which the castle stands. The ground is a thick moss-like grass, soft to touch and spongy to walk upon. Thankfully this world itself hasn't suffered under the king's regime. While we wait, me in the guise of one of the large trees that meet the grassy hill, she tells me stories of the lives of those who have disappeared or been violated by his rule. What she relates is astounding. The king doesn't allow a soul to disagree with him, and expects all those under his rule to provide all they can to him, with little return. Aside from what he has done to me and mine, he's a wicked ruler and one I doubt will be missed. She also has news that gives me even more confidence about our mission today; there are those in the castle who will turn a blind eye, and possibly even raise arms beside us if need be for the good of the realm.

Misa has turned herself into one of the castle guards, complete with faux magic-inhibiting shackles for my wrists. She is imposing in her gold and silver armor that encases her muscular body. This new body is a far cry from the lithe woman I saw before. The realism of the façade will make it easy for me to take on my role as well. Indeed, we are the perfect vision of a good soldier having successfully tracked down and captured the king's escaped prisoner. All that's needed now is the go-ahead from Verus through the signals she sends to Misa's bracelet. Each passing minute is filled with dread that it will glow purple, the color warning us of danger. I stare at her wrist more often than look at the landscape around us. I'm eager to see my mom and to end this once and for all, but we will not risk charging in blindly.

More minutes pass before I see a glow out of the corner of my eye. On Misa's manly wrist her bracelet glows a stoplight green, and my lips stretch into a wide smile.

"Green means go, yeah?"

Tilting her head my way, Misa's now-deep voice answers me.

"Yes, how did you know?"

There's another reminder that I'm not in Kansas anymore. All roads in Avalon must be merely dirt and stone, and they definitely lack any traffic lights. "Lucky guess?"

My slight shrug turns to muscles firing at the ready. Misa's energy rolls off her as well; she's ready to have her freedom from the man who tormented her true love and threatened both of their lives. She lifts her chin at me, the question silent between us. Hell yeah, I'm ready. It's easy for me to take on the appearance of an angry, tired, and beaten soul being brought to her doom. Making sure we aren't seen coming out of thin air, we check our surroundings just before Misa drops our illusion and prods me not so nicely in the back with the tip of her sword while we make our way to the castle. We chose our soldier well, a friend of Verus's who is known by all within the kingdom to be a good man who only wants to see his world restored to peace, harmony, and protected by a less psychotic ruler. It's not much to ask for, right?

"Jin! Jin, you've found her. Well done. The king will reward you greatly, no doubt. Shall I accompany you?"

Stopping in front of the castle, 'Jin' shakes his head. "The king's orders were to keep her escape quiet, to avoid causing a stir. I'll take her in alone. Stay here. I'll share the story of her capture with you all over a tankard tonight." Hear hears greet us and the two guards open the castle doors wide for Jin and me to enter. We move swiftly, Jin nodding and speaking quickly to anyone else we come across. Lestan's plan must have worked, because those encounters are few and far between. The castle is quiet, almost tomblike now that everyone is searching for me across the land. Lestan had told us we would find them in the smaller throne room. Misa drives me there now, my stomach tickling with flutters as I prepare for the end of this insanity.

"Are you ready?"

"I'm always ready."

Banging on the door, Misa calls to the king and is answered by a command for us to enter.

"I'm sorry about this."

What? Before I say a word, she throws open the door before kicking me so hard in the back with her foot that I go flying into the throne room, unable to keep my balance. I hit my knees hard on the ground before my palms smash into the floor, jarring my handcuffed wrists so badly that I swear the bones should have cracked. My mouth even kissed a bit of floor and I can taste tangy blood from where my tooth pierced my lip. Damn, she's really into her role. I better step it up a notch.

From atop her throne, my mother's cry is heart wrenching. "Alex! Alex, oh Alex, I'm so sorry."

I can see her between the strands of hair falling over my face. She sits beside the king on a gaudy velvety pincushion-like chair adorned with

185

carved wood. He's placed shackles on her wrists similar to the ones I wear, but I can tell her magic is truly shut down, unlike my own. 'Glena' is close enough to sit on her if duty calls, undoubtedly ordered there in case the doctor needs to act quickly. Verus has once again slipped into her Glena skin and wears a wicked smile on her face that reaches its highest level of disgust once her nose crinkles at me as well.

On the opposite side, Lestan stands coolly near his father with his back against the wall next to a tall rectangular window. He looks stunning standing there, his arms crossed over his chest, but his eyes are most wicked. The prince stares at me like a piece of meat—his piece of meat.

"Tristan. Let her go. I'll stay here with you, just please, let her go."

I struggle to my feet as my mother's pleading continues. It's a bit difficult in these handcuffs. This is not how I pictured my first time being bound would go.

"Ah, Tristan, there you are. Is this where you've been hiding? And here I thought you'd be out in your world, hiding with the bugs and beetles and under the dirt like the vile creature you are. But no, you send your thugs after me instead of coming for me yourself. You coward." He's amused as usual, chuckling at me, no doubt enjoying the show. "I'll say this once to you, you phony king of Avalon. Let my mother go or you will pay."

My mother struggles against her restraints before Verus slams her against the back of her chair with a growl, demanding that she mind her place.

"Alex, no. Don't worry about me. Go home. Live your life. This I owe you for all I left you to face on your own. I'll stay. Tristan, I'll stay. Now let her go like you promised. I just needed to see that she was okay. Let her go home and keep your word that she'll never be bothered by you again."

Tristan's fingertips come together just before he touches the tips to his lips. "Yes, I did say that, didn't I? Well all right then. I'll let her go and I vow to never harass her again once you give yourself to me, now and forever. Your word will be bond, Stacy, one that cannot be broken in Avalon."

While looking at me, Stacy Conner, the woman, my mother, whom I've seen at her weakest and her strongest, nods.

"I don't hear you, Stacy. With more feeling please."

"Yes. I will stay here with you, forever. Now let her go."

I want to turn to Lestan, to give him my shriveling *what the fuck* gaze. He didn't say anything about a bond. Now she's stuck here? What if we fail? Well, that's just stupid. If we fail, we're all dead anyhow.

"Very well. Eila. You are no longer bound here by my will. You may go." He waves at me with his velvet-clad arm. "Oh, but wait. I must have forgotten. Lestan, you wished to have her stay, did you not? Oh my, how could I have neglected to recall such a thing? Oh well. I kept my end of the bargain. The rest is up to my son, you see."

Whipping her head toward her ex, my mother's eyes bore into him with such hatred that I wonder if anyone will keep her from giving him the final deathblow. "You son of a bitch, and you wonder why I left you all those years ago. I'll never love you. Never."

I see Tristan's hand flinch, and I lunge.

"If you lay one hand on her I swear I'll . . ." And now I'm immobile. What in the hell? Looking down, I see true wild vines wrapping around my legs, twining around my arms and inching up my neck. Lestan. I see his focused stare and moving fingertips. He's controlling these plants, his power finally revealed, and very fitting I might add. Now if I could only calm my rising panic that would be great. I mean, he's on our side, right?

"That's better. Now Lestan, my son, do you still wish to have your Eila here with us or have you grown tired of her insolence? I know I have."

Lestan strides over to stand before me, using his finger to force my chin up so I have to look into his eyes. "I will not keep her here if she doesn't wish to be by my side. Her treachery in the past haunts me still, and I do not wish to have her as mine unless it is of her own free will."

Laughter pours out of me uncontrollably, although it hurts a bit against the tightness of his vines. "This you ask me while you ensnare me with your botany experiment. I've proven it to you over and over again, Lestan, Justin, whoever you really are. I do not love you! I will never love you! Especially now that you've sided with your father who has tortured me, killed and harmed countless others, and is an overall sociopath. So no, lover boy, I will *not* stay here with you. You and your father can go to hell!"

The rage in his eyes fills me with a dreadful emotion, and try as I might, I don't think I can hide the large swallow of air I force down my throat. Yet it's the tears that I see next, the ones that pool and quiver within Lestan's eyes that nearly crush me. I'm only playing a part, but it must feel all too real to him, something that is just as much my fault as his.

"So she can go then. Right, Tristan. You heard your son. He won't hold her here as you do me. Allow her to return home."

The king stands and moves to where Lestan's might traps me in place. This is what we want, to get him away from my mother so Verus can free her before we take him down. It's so close I can taste it.

"You're not going anywhere, you rotten bag of flesh and bones. You dare defy my son's wishes and then believe we will let you go? No. I have what I want now, thanks to you, your weak friend, and the love your mother has for your pathetic existence. Say goodbye to Mommy now. As far as I'm concerned, you won't be missed."

Raising his ring, he touches it to my forehead. The powerful green glow brings an increasing tightness to my temples and I scream out at the vicious pain. He's taking something from me. My memories? My life?

"*No!*"

Seconds after I release my scream into the face of the man I can only wish dead, the pain stops. My closed eyes snap open and I see Tristan's face, frozen even though tears fall from his eyes. The plants that imprisoned me fall away. Verus, now in her own form, is touching her father's shoulder. It's obvious now. She's using her ability on him, making him fully experience something horrific and wretched from her own past as if he had been her. Though it isn't for him, I feel a deep and painful sorrow. Sorrow for the young woman in front of me who suffered through whatever awful thing it is once again. Verus stays strong, gladly reliving it so that her father may pay for his sins.

Though his tears fall, I can see movement, and I fear his great power is breaking the hold she has over him. I call out in warning just as my mother, now free of her shackles, grabs hold of me, moving both of us away from the brewing battle. Lestan turns his power onto his father as well. Not only vines and branches come this time, falling in from the windows, moving from the potted plants in the surrounding room, but also insects of all types. Spiders, centipedes, menacing creatures I've never seen before, climb up his body, into his royal garb, and inch closer to his face. My skin crawls watching the hundreds of small legs take over the king's body. Unflinching, Lestan watches as his father's eyes clear now that Verus has backed off, shaking a few lingering critters off her hand and standing beside her brother. Their father's eyes grow wide in horror and fury. He's been deceived, tricked, a coup by his own blood will take him down and he can't do a thing about it.

"Lestan? Verus? How can you? I gave you life and everything you have ever wanted, and yet you dare turn against me. For what, for earth humans? You will regret this, I swear it."

Inching closer to his father, Lestan unleashes on the man who's brought nothing but sadness and control to him since he was a small boy. "No Father. Not just for them, but for our mother. You banished her when she grew too powerful and when she didn't agree with your sadistic choice of rule over Avalon. Then you told her two children that she had died. What a cruel joke. What a nasty form of control. You've run the world through fear and lies, and your people will know the truth behind your mockery."

Tristan's fury begins to melt into real fear. His time is up and he knows it. My hands, free now from the phony restraints, touch a furry head and I look down to see a spindly haired dog below me. It has Thatcher's eyes. I smile at my friend, then we turn to watch the show, the final act to the mad king's reign.

"Wait, wait my son. I can change. Please, just give me a chance to prove it to you. This isn't my fault. Gaia made me what I am. I am in her image. She loved and craved power during her rule, but I can stop. I promise I can stop. With your help. With the help of you both. My daughter, my Verus. Don't do this. I will give you and Misa my blessing. That's what you want, isn't it? You can't kill me. I'm your flesh and blood." He's begging now. "Your mother. I can find your mother, reverse the banishment, I swear to you."

189

"But you can't, Father, can you? You've driven her somewhere only she could come back from, and we fear she no longer truly exists, having become one with the tree goddess Terra. You drove her there when you took her children and her life, and nothing you say now can change that, for us, or for the others you have hurt. And Misa and I don't need your blessing." Misa's soldier cloak drops away and she takes Verus's hand, united now—as one.

Woody branches reach Tristan's neck and begin to squeeze. His eyes bulge and dart wildly around the throne room. Watching a man die in this way is too much to bear, even if I hate him with every fiber of my being, so I look down while his screams echo throughout the room. Then a scent hits my nose.

"Is something burning?" My question is low, only to Thatcher and my mom who scan around looking for the source.

"I smell it as well." Thatcher moves from my side to get closer to the king.

"No, Thatcher. Wait!" But it's too late. The king's ring is afire with a thick, bright green laser-like glow that shoots from where his hand is pinned to his side, striking Thatcher's chest and then tearing apart the plants under Lestan's rule. Lestan throws an arm up and back, pushing Verus and Misa out of the way. I rush to Thatcher, despite my mother's cries of warning, sending my healing power into him as I pull him away from the growing threat.

Lestan's control over the flora and fauna wanes when the king's entire being sets aflame. Leaves instantly catch fire while little bodies crackle, releasing tiny screams as they burst into flames. Ash falls, creating a death-fueled circle around the king. He charges at his son, a living flame of fury and uncontainable force. Gaia's dark green magic is alive in him, but it looks sickly instead of vibrant.

"You disappoint me, my only son. I had such high hopes for you. But you are spineless, and you will never know what you could have become. I've let you die once, but this time I will make your death permanent." Lestan's back is against a wall and he's powerless. Anything he commands to attack his father burns upon impact. If the king gets his hands on Lestan, he'll face the same fate. I can't let that happen. I won't.

190

My mother touches my arm, her eyes giving off her bright blue fiery glow. "I'm with you." She sprints to the other side of the room to where Tristan can see her clearly while I creep slowly to the king's back.

"Tristan! If you kill your son you will *never* have me. I would rather die than stay here with you." Where did she find a knife? She holds a deadly blade to her wrist. That gets the king's attention.

"Fool! You cannot kill yourself, Stacy. You are bound to me and that doesn't allow you to take your life. Why do you think my wife is still alive? Even after all I did for her she begged to die, but our bond would not let her. It never will."

While he's distracted, I yank the pins from my hair and will my fighting staffs to life. The small metal projection isn't enough and I pull on Gaia, willing her to stretch the metal to even sharper deadly lengths. The king grabs the sides of Lestan's head, causing the prince to release bloodcurdling screams. He's going to kill him. I have no time to think. I need to act now, to save Lestan, to save us all. Lestan's eyes lock with mine. They plead, perhaps for me to escape, to leave him to die, to accept his fate, but that is something I cannot do. Knowing the flame will burn me, I push healing energy into my skin so it can instantly repair itself.

Then I attack.

Slicing down low, I sever both of the king's Achilles tendons. He drops to the floor. Like a mirror image, Lestan plummets as well. The king, now on his knees as the fire continues its deadly flame, protecting him, tries to turn his head to see me, but his pain is too great. Walking around him, I kneel so we are face-to-face. I don't see a man. I see a monster. I lean in close, allowing his flame to lap at me, to burn against me while Gaia fills me once again. He won't see fear in me, but I will be the last thing he sees.

Dark thoughts enter my mind and I know Gaia's power shines through me. I can see it reflected in the king's eyes. Are we truly alike after all?

"There you are, Eila," he says. "You see it, feel it, don't you? We are both children of Gaia. Join me. You know you want to. Kill me and feel your real power over life itself. I will come back, even more powerful than before, just as Lestan has. We will all rule together."

If I kill him what will happen to me? Will I become just as he is? Evil, power hungry, and crazed?

There is a whispering echo in my mind. "*No, my child. I have learned from my mistakes, from what I twisted him into. Know this: I have now abandoned him, but I will never abandon you.*" Gaia's ancient voice speaks to me, sending me more of her power to fight the flame that is now covering my body, allowing my skin, my flesh, to burn and repair over and over again.

I feel fucking invincible.

Uncontrollable rage fills me when I look at Lestan's burnt body. He's trying to say something, but it's hard to hear him; his voice is cracked from the damage to his throat and lungs, but his ruined lips mouth the words *kill him.* Giving Lestan an answering smile, I turn back to his father and rise to my feet. Holding the twin staffs pointing down against my sides, I prepare to raise them one last time.

"I will never be like you, Tristan. Never. You are forever damned." Crossing the staffs over my chest, I bend down to the fallen king, looking him directly in the eyes before I thrust the staffs out. The blades slice easily and swiftly across his neck. Blood gushes in dark red waves as his green fire dies. Strangled breaths signal his end, but his eyes grow even more fearful when my mother comes to stand next to me, raging blue fire dancing on her fingertips. She glares at him.

"You are never coming back. When I'm done with you, there'll be nothing left to bring back. Do you hear me? Nothing."

With a final, strangled breath, Tristan's life ends. A crackle, like lightning, bursts from my mother's hands and Tristan's body is engulfed in her flame, crumbling under the heat and becoming ash before even that disintegrates into nothing.

Uncontrollable shudders force me to the ground. I've killed someone. Such power has been wielded at my command. I feel so cold. She said she wouldn't leave me, but I feel abandoned by Gaia right now.

Wrapping her arms around me, calming me, my mother talks soothingly. "You had to. Alex. It's okay. You did what was right. We all know that. You're going to be okay." The fire has died in her eyes, but a flicker of trepidation replaces it. Does she believe her words or does she fear for me now as well?

Something else is more important though, so I squeeze her hand and pick myself up off the floor. Lestan.

Verus has a hand on his ravaged shoulder. His eyes, though glazed, look joyful. She's taken him somewhere sweet and pleasant, somewhere he can't feel the pain. Taking a deep breath to calm myself, I send my healing power into Lestan. Bright green vines reach out to him, with no trace of Gaia's intense dark green power. I search inside him first, checking for organ damage, and internal bleeding. Next, I will the dandelion seeds to dance along his skin, repairing and stitching him back together. But I need to see how he is mentally before I ease up, so I signal Verus to remove her hand. Horror replaces happiness and his shriek echoes into the room. He's not okay. Not in the least. He's terrified. Confused. Digging deeper into my being, I plead for my father's pure Healer power, and when I see the small starburst before my eyes I send it directly into Lestan's mind. The screams cease and his eyes close. Once his breath is evening out, I slump forward, my body demanding to relax.

"He's going to be okay."

Verus starts to weep with relief and Misa comes to sit with us on the castle floor, holding Verus and murmuring to her. I start to move, but the princess reaches out and grabs my hand, squeezing it gently. "You saved us. I can never thank you enough for what you have done for all of us. If you should ever need us—need anything—do not hesitate to ask."

I squeeze Verus's hand in return and give her a smile, then stand and watch Lestan as he sleeps. Mom and Thatcher join me and I kneel once more to hug Thatcher, who is back in panther form.

"Thank you my friend, for everything."

Rumbling purring jiggles my hand as I stroke him and even manages to rattle my chest. "Please stay in our lives. Now that the king is gone, allow us the opportunity to honor you back in Avalon, so you may see the real beauty of this place."

Scratching his ears, I hold back my tears and plaster on a smile instead. "Of course, but maybe not right away." We both laugh.

"Do you want to stay till he wakes?" The question has bounced around in my mind, and even though I know my mom wishes to leave this place as much as I do, she's kind enough to ask.

"I was hoping he'd wake right away, but the damage was severe and he needs rest." There go those tears again. Does he have to try to die on me twice in such a short amount of time? It's more than a girl can handle. I look at Thatcher. "Please tell him goodbye for me, and that I'll be back. To check on him, and to take you up on your offer."

Misa and Verus hug me while Thatcher leans against my legs. I break from the embrace and kneel in front of Lestan once more. I kiss him softly on the cheek before whispering, "It's over. He's gone. I'll see you soon, I promise." One last kiss then I move away, holding hands with my mother as we walk out of the throne room while guards come rushing past. I think of home.

CHAPTER 18

Home

I sat staring blankly–
Oblivious to tones as they struck my tympanic membrane.
You walk away, the words resonate–
As if a past I lived unclearly.
Not fear, as of the roaring tiger or striking shark,
but avoidance.
Just as the rocky cliffs crumble toward a series of torturous waves,
so do your words as if earthly matter themselves.
I close my eyes in the moment contemplating within my being . . .
the reality of your existence.

⁕

Soft rumbling on my chest wakes me, and my lids open only to come face-to-face with a very droopy-eyed Pitter.

"Oh, I woke you up? What do you think I am? This is a bed, you see?" Poking at the mattress with my fingertip, I'm hoping he'll get the point, but his eyes close and he falls back to sleep on my chest instead. "Well fine then, I can fall back asleep too. Watch this." But my closed eyes pop right back open. Ugh, my head's foggy but I know I can't fall asleep again. I had fallen face first into Sandra's guest bed. Ryan said he'd keep watch over me, but he isn't here now.

I can't shake the sadness weighing on my heart that though he's happy to have me home, things aren't going to be the same between us.

He lay down next to me last night, but he was distant. Not only did his mind become a tool for the Fae king, he also watched me entangle my life, and body, once again with Lestan's. If I was in his shoes, I might think of putting a stop to things as well. I knew the moment he left my room; he thought I was sleeping when he whispered into my ear that he loved me, and that he'd prove it by making sure he wasn't the cause of further threats to my life, or to those I love.

Once again, he feels our relationship has led to more danger. Though, having dealt with this hardheaded logic from him before, I plan on squashing his worry again. I'm always going to be a target. It's the life I have chosen to lead as an Earthen Protector and Healer. I'll need to remind him that I made the choice to remain in Avalon, not him, so I'm the one responsible. Oh, and that dead psycho king. Not to mention, my mom's a big girl. Once she heard Tristan's name, she and my father went to Vex and healed him enough for a one-way ticket for my mom to Avalon. Of course she says she knew we'd all be fine, but I'm not so sure. One thing the Fae king was dead on about, my mom has changed, and this time around she's going to help me as much as she possibly can.

Aside from my relationship drama, my homecoming was topped off by the looks I got from everyone when they found out I had killed the king. Valant clapped wildly, of course, while the others looked the way I was feeling—fearful, sad, and worried. I asked to go to bed after that, and they were pretty quick to send me on my way. Demon kills are okay, I guess, but Fae kings seem to be another story. Or maybe they could see and sense that I've changed. And I don't think whatever it is can be reversed. Yet I've harnessed great power before, so I can control whatever this is—right?

Getting up slowly, I shuffle into the kitchen, still in Sandra's borrowed jammies, to make some tea.

"Morning! I have some hot water ready."

Sandra's a saint, but how did she know I was getting up? I think someone's keeping her Seer eye on me. I gratefully take the mug and dig amongst the tea packets. Once satisfied with my choice, I move toward the patio but she stops me with a light touch on my elbow. "He's out there. I think he's meditating or something. I'm not sure, but it might be best to leave him alone for now. Having your mind invaded like that is a lot for a person to handle. Maybe Jax can help him through it some, having been there himself. They seem to have become fast friends, which is good, right? Think of how much fun we'll have on double dates."

Well, I don't know where Ryan and I are at now, but I take a sip from my mug and smile at one of my oldest friends. "Oh, don't forget how much fun they're going to have. I mean, to have both of us together, at the same time? Now that's entertainment money just can't buy."

Laughter can cure so much, or at least have you forgetting about your woes for a while. But you know what doesn't help? Demon pop-ins.

"Now how are we feeling this morning, eh, killer? You're looking almost as good as new. I'm happy to help out a bit more if you'd like to rehash everything for your pal Valant. I'm starving, you know. It's been hard with you so far away and only scraps here and there."

Walking up to him with a wide smile, I get close enough to give him a hard punch in the arm.

"Ouch. What was that for?"

"Do you have to start in already? Caffeine first, please."

Even though I turn away, he follows close behind.

"So that's a yes." I wheel around on him and he backs up, smiling mischievously.

"Later then. Got it. This place is too crowded anyway, especially with the stench of worry and pining love. It's been awful. See you around. Call your friend Valant when you're ready. It'll be good for both of us, I promise." Looking proud of himself for what he sees as very pleasant Demon behavior, he starts to slowly disappear.

"I have not forgotten our agreement, Valant. Don't worry."

Well, that's odd. He actually seems genuinely relieved to see me. His small nod warms me, but then the needle-like teeth glint one last time and I remember what I'm dealing with. Demons don't care for anyone but themselves.

"I must be kidding myself, thinking more of Valant, right? Though he did assist me more than once, but he's not helped me plenty as well. Regardless, we have an agreement and I'm looking forward to spending some time with him, especially after learning from Gaia that she created the Demons as well. It should make for good banter while he eats." Sandra stops mid-sip, nearly choking on her coffee. "Sorry. Geez, my life really grosses me out sometimes." Laughing, we walk arm-in-arm to the couch, giving Ryan time to Zen out and letting some silence into the room as the ocean breeze moves through her house.

"I've missed home."

"We all missed you too."

Logan and Jax saunter in, talking about sports teams and arguing about players. It's as if nothing happened, and that's just fine with me. The one thing that is definitely going to take some getting used to is Sandra having a serious boyfriend. I can almost hear the sobs from the men of San Diego. Bless the man who can tame that girl.

The smells of breakfast cooking waft through the house, and even Ryan can't resist the call. We grab plates of food, courtesy of chef Jax, and perch here and there talking about anything and everything normal. Even Ryan seems to blend into the casual atmosphere, not being as enigmatic as usual when he's around people. Breakfast has a way of bringing people together. But it's the sudden clatter of Logan's dish and the sharp movement under his skin that brings us out of this normal life facade and back to dangerous reality. Logan's eyes fall on me, and not as softly and as sultry as they have since I've returned. No, these hold danger and warning.

"What did Lestan say about the person he became while he was here?"

Now that's an odd question to ask. "Nothing really. Why? What's wrong? I figured he just changed his appearance."

Before he can answer, the doorbell rings and we all freeze. Sandra starts to tear into Logan a bit, about how he's using his Sight as an alarm of sorts again, and isn't he worried after what happened before. She walks to the door with Logan and me in tow, Logan telling her that Yi keeps him aware and that this time it's safe. Ryan moves to the window while Jax stays where he is, casually chewing on a slice of bacon. Looking back, Sandra mouths *police* and we try to act nonchalent, moving away from the door so Sandra can open it without us all looking super suspicious.

"Good morning. I'm Detective DeFain and this is Detective Press. Are you the homeowner, Miss Oman?" Sandra slips into the lovely, innocent demeanor that no man can resist.

"Why yes, detective. How can I help you this beautiful morning?"

"We're looking for a friend of yours, a Miss Alex Conner. We heard that she stays with you from time to time. Is that correct?"

I go to the door, already having sensed this was going to be about me, and push it open a little further so both Sandra and I can stand in the doorway.

"I'm Alex Conner. Is everything okay? Is it my apartment?"

Two officers stand outside. They don't look to be ready to take me in, but one never knows.

"No miss, your home is just fine, but I'm afraid we have some bad news. Do you know a Professor Justin Harris? We've learned from his coworkers that the two of you were close. Is that right?"

I can't breathe. *Breathe, damn it. Act natural.*

"Yes. We dated off and on. Is everything okay? Is he okay?"

The officer takes on his bad news stance. "I'm sorry to say that he was reported missing some weeks ago. His truck turned up at his house a few days past, but his coworkers claim it was not there before. We assumed he must be around, so we searched and we found him. I'm sorry to tell you this, Miss Conner, but Professor Harris is dead."

What in the hell is happening? Confusion buzzes in my head like aggravated bees. It's not Lestan, not again, but that means there's a real Justin? But how? What happened to him? Tears come because they need to come, damn it. I can't stand here acting normal when a man they know I was intimately close to is dead, no matter how I know that it isn't the Justin I knew. Please tell me it isn't, that this isn't some cruel joke or the last act of a dead king.

"We are sorry for your loss, miss. His colleagues thought we should inform you since he has no kin that we know of. I know this isn't the time, but please come to the station sometime soon and talk with us."

Here we go.

"Anything you need? Do you think someone hurt him?" The two officers glance at each other, seemingly unsure of what to say, but it doesn't feel like they think I'm a suspect, not even a little bit. My god, what does that body look like?

"It's more about your protection. You see, the body we found, it's Professor Harris all right, but he's been gone for a long time. Approximately a year, it seems. But from talking to the people at SDSU and in his greenhouse we know that he was around, alive and well, up till a month ago. Now we aren't sure—our pathologist is calling in some help in case he's wrong—but we think an imposter may have killed him. That could mean you're in danger as well, Miss Conner."

Tristan had to have done this. He killed someone and had Lestan take his place. It had to be him. Unless it wasn't, which would mean this was Lestan's doing. A chill creeps into me and I can't control the shaking. Sandra wraps her arms around me, pulling me close and talking to the detectives for me. Apologies and sorrys are exchanged and cards are taken, and the door clicks shut behind us.

Sandra moves me back to my room. I think I kicked Logan out of it, but he didn't seem to care. I hear voices in the room but I can't make out words. Did Lestan kill an innocent man? And if not, did he know his father had? I mean, how stupid could I be? It's not like they have the power to create a whole life, an entire person so ingrained in the world that was not their own, unless Lestan had been here that long, waiting and biding his time. But no, that wasn't the case. There was a real Justin, a living breathing Justin, and Lestan replaced him. Oh goddess, did I ever meet the real Justin? Is that why he was chosen? Because I was seeing him? Or was it Lestan the whole time? Either way, his blood is on my hands and I want some answers.

"I need to talk to Lestan." Ryan's voice roars to life above the others.

"You are not going back there. Not now. We need to figure this out. You aren't a suspect, so we don't have to worry about the police."

Ryan's words freeze any more tears from being created because now I am pissed. I sit upright. "Do you think I'm worried about the police? Somebody is dead because of me, and I may have brought back the man who killed him. That is what I care about, and not only for me, but I left him back in Avalon with his sister and Misa. With Thatcher. They may all be in danger."

"Or not." Logan doesn't flinch when I turn my glare on him, but Yi does pull on his skin. "You know what his father is capable of. Lestan may just have been a pawn. I know you've thought of that as well."

Easing my glare from hell down a few notches, I slump a little in exhaustion. All of the astral traveling has taken a toll. I catch Ryan's eye and see him shifting for the door. Great, he's leaving and we've barely even talked. He's going to bail on me again. Hasn't he figured out by now that that never works?

"Yes, as a matter of fact, I have thought of that. It's my belief, but I don't want to be blind. I need to talk to Lestan." Raising my hand to squelch the argument from all four of them, I continue. "But not right now. I'll call the detective in a couple of days and go down to find out what they know. But after that, I need to contact Lestan."

I wish I could close my eyes and have everyone disappear. Sandra, who's been watching me, and like the good friend she is, rises off the bed and starts to move everyone out of the room.

"Logan? Stay, please? I need to know what you saw. Ryan, I'd like you to hear this as well."

I turn around. I know I don't want to see his face when deep in the pit of my stomach I can already sense what his response will be.

"You can fill me in later. I need to take a walk." He turns away before my retort leaves my lips. What I should do is go after that man, make him look me in my eyes so he can see that I need him. But I don't do it. The ring that bonded us disappeared between the king's fingers, crushed by the damage he did to it and to the two of us. Can we come out of this, like we have all the other times? Part of me knows we can, and the other part knows nothing. My life truly needs some serious fixing.

Logan closes the door behind him and joins me on the bed. We look out the window to where the ocean waves break against the La Jolla rocks. From up on the hill the view is magnificent, and I almost forget the worry weaving through my mind.

"What did you see, Logan?"

Yi answers by screeching and tearing from his flesh. The action causes Logan to fall against me slightly as the eagle's great taloned feet push off his arm. Our faces close, our lips nearly touch, and I feel a sizzling spark between us before I pull away.

Logan shifts more upright. "Yi warned me and I got flashes of a vision. I saw that the police were coming and that Justin was dead. I don't know how, but I know he's been dead for a while and someone put him in the ground under his plants behind the greenhouse."

Yi is flying around like crazy, finally screeching and flapping as he hovers, staring at the floor under where my pillow is on the bed. I follow his gaze and lean to the left until Logan grabs my arm. He shakes his head at me in warning and leans over my legs, looking beneath the bed. How can something so simple make my skin and girly parts tingle like this? His chest merely brushes my knees and I'm on fire. *Get a grip Alex. Ryan, remember? Have you forgotten how you feel about that man already?* Looking at Logan, I curse at my conscience. Can you blame me? Look at him! He's still in his pajama pants and a tight blue T-shirt. I lick my lips, imagining his mouth pressing against them, but then shake my head as I see him grab something from underneath my bed.

It's a statue, a black panther, and with a note attached. I take it into my hands. The figurine, which is as dark black as a moonless night, is unexpectedly warm to my touch. Seeing my wide eyes, Logan joins me again on the bed. "I know, it feels surprisingly warm, right? I mean, for stone, which it appears to be. Be careful with it. I've had some experience with odd objects." Yi lands upon the bed, weaving his head and eyeing the panther. It looks just like Thatcher, majestic and beautiful.

"I think it's a present." I open the note and read its contents. "It's from Lestan. He says it's both a gift to remember them by and also a way for me to reach him should I ever need his help." Touched, I forget about the dead man under the ground, no, he's being poked and prodded in a freezing coroner's lab, isn't he. The stone panther begins to shake in my trembling hand, prompting Logan to take it from me and move it onto the dresser across the room. The warmth from it travels up my arm and fills my body. It's as if Gaia fills me again, although I did not will her to do so, but the power feels good this time and adds intensely to the lingering feelings from Logan's innocent brush against my knees. When he turns back to me, his eyes flicker with surprise then turn to pools of lust when they meet mine. He makes his way back to me. Before sitting down he touches my face, lifting it up and caressing my jaw.

"You are so beautiful, but I really think you need to rest." My smirk is followed by a slight giggle as I reach for his other hand and pull him onto the bed. This time it's my turn to touch his face. Yi screeches and flies back into Logan's arm, pushing him closer to me once again. "What about Ryan?"

"A lot has changed since I've been gone, and I cannot resist you. I don't want to. Are you okay with that?" The words come out of me in a rush before I'm able to slam on the brakes. My sweet, caring conscience is pushed aside as power deep in my core flares to life and smothers her thoughts of Ryan, refusing to be denied.

His answer comes in a crushing kiss. His lips are soft and I quiver in the heat that flames between my legs. Unable to hold back, I release a moan and Logan's hand comes to my mouth, pressing a finger to it and looking at me with a glint in his eyes. A red fire sparks from his irises. Goddess, he's making me squirm. Staring into his eyes, the eyes of my best friend's brother, I see mine in their reflection. They hold the green glow of my power, but wait, I also see Gaia's darkness creeping amongst my bright emerald tone. My hands freeze. What am I doing, losing control again with a boy—okay, more like a super hot man—when Ryan has been there for me all along, and I for him? My time in Avalon has affected me, and I need some time to figure things out and get my powers, and emotions, under control. Breathing heavily, I blink a few times, trying to dial the goddess back, when I hear a thumping. We both turn to look at the panther statue on the dresser in the corner.

"It must have been my imagination," we both say, and then we are springing to action and moving to the tiny Thatcher.

"Hello?" I shrug at Logan. Nothing answers. I feel stupid and we laugh out loud at our skittishness. What I am sure of is that whatever just happened between Logan and me was driven by something deep inside me. A part that doesn't give a fuck, a part that scares me, but a part that also makes me feel extraordinary, amazing, huge. The questions are, can I control it, and will I ever want it to stop? I stand next to Logan, breathing deeply, my shoulder touching his. He knows all about having a great power within him and how to control it; maybe he can help me. If I can keep myself in check around him long enough, that is. I douse myself with thoughts of Ryan, of what I am doing to him, to us. Maybe I do need some time to myself; being in a relationship with the craziness of my life may just not be possible.

Breaking the spell between us, and perhaps knowing we have both pushed past our self-control a bit too far, Logan speaks. "I meant to tell you, well, before all of this happened, that I think I found something in the files to help your father. We've been trying to find information on your mom's boss, and on the guy Bryan Malon who disappeared with your dad, so when I saw it I thought it couldn't be a coincidence."

Suddenly very curious, I stop gawking at his mouth, having once again become mesmerized by the scar on his upper lip, and look him in the eyes with professional interest.

"There are notes about a boy named Bryan. Do you know if he was in and out of therapy? It looks crazy, like there was some sort of group trying to reverse the lust for power that turns them toward the other side, to being an Absolute Protector. It's the only note I saw about the program, but Bryan was specifically interested in Demons and Avalon, which he said holds tremendous power. They said he was cured though, and gave him a clean bill of health." Bryan, the man behind the spell that sent both him and my father to another dimension, to a hell we still don't fully know all about. "What's even more interesting is who was looking at those same files when I broke into the Council's system." Now he has my undiluted attention. He's breaking laws for me. That's sweet. "Your mom's boss, Lawrence Reed. He not only looked at files, he also removed some, lots of them, and they all had the same name attached to them, Bryan Malon."

My hands curl into fists as my brain starts to tick around wildly. I always thought Bryan was the cause of everything that happened to my father and my family, and now this Lawrence Reed guy, who was pulling my dad and mom's strings in the Council, tried to erase anything to do with Bryan?

"Of course Lawrence Reed disappeared when I killed the Demon. Every trace of him gone." Everything except his fancy cigar that linked him to the man my father and my mother were both working for, unaware of each other.

Logan smiles, that red glint in his eyes again as he takes my hand. "No one ever really disappears without a trace."

"Well okay then, Agent Oman, let's go find us a snake. Let's find Lawrence Reed."

THE END

THANK YOU FOR READING

Only: The Alex Conner Chronicles Book Three

Be sure to pick up the other books in the ongoing Alex Conner Chronicles series and stay tuned for more books this year!

Trust: The Alex Conner Chronicles Book One
Truth: The Alex Conner Chronicles Book Two
Forbidden: An Alex Conner Chronicles Novella
&
My first YA Epic Fantasy/HEA Romance novel
Eve of the Exceptionals

KEEP UP WITH PARKER SINCLAIR:

Sign up for my newsletter here: *www.parkersinclair.net/contact*
Email: *mail@parkersinclair.net*
Webpage: *www.parkersinclair.net*
Purchase my books: *www.parkersinclair.net/buy-a-good-book*
FB group page: *www.facebook.com/groups/236408996753314/?ref=bookmarks*
Amazon Author Page: *amzn.to/1XIDwzO*
Facebook Fan Page: *www.facebook.com/ParkerSinclairbooks/*
Instagram: *@ParkerSinclairauthor*
Twitter: *@Parker_Sinclair*
Goodreads: *www.goodreads.com/author/show/9860680.Parker_Sinclair*
Blog: *www.parkersinclair.net/blog*
Youtube: *www.youtube.com/channel/UCWQE3qvMyB5DEZ9wwdz8rOQ*

About the Author

Ms. Sinclair gives credit to the development of her imagination and passion for writing to multiple childhood destinations lacking indoor plumbing. It may sound odd, yet when your journey to adulthood consists of numerous backpacking, camping, and hiking trips to the most out-of-the-way and breathtakingly beautiful places in North America, the creation of games, worlds, and characters are the results. She would never trade the childhood her parents gave her, and she thanks them for raising her to have her own thoughts, dreams, and bountiful imagination. Oh, and she wishes to thank them for teaching her that one should never leave their jeans on the floor of an everglades campground shower—lest they do the dance of the scorpions in the pants again!

While attending college, Ms. Sinclair studied biological sciences and psychology, specifically animal behavior, but her love has forever been to write. There are boxes in her house filled with notebooks, journals, and logs with poems, stories, lyrics, and personal rants scratched into them with pencil, marker, pen, whatever she could get her hands on. Words demanded to be thrown out of her mind and onto paper by any means necessary. Ms. Sinclair's studies have contributed greatly to the worlds, characters, and stories she creates, proving that no matter what path you take, it will all be part of where you end up—sometimes in spectacular ways!

Since 2007, Ms. Sinclair has called Virginia Beach home where she is a licensed professional school counselor and a full-time writer.

Made in the USA
Columbia, SC
12 July 2017